Love and Roses

Love and Roses

THE ABUNDANCE SERIES
BOOK 3

SALLY BAYLESS

KIMBERLIN BELLE PUBLISHING

Printed in the United States of America
First Printing, 2018
ISBN: 978-1-946034-05-2

Kimberlin Belle Publishing
Contact: admin@kimberlinbelle.com

Scripture quotations are from New Revised Standard Version Bible,
copyright © 1989 National Council of the Churches of Christ in the
United States of America. Used by permission. All rights reserved.

Publisher's Note: This is a work of fiction. Names, characters, places,
and incidents are a product of the author's imagination. Locales and
public names are sometimes used for atmospheric purposes. Any
resemblance to actual people, living or dead, or to businesses,
companies, events, institutions, or locales is completely coincidental.

Cover Design © Jennifer Zemanek/Seedlings Design Studio

Chapter One

Nate Redmond edged the big black mutt out of the way, set the bag from the veterinarian on the landing at the top of the stairs, and dug into his pocket for the key to his new apartment.

The landlady had said the place over the florist shop was adequate, but nothing top of the line. Not a problem. He didn't need top of the line.

What he needed was a fresh start.

Hopefully he could find it here in the little town of Abundance, Missouri, while working for Uncle Al at his law firm, Redmond and Associates.

Nate turned the key in the lock, and the dog nosed the door open and trotted inside.

"Making yourself right at home, aren't you?" Nate brought in the bag from the vet.

A wall of hot air heavy with humidity and ripe with the smell of fresh paint and unwashed dog surrounded him.

The first step of moving in had to be to turn on the air conditioning.

Only there wasn't air conditioning, not even a window unit, which the landlady had neglected to mention. All she'd talked about was how the place had just been painted.

Granted, the paint was new, the walls a creamy white. Everything else—from the ugly brown carpeting to the outdated plumbing—looked as if it had been around since the 1940s. Back when HVAC meant a radiator and an oscillating fan.

On the plus side, though, the lease had been fine with pets.

Nate took the bowls he'd bought at the vet out of the plastic bag and gave the dog some water and a small amount of food. "Don't give him too much too fast," the vet had said.

Nate tried to open one of the living room windows. Stuck. He tried the other one. Also stuck. He made sure the latch was completely open and tried again.

The window didn't budge. The less-than-fragrant air in the apartment had to be a hundred and five degrees.

He ran a hand through his hair and studied the windows. Were both frames warped?

No. They were painted shut.

He strode toward the bedroom. If those two windows were sealed shut as well—

They slid up easily.

All right, this was manageable. He shoved the bedroom windows open as far as possible and headed back to the moving van for his laptop.

Halfway down the exterior metal stairs, he paused and looked up and down the street. A bird sang in a tree that grew in a circular opening in the sidewalk. A small cluster of men in ball caps stood near a diner, apparently the place to be on the first Saturday morning in June. Here and there, a shopper strolled down the sidewalk, and outside the antique shop past the tiny alley, a woman watered two large planters of pink flowers. There were no honking cabs, no diesel fumes from buses, and—although most of the street parking was full—no throngs of people on the sidewalk. Probably normal for here. But to him it was weird. Just weird.

Nate checked his parking from all sides to make sure he was within the lines and got his laptop from the front of the moving van.

The woman at the antique shop flashed a wide, pretty smile. Her light-brown hair was pulled back in a ponytail, and her eyes were kind and unguarded. She gave him a little wave and returned her attention to her flowers. In her pale green T-shirt, jean shorts, and those little white tennis shoes like women wore fifty years ago, she looked, in all the best sense of the phrase, like the girl next door.

But not the next door he was used to. He returned upstairs and set his laptop on the kitchen counter. "What do you think of this place, Blackie?"

The dog ignored him, licked up a tiny crumb of food that he'd missed, and flopped down on the kitchen floor, panting.

"Hmm, not a Blackie, but you do need a name." Earlier this morning, Nate had been so busy following the GPS and driving the moving van, which still felt enormous even after the trip from New York, that he hadn't come up with one. Maybe... "Shadow?"

The dog didn't move a muscle.

What was another good name for a black dog? "Ember?"

No response.

"Bear?"

The furry black head lifted, and the dog trotted over.

"'Bear' it is." Nate rubbed the scruffy fur on the dog's neck.

He'd never pictured himself with a dog. At least not until he pulled into the rest stop a couple of towns over and found the attendant yelling at the stray that was eating potato chips out of the trash can.

"Stupid thing's been here for days," the man had said, with a gleam in his eye. "The boss even advertised to try to find the owner. Animal control better hurry up and get here. Ain't nobody wants this stray."

Five minutes later, Nate was back behind the wheel of the moving van, black dog at his side.

When he spotted the sign for the vet's office at the edge of town and found them willing to see the dog right away, it had seemed like a sign that adopting him was the right thing to do. Except for being hungry, Bear had gotten a clean bill of health. The vet said, judging from the animal's demeanor, he hadn't been mistreated. But he did need a new home.

A lot like Nate.

Moving to Abundance, taking a job in his uncle's law firm, adopting this dog—he was doing the right thing. His plan to rebuild his life was a good one.

He petted the dog's ears. "Well, Bear, before I unload, we need a window-unit air conditioner, and I need to buy you a brush and some dog shampoo."

His phone rang.

Nate pulled it from his shorts pocket, checked the display, and after another ring, answered.

"Did you get there?" a familiar voice asked. For the past six years, Jessica Wilson had been his colleague at Spillman, Hector, and Associates. And for almost a year, until several months ago, she had also been his girlfriend.

"I'm here." He leaned back against the kitchen counter.

"It's not too late to turn around and come back." Jessica's words had that same caring tone that served her well in the courtroom, a tone that said she wanted what was best for all involved.

Which wasn't always the case.

"I think relocating to Abundance is going to work out well," Nate said.

"Really? Does that town have major league baseball? Or a great live music scene? Or Thai food?"

All things he would miss. "No, but—"

"You're not even going to be able to buy those sour-cherry candies you like."

"Abundance has UPS." Which better be zipping its way toward him, since he was almost out of his favorite treat.

"This whole idea is crazy. I know Spillman would take you back if you asked. He, of all people, has to understand about—"

"I'm not moving back, Jessica. I'm going to adjust."

9

Really, he was. He had to. "I'm sure there are all kinds of things to love here in Flyover Country."

"Wouldn't you rather work at a firm that handles something more exciting than Farmer Joe's last will and testament?"

"This is where I need to be." It was time for her to accept that. Ever since she'd broken up with the guy she dated after him, she'd wanted to get back together. Which wasn't at all what he needed. "Besides, I'm sure you'll be seen as an even bigger asset at Spillman without me there showing you up."

"Like you ever could." She sniffed. "I'll give you two months. You'll come crawling back to New York. No way are you going to be happy in the middle of Missouri." She hung up.

Nate shoved his phone in his shorts' pocket and walked from the kitchen to the living room. The stained Formica countertop, the stuck-shut windows, the oddly empty street outside—none of that was a problem. Of course he could be happy here. He simply needed the right attitude. And an air conditioner. "Bear, ready to go shopping?"

The dog raised his head.

"C'mon. You seemed to enjoy hanging your head out the van window when we were on the road this morning."

A child's voice sounded from the hallway. "Dogs like that."

Nate turned toward the bedroom.

A little girl, maybe three or four, with big blue eyes and short, reddish-gold curls, peered out at him. "They always look happy riding in cars."

"Uh, hello." How did she get in here? He glanced toward the apartment door and back at the girl. True, he had left the door unlocked when he went down to check his parking and get his laptop, but he'd only been gone a couple of minutes. "Who are you?"

"I'm Emma. I live next door." She walked out of the bedroom, her tiny, glittery flip-flops slapping the carpet. "Can I pet your dog?"

Abby Hamlin Kincaid washed the granular fertilizer off her hands in the kitchen sink, then walked through the storage area and into her antique shop. She sat down at the computer on the desk behind the counter and checked her online store. Fabulous! She'd sold the milk glass punchbowl. As soon as payment cleared, she could package the bowl and send it to its new owner.

But hold on…She went to the bottom of the stairs and leaned her head over the rail, one ear cocked toward the second floor. Before she'd gone out to take care of her petunias, she'd told Emma she could watch one show, an educational cartoon. Music for a program aimed at older kids trickled down the stairs from the family room on the second floor.

"Emma, you need to turn off the TV and come downstairs. It's time for us to fix lunch."

Emma didn't answer.

Abby started up the stairs. Apparently it was also time for a reminder that when she said one TV show, she meant only one.

The cowbell on the front door clanked.

"Hello?" a deep voice called.

Oh, a customer. She'd be right down to help them as soon as she got Emma. Abby turned on the stairs to invite them to look around—

And nearly lost her balance.

Emma stood in the doorway beside an enormous black dog and the guy who'd been moving in next door.

"Are you missing someone?" The man angled his head toward Emma.

"Emma," Abby gasped, her heart caught in her throat. She rushed down the stairs and pulled her daughter close. "I—I thought you were upstairs watching TV."

"I went next door to see the dog." Emma's voice didn't hold a single note of guilt, as though leaving the house on her own was something she did every day.

Abby leaned down and looked her in the eyes. "You did what?"

"I saw the dog out the window. He looked sad."

"Sad?" Abby's single word came out in what might have been a screech.

Emma shrank back, and the man's eyes widened.

Okay, so it was a screech. But Emma was three years old. She'd left the house all by herself. Crossed the alley. Gone into a stranger's apartment.

And Abby hadn't even known.

This guy had brought Emma back. What if he hadn't?

"Bear probably did seem sad." The man looked as if he wished he was somewhere else. "He's had a rough time. I just adopted him this morning."

Abby studied the dog more closely. That explained why a guy who seemed like he'd own a purebred with a coat that gleamed instead held the leash of a mutt with fur that hadn't been brushed in weeks. It didn't explain what her daughter had been thinking or—

"I'm Nate Redmond, by the way." The man stuck out his hand.

"Oh." Abby shook his hand. "Abby Kincaid. And I guess you've met Emma. I'm so sorry. She is a little adventurous, but always before when I've let her watch TV, she's been totally engrossed."

"I guess you'll have to set some clear boundaries, so she doesn't wander into traffic and get hurt."

His words, by themselves, might not have been so bad, and considering what had happened, might even be justified. But something about his tone implied that he knew more about raising her child than she did.

Based on what she'd heard about her new neighbor, though, she doubted it. Neva, the owner of the flower shop, had said her new tenant was single, no kids, never married, all of which the florist had mentioned more than once while giving Abby a pointed stare.

Abby had ignored her.

A relationship was the last thing she needed. People kept trying to set her up, saying it had been a long time since Eric died, suggesting that God might bring her a second chance at love. But she wasn't interested.

Particularly not in someone who didn't even seem like he'd fit in around here. She re-centered her wedding and engagement rings on her finger and studied the newcomer. A navy polo and khaki shorts. Brown hair, dark blue eyes, and short stubble over a chiseled jaw. This guy belonged in a magazine ad for preppy sportswear, hanging out on some expensive sailboat. Not in her sweet little hometown.

Emma sidled back over to the dog and petted his head.

Abby put a hand on Emma's shoulder and steered her back beside her.

"Mommy, where's Flyover Country?"

Abby turned to Emma. "What?"

"Flyover Country." Emma tapped Nate on the arm. "Isn't that what you said?"

Abby raised her eyebrows at Nate. So he was one of those folks who thought people in the middle of the country weren't worth noticing. Definitely not going to fit in.

He at least had the courtesy to look guilty.

"We'll talk about it later, pumpkin." Abby turned to Nate. "Thank you for bringing Emma back."

"You're welcome."

The dog began to whine.

"It sounds like Bear and I need to leave," Nate said.

Emma waved to the dog as they walked away, and Abby closed the door. Time to have a serious discussion with her daughter and come up with the right punishment—something that wouldn't be cruel, but would definitely get the point across that leaving the house alone was a very bad thing to do. Nate's concern that something could happen to her was all too valid, and Abby couldn't bear it if something happened to Emma. Couldn't even think about it.

Would it work if she put Emma's toy kangaroo in timeout for the day? If she took away TV for a week? Abby would figure it out.

And she'd put a cowbell on the side door and the door that led to the screened-in porch as well.

Because, no matter what her new neighbor thought, Abby was a good mother.

Chapter Two

This was the tricky part.

Nate kept one hand on Bear's shoulders as he opened the tub drain. "All right, boy, stay calm." He grabbed the towel from the hook behind the door and draped it over the dog's back. Excellent. He could rub Bear as dry as possible before giving the dog a chance to shake.

By the time the water—and more hair than Nate wanted to admit—had drained from the tub, Bear was mostly dry. Nate not so much. He released his grip on Bear and shielded his face with the towel.

Bear's tags jingled and droplets sprayed out, but it wasn't that bad.

Nate opened the bathroom door.

Bear leapt from the tub and galloped out of the bathroom.

Wait, what if—

Nate raced behind Bear into the bedroom.

The dog, however, didn't shake again. Instead, he wandered to the window, near some boxes Nate still needed to unpack, stared out at downtown Abundance's Sunday afternoon, and gave a half-hearted woof, a warning to any squirrel on the block that he was back on guard.

See? Nate was figuring out this pet-owner stuff fast.

He wasn't a total idiot, despite yesterday. Yesterday, if he'd had a brain, he wouldn't have been so quick to criticize his new neighbor. The idea, though, of a little kid able to wander into the street had flat-out terrified him and made him forget about social niceties. He knew all too well how a child could get hurt.

But he needed to get off on the right foot, not annoy people. Uncle Al had made it clear that the people of Abundance wouldn't care how great a hotshot Manhattan lawyer Nate had been. If someone didn't like you, they didn't want you writing their will.

Al even expected him to attend church. Nate had gone this morning for the first time since he was a little kid. He was pretty sure God had no use for him, but at least the music was good. If sitting there for an hour a week was what it took to make it as a lawyer in Abundance, he could handle it.

Yeah, part of him would like to hop on a plane for LaGuardia and race into the city, even run out for lunch with Jessica, but he needed to succeed here.

Which meant he needed to apologize to his new neighbor.

Bear turned back from the window. The dog looked better already. Once his fur was dry, Nate could brush him and the two of them could take a walk through downtown.

"Ready for lunch, Bear?"

The dog followed him to the kitchen and Nate put a small amount of food in his bowl, once again carefully following the vet's instructions to get Bear reacclimated to eating regularly. Then he changed into a dry shirt and shorts and went to talk to Abby. "Be right back," he called out.

He'd apologize, take Bear for a walk, and get ready for tomorrow, his first day at his new job. It wasn't New York, but still, the idea of settling into a new office, meeting local lawyers in the area, and feeling useful again was appealing.

He could make this Abundance plan work. The apartment had turned out okay. Even though it was June, the window unit air-conditioner had been on sale. The guy who Al had sent over last night to help haul the couch, recliner, and mattress upstairs had been an enormous help. And, who knew? This Abby woman and her husband might even become his friends.

Nate was ready to swing open the door of the antique shop when he noticed the sign said *Closed*.

Hmm. Maybe she just ran out for a few minutes. An antique store would be open on a Sunday in New York.

Someone inside the shop giggled.

He knocked.

Emma opened the door, Abby at her side.

The little girl peeked around him as if checking for Bear.

Abby, however, looked at Nate. A flash of

embarrassment passed through her hazel eyes, and she whisked off a hat.

Well, sort of a hat. It was a tall, sparkly purple cone with see-through purple ribbons coming out the top. The sort of thing a princess might wear in a movie. Only, in a movie, a princess wouldn't have her light-brown hair in a ponytail or wear what appeared to be an old purple prom dress.

Emma wore a similar outfit, only smaller and pink, with her glittery flip-flops.

"Um, hi, Nate," Abby said.

"Hi, Abby. Hi, Emma. I wanted—"

"We're not Abby and Emma," Emma interrupted. "I'm Princess Aurora and this"—she pointed dramatically at her mother—"is Princess Felicity."

Nate struggled to keep from laughing, then bowed and kissed the air near Emma's hand. "Prince Nathaniel Redmond of the neighboring kingdom, at your service."

Emma burst into giggles. After a few seconds, she stood up taller and gestured toward the front room of the antique store. "Welcome to the palace."

He glanced at Abby. "If you don't mind, I would like a chance to speak with you."

She hesitated a second, but led him into what at one time might have been a parlor and was now an antique showroom. "Come on in."

The shop was nice, if one liked that kind of thing. He preferred modern furniture, but the pieces looked to be high quality. Some of them might even be that milk-glass stuff that Jessica had searched for last Christmas. And the place was restful. A grandfather clock ticked slowly. The hardwood floors had scratches and worn places, as if they were original. The flowered wallpaper had faded to mostly a soft yellow, very similar to the paint outside. The shop even smelled amazing, faintly of lemon furniture polish but mostly of bacon.

Abby bent down to Emma, slid a ring with a huge green stone off her finger, and removed a necklace with similar stones, all too large to be real. "Princess Aurora, could you take the royal emeralds back to the jewelry case for me and get the royal amethysts? The purple jewelry? I think it would go better with my dress."

"Okay." Emma took the ring and necklace and dashed toward the stairs.

"Remember what you learned in royal deportment class about how a princess walks," Abby called.

"Oh." Emma straightened her back and held her head high while she picked up the edge of her skirt with one hand. She rested the other hand on the rail and glided up the stairs.

"Impressive." Nate turned to Abby.

"I know. She loves the whole princess thing. A few pretend princess-deportment classes work so much better than telling her not run on the stairs."

"So I see." Abby sure didn't seem like a mother who would let her child play in the street. "Abby—" He glanced back to where Emma had been on the stairs. "I was out of line yesterday. Clearly, you and your husband are great parents."

For a second, she stood very still. "It's just me," she said in a small voice. "My husband passed away."

"Oh." Nate winced. Talk about saying the wrong

21

thing. "I'm sorry."

Abby raised her chin. "It's okay. You didn't know. And from what you saw yesterday," she said in a stronger voice, "I wasn't a very good parent. But Emma and I talked about it. She won't go out again without telling me. She certainly won't show up in your apartment to bother you."

"She wasn't a bother. I was just worried she'd get in the street. She's a really cute kid."

"Thank you." Abby's tone grew warmer.

"Bear loved all the attention she gave him."

"It's very kind of you to take in a stray."

Nate shrugged, his brain still processing the fact that Abby was widowed. He'd seen the wedding ring on her finger and assumed—

"I heard you have family in town," she said.

"I do." One of those family members, probably Aunt Vivian, might be able to tell him how long it had been since Abby lost her husband, a detail that suddenly seemed important. "Al Redmond is my uncle. I start work in his law firm tomorrow."

"You're a lawyer?"

"I am."

Abby's facial expression didn't change, but her tone had cooled ever so slightly.

Surely she wasn't one of those people who thought all lawyers were slimy. Because they weren't. He'd made such a mess of his personal life. Being a lawyer was one of the few things he was proud of. Maybe the type of law he'd been practicing in New York wasn't exactly serving mankind, but he'd been good at it. And honest.

"How nice," she said in that same tone, a tone that made it clear she didn't find it nice at all. "Well, it's been lovely talking with you." She took two steps toward the entrance and laid a hand on the doorknob.

Hmmm. A not-so-subtle hint that it was time for him to leave the palace.

Two minutes later, back in his apartment, he looked around for Bear. Not in the kitchen, where his food bowl was licked clean. Not on the black leather couch. Good. They'd had that discussion last night. Those pointy dog toenails couldn't be good for leather.

"Bear?" Nate stuck his head in the bedroom.

There, sprawled out across the comforter on the bed, surrounded by a damp area where the fabric had wicked the water from his fur, was Bear.

"Bear, off!"

Yeah, Nate was really smart. No problem giving the dog a bath. Except that now his bed was soggy and smelled like wet dog.

And what had he been thinking, wondering how long Abby had been a widow? She didn't need a man with his baggage.

Besides, the woman had a thing against lawyers.

Oh, sure, here in Abundance, life was just great.

"Emma, we're leaving in fifteen minutes to visit Grandma Doris. Go up and put on your shoes."

Emma leapt up from the floor of the antique showroom, where she had been coloring. "Grandma told me at church this morning that her neighbor's cat had kittens." She dashed toward the stairs, her strawberry-blonde curls bouncing.

Perfect. Emma could see the kittens, and Abby could have a quiet Sunday evening talking to Eric's grandmother Doris.

Abby couldn't reminisce about her husband with her parents anymore. Lately, every time she did, one of them mentioned a different man Abby should have coffee with.

And she certainly couldn't discuss Eric with his dad, not with the way Hubert felt. She rubbed a hand over the back of her neck. That situation was a mess. Things weren't only awkward between her and Hubert. There was also a strain between him and his mom. But Doris Kincaid never wavered, always treating both Hubert and Abby with love.

Thankfully, Doris was delighted to tell stories about Eric and about her own husband, Zane, who had passed away fifteen years ago. If she hadn't been, Abby would have had to remember Eric alone.

She updated one last thing on her online store and went to the kitchen, the only family space on the first floor, to get her purse. She stopped by a photo on the wall of her and Emma and Eric, when he'd first gotten out of the Army. When Emma had been tiny. When Eric had been handsome and proud and glad to be home.

Before that horrible day a week later when he was killed.

So unfair. So incredibly unfair.

Poor Emma barely got to meet him.

If he'd had a chance, Eric would have been a wonderful dad. He'd have taught Emma how to play softball and how to ride a bike and how to drive a car. He'd have been a rock for both her and Emma to lean on. That had been Eric. Strong. Solid. Honorable.

She kissed one fingertip and placed it over his heart in the photo. If only he'd never gone to Kansas City, never run into that convenience store, never tried to stop that drug addict from robbing the place.

He would have been here today, seen his girl all dressed up as Princess Aurora, and pretended to be a prince...

She picked up her purse and looked back at the photo. No. She could easily imagine Eric teaching Emma to catch a ball, but she couldn't quite picture him playing pretend.

Like Nate had done.

Her stomach tightened. Why was her brain swirling the two men together? What was she doing even thinking of another man, especially a man who was a lawyer?

Never, ever, would she forget the way the defense attorney had gotten the case against Eric's killer thrown out. Everyone in the courtroom had known the man was guilty.

Oh, yes, that lawyer's tactics had followed the letter of the law. She'd asked, repeatedly, and been told that everything he did was legal.

That didn't make it right.

He'd taken the heartache of Eric's death and quadrupled it.

By itself, losing him had been horrible. But her anger at that lawyer, at the judge, at the whole legal system had only made things worse. And the feeling of powerlessness, the knowledge that she could never find justice for Eric, had nearly broken her.

Because of that defense attorney, she'd had to fight her way not only through the emptiness and the ache that filled her chest for months but also through the hours that she lay awake in bed with heat rolling off her in waves and her muscles clenched, until, at long last, when the clock said three or four or five, she circled back around to grief and sobbed herself to sleep.

For a handful of minutes until Emma woke up hungry.

Abby blew out a long breath.

She'd thought hard about this. And prayed about it. A lot. When she kept her emotions out of it, she could see the truth.

The justice system had failed her. Most of the time, though, it worked properly, and that required someone to defend the accused. The defense attorney had been doing his job.

The problem was not the lawyer.

The problem was the addict who'd killed Eric.

So she shouldn't be rude to her new neighbor just because he was a lawyer.

But still, thoughts of Nate shouldn't intermingle with thoughts of Eric.

She hitched her purse higher on her shoulder. The best way to remember Eric—and not have those memories confused—was by visiting his grandmother.

Half an hour later, Abby pulled into the driveway of Doris's small ranch-style house. She opened the minivan door to let Emma out and grabbed the plastic bag from Cassidy's Diner.

Doris swung open her front door. "Emma and Abby! Two of my favorite girls! Come on in!" The older woman's white hair curled in damp ringlets, as if she'd just gotten out of the shower. She spread her arms wide, and the sleeves of her bright turquoise caftan flowed down like the wings of a five-foot-two bird. A bird that was too frail after suffering through that virus that was going around, but too stubborn to take it easy.

Emma raced ahead for a big hug.

Abby raised the bag from the diner. "Cassidy's fried-chicken family dinner, exactly like you requested. With a big slice of peach pie for us all to split. I couldn't resist." She strolled up the sidewalk, growing more relaxed at the sound of the crickets chirping and the smell of the honeysuckle blooming beside Doris's porch.

Doris led them inside, past the living room with its outdated blue-plaid couches, and toward her big, round dining room table, covered in a red-checkered vinyl cloth, already set with Corelle plates, two glasses of ice tea, and one of milk. "You can't imagine how thrilled I was when you suggested bringing dinner over. I wasn't a bit interested in cooking, not after weeding around my watermelon plants. Quentin Waller is not going to beat me at the county fair this year."

"How are your watermelons doing?" Abby pulled containers from the diner bag. Doris shouldn't be weeding outside on such a hot afternoon, not until she was completely better.

"They're doing great. I have my regular vines, and I have the five plants I started inside back in March, remember? From that special seed I sent away for?"

"I remember." Abby had set up the lights for Doris to sprout the seeds inside. She also remembered the last time she'd tried to tell Doris to take it easy. She might as well save her breath.

"There were six good seedlings, but I lost one when I transplanted." Doris's eyes clouded, mourning the loss. "What with you going on that buying trip to that flea market over in Kansas, you haven't seen them in weeks. At least one of them ought to produce a melon big enough to make Quentin stop crowing about his prize corn from last summer."

"He was rather proud of it," Abby said.

"Rather? He was downright annoying." Doris jerked her head. "Sometimes I wish he'd move to the next county."

"But Grandma," Emma said in a shocked tone. "If Mr. Waller didn't live next door, I couldn't see the kittens."

Doris rolled her eyes. "I'm sure he'd make sure you saw them somehow. Those cats are just one more thing for him to talk about. If he's not dragging me over to see them when they venture down from the barn loft, he's stopping by with photos that he took on his phone."

Abby suppressed a laugh. Was Doris ever going to realize that Quentin Waller had a crush on her? Or was she simply not willing to admit it?

"Hmm. Let's take a look at you, Miss Emma." Doris peered across the table. "You seem to be getting bigger than the last time you were here."

"Really?" Emma sat up taller in her chair.

"Oh, yes," Doris said. "You're going to be taller than me next time I see you." Eric's grandmother said this every time she saw Emma. But Emma adored it.

And so did Doris.

Dinner was wonderful. Abby loved watching the dear woman and Emma together, and loved listening to stories about Eric when he was Emma's age.

At last they finished the meal and Emma noticed Mr. Waller in his yard next door. "Mommy, can I go see the kittens?"

"If Mr. Waller says it's all right."

"You know he will," Doris said. "I'm sure that's why he's out in the yard. They're probably venturing out of the barn, and he's hoping Emma will come over."

Abby went out with Emma and talked to Quentin Waller. Doris was right. The older man was eager to show Emma the kittens and promised to keep a good eye on her.

"You can only stay a few minutes," Abby called to Emma as she started back to Doris's. "We need to leave for home pretty soon."

"Okay," Emma said.

"Abby." Doris stood up as soon as Abby came back in the house. "I want you to read this letter I got." She picked up an envelope from the sideboard, sat down, and slid it across the table. She leaned in toward Abby, looking eager for her thoughts.

"Let me see." Abby took a seat and adjusted the chair's lumpy, plaid cushion, then pulled out the letter. "Dear Mrs. Kincaid," Abby read. "For years, Abundance has benefitted from your family's generous gift of the land that became Rose Park. At this time, however, an exciting new opportunity has presented itself. As you may know, the community has a need for more recreational space, in particular, for a larger tract of land that can be developed into park space that would allow for a ball field. We have been approached by a firm that wishes to develop Rose Park into a shopping area and will pay quite handsomely for the land because of its location. Although we are reluctant to sell Rose Park, we feel the potential proceeds from this opportunity are too great to miss—"

Abby's mouth dropped open. "They can't do this!"

"It is their property," Doris said in a resigned tone. "And they say wording on the deed gives them the right."

"But to sell Rose Park, the land your father-in-law donated in honor of his wife? It seems, well, almost illegal." And sneaky. Abby had filled out the park survey that the city posted online, marking the equipment and sports fields she and Emma would use. Nowhere did the survey mention getting rid of Rose Park. She'd even sent a separate email, excitedly suggesting which things she thought could be added there. "That park isn't just important to our family; it's an important part of our town's heritage, of our values."

Even before Abby started dating Eric, she knew that the park was named for Rose McFee, who, as a wealthy young widow, had moved to area in 1941 and established The Rose Hotel. Despite the attitudes of the time, Rose had shown every person she met—both in her daily life and in her business dealings—kindness and respect, no matter their race or color. Her actions often surprised the people of Abundance and sometimes drew their anger.

Rose didn't let that stop her.

Eric had told Abby more of the story. Rose further surprised the town when she remarried, to a man ten years her junior, Simon Kincaid, and early in 1942 gave birth to their son, Zane, who became Doris's husband. Rose McFee had been Eric's great-grandmother.

Abby tapped the letter. "This part lower down about how the roses in the park are barely blooming…"

"I know when I had that virus that you tried what the man at the nursery suggested."

"It didn't work."

Usually, when the weather was good, Abby picked up Doris and they worked at the park once a week, taking care of the roses, repainting the benches, doing whatever small things they could. Once, a Boy Scout had redone the gravel path for an Eagle Scout project. Other than that, though, nobody else seemed to care about the park. Certainly not the city. But as much time as Doris and Abby had spent there over the years, someone should have at least talked to them in person about the plan to sell the park.

"I've been looking at my checkbook, trying to figure out how I could afford to have that tree trimmed like we talked about. I know the reason those rosebushes are doing poorly is that they don't get enough light."

Heat rushed to Abby's cheeks. "That's way too expensive. Anyway, the city probably wouldn't want us to do that. Besides, we've told them that's why the roses have weakened. They should have trimmed that tree. They own the land."

"I guess that's their point. They own it. They can sell it. For this new development…" Doris's lips thinned.

31

"You know, Rose Park meant a lot to my Zane. And it means a lot to me."

"I know." Abby reached across the table, gave Doris's hand a squeeze, and felt the thin gold band that Doris never removed. Abby glanced down at her own wedding ring. The park had meant a lot to Eric, too. He'd even proposed there.

So many of her memories of Eric—not just from that one special day, but memories of picnics and walks and stolen kisses—were tied to Rose Park.

"Zane was incredibly proud of his mother," Doris said. "I'll never forget his face when a black man got up at her funeral and said that one day, right after the hotel opened, Rose hired his father to be a dishwasher, along with a German immigrant woman whose husband had abandoned her. Rose paid them each the same as she paid a white man. For both of them, it meant they could feed their families."

"Eric told me stories like that," Abby said. "Rose must have been an amazing woman."

"She was. Zane's dad didn't want her example to be forgotten. That's why, after she died and the hotel burned, he donated the site for a park."

"And Abundance wants to sell it. Unbelievable." Abby crossed her arms over her chest.

"I called Terrence."

"And?" Abby leaned in. She'd only met Eric's uncle a few times, but he seemed like a good man.

"He said there wasn't much he could do from out in Arizona. Especially not now, when he's buried in work." Doris began scraping and stacking the plastic containers from the diner. "Maybe I'll talk to Hubert about this. He might help."

"Good idea." Abby tried to sound positive, but most likely Eric's dad wouldn't help. Almost four years after Eric's death and Hubert was still angry. At Doris. And even more so—at Abby. If only—

The screen door banged and Emma dashed in. "Mommy, can I have a kitten? Pleeeeeease?"

"Emma, I'm sorry. You know we can't have a cat. I'm too allergic."

"But—"

"No buts, Emma. We can't." If she lived with a cat, Abby would have to buy antihistamine by the case. And, as Abby had told Emma many times before, an antique shop—with all those breakables—was no place for a dog.

Emma's lower lip tripled in size.

Abby hurriedly cleared the table, throwing away the two empty Styrofoam tubs and setting the plastic takeout containers by the sink. Doris would want to wash them and save them. "I think we'd better go," Abby said as she came back in the dining room.

"Surely we could cheer Emma up before you do," Doris said. "I was hoping I could show you my watermelon plants. Maybe I could get out those—"

"No," Abby said hurriedly. She knew what was coming. She had to cut Doris off before she could say *finger paints*. Emma was too tired and it was too late.

Abby hugged Doris goodbye and bundled a grumpy Emma into her car seat.

Visiting Doris had started out so nicely, but it hadn't ended well. Not only did Abby feel bad because Emma couldn't have a kitten, but that letter was terrible. How could Abundance sell Rose Park for development?

That park was part of the town's history.

It was Emma's heritage, given in honor of her great-grandmother.

And it meant so much to Doris.

And to Abby.

Chapter Three

"And this is your new office." Jewel Brickner, Uncle Al's secretary, spoke in a proud tone as she led Nate into a small, drab room on Monday morning.

Down the hall, the lobby for Redmond and Associates was impressive, with furnishings fitting the historic home that the building once had been. Nate's office had the same wide molding, but that was where the resemblance ended. Here, the carpet was cheap, the desk would have been given to a clerk in his old firm, and the chair didn't even have arms. The single window looked out, not on Manhattan from thirty stories up, but on rainy downtown Abundance from the first floor.

Quite the change he'd made.

"I do hope you like that chair," Jewel said. "I drove down to Columbia and sat in all the display models at the office supply store to pick it out."

Nate mustered up as much appreciation as he could.

"Thank you." The woman had done her best. "I'm sure it will be quite comfortable."

"I wrote down the password to the office Wi-Fi." She pointed to an orange sticky note in the middle of the computer monitor.

He squinted at her hand. Her fingers were plump, and every other nail was painted with red and white stripes. The alternate nails were navy blue, each decorated with a small white star.

Jewel waggled her hand. "In honor of Flag Day, coming up soon."

Nate didn't know how to respond. No secretary at Spillman, Hector, and Associates would dream of leaving a password on a sticky note or having her nails painted like miniature flags. But Jewel's nails did match her too-tight red pants, navy-and-white top, and the large patriotic bow in her bleached-blonde hair.

Not the secretary he would have expected to find working for Uncle Al, the small-town standard bearer for the three-piece suit.

"I'll leave you to get settled. Al had me put those files on your desk for you to read. He had an unexpected client come in early this morning, but I know he wants to talk with you soon." With a flutter of her sparkling nails, Jewel left.

Nate loosened his tie, hung his jacket on the hook on the back of the door, and sat in his new chair. After a couple of adjustments to the seat height and recline, it actually felt better than the chair he'd had in New York. See? Things weren't that bad. The office, though not what he was used to, was clean and adequate. Like his apartment. Probably exactly what he needed to stay focused on what mattered.

Ten minutes later, he slumped over the desk, chin in his hands. A divorce, a land transfer, and a will that could be handled with a form off the Internet. Nothing even one iota of interest, not one ounce of meat to sink his teeth into.

Al's sons, who'd once been in practice with their dad, had moved away after they married. Both had claimed that life in Abundance didn't fit their wives' careers. Nate stared at the cases on his desk. Maybe his cousins had used their wives as excuses to escape.

Jessica was right. His skills were going to be seriously underutilized here.

But a fresh start, one where he focused on the good he could do as a lawyer, rather than billable hours, might help him sleep better at night. Might even get a certain new neighbor to say the word *lawyer* without twisting up her face as if the syllables were sour.

Nate opened the top right-hand desk drawer. A stack of yellow legal pads, a box of pens, and three packages of binder clips awaited. He pulled out a pad and a pen and opened the first folder. Time to make a few notes.

He'd barely angled his paper into position when someone knocked.

"Come in."

"I almost forgot about your package that was delivered on Friday." Jewel handed him a box.

"I'm glad it got here." Nate opened the package and pulled out the bag from inside. Two pounds of sour-cherry hard candies, his favorite. He undid the twist tie and held the bag toward Jewel.

"Oh, thank you," she exclaimed as she took one. "Don't mind if I do."

"I love these things. I used to have a glass jar for them on my desk in New York, but I haven't found it yet in my boxes."

"I have just what you need."

A minute later she returned with a jar with a lid, almost identical to the one that was somewhere in his moving boxes.

Nate filled it and stashed the rest of the bag in his desk to take to his apartment. Before he put the lid on he held the jar toward her. "One more for later?"

"Thanks." She took another candy. "By the way, Al wants me to tell you that he plans to take you to lunch across the street at Cassidy's Diner. And you should know that every Friday I bring in hot doughnuts. Al pays, but I pick them up from the new shop across town."

Nate tapped the jar. "Thanks for this."

She waved a dismissive hand. "Al wants you to come in and join him. Says he'd like your thoughts on something. Probably about the work for Sullivan Enterprises. I just put through a call from the son, Cooper. He and his dad hired the firm to handle some negotiations related to the new park."

"New park?"

"Boy, do we need one." Jewel planted a hand on one hip. "The kids ought to have a decent ball field and some playground equipment that wasn't made in 1978."

A spark of excitement flared in Nate's chest. The town didn't even have a decent ball field? He slapped shut the file folder on the desk and got to his feet.

This park idea was exactly what he'd hoped for when he moved to Abundance—an opportunity to live out his values, a way to use his legal skills to do good, and a chance to make a contribution he could be proud of.

Abby waved goodbye to a customer carrying a large Antiques in Abundance shopping bag and sank into one of a pair of green armchairs in her showroom. She turned to her sister, Kristen, who was snuggled up on the loveseat next to Emma, reading her a story.

"The end!" Kristen closed the book with a decisive thump and brushed back her blonde hair.

"Can you read it again?" Emma said.

"Not now," Abby said. "When I went up to the storerooms to find a necklace for that last customer, I noticed that all the stuffed animals in your room had jumped out of your toy tub and onto the floor." She tilted her head as if to imply she wasn't sure how they managed it. "They are so bouncy sometimes."

Emma grinned.

"I'm going to set the timer on my phone for ten minutes. I want to see if you can convince all of them to jump back in."

Emma's grin disappeared.

But she did need to pick up her toys. "Maybe if your big green frog goes first, he can show them how it's done. Maybe if they jumped in backward…"

"Backward?" Emma giggled.

Abby set the timer, and Emma headed toward the

stairs, singing about her green frog.

"You are an amazing mom," Kristen said.

"She's an easy kid. And she obviously adores her Aunt Kristen." Abby sighed. "I'm so glad you moved back to Abundance this spring." Abby had gotten a little lonely, especially after her cousin Becky got married at Christmas. With her best friends, Tess and Stacey and Becky, all busy with their husbands, she'd felt left out.

"Being back here is working out great," Kristen said. "Especially financially."

"Good," Abby said. For once, her logic and Kristen's matched. There was no reason for Kristen to pay the high rent on a big-city apartment now that she was freelance editing. "I never understood why you'd want to move so far away from family in the first place." Ever since Abby had gone away to college, she'd known that she wanted to return to Abundance as soon as she could.

Which hadn't gone over too well with Eric's dad.

Was there really a chance he would help Doris save Rose Park?

"You won't believe what's happened," Abby said. Quickly, she explained to Kristen what the city planned to do to the park. "Doris said she'd call after she talked to Hubert, but…"

"You don't think he'll help."

"No. He's still mad at her. And at me."

"It wasn't your fault Eric got shot."

"I'm the reason Eric planned all along to leave the Army, because I wanted to live in Abundance. The way Hubert sees it, if Eric had never married me, he wouldn't have been in Kansas City that day."

"That's utterly ridiculous. That shooting was a random thing. It wasn't in any way your fault. Besides, even if he'd stayed in the Army, he might have come home to visit and gone to Kansas City. And it wasn't like his job in the Army was without risk."

"I know." Abby savored Kristen's adamant support. The world was so black and white to Kris. "Hubert just needs someone to blame. Sometimes I handle the situation with him okay. I mean, I know he's grieving. Losing Eric's mom to heart disease and then Eric...it nearly killed Hubert. But I can't stand how he takes it out on his own mother, all because Doris stood by Eric when he said he wanted to marry me. And—"

Abby's phone rang and she answered it.

"Abby, it's Doris. Hubert says the local businesses are all excited about the shopping area that will go in where Rose Park is."

"Greed is no excuse for the city to sell something that was a gift," Abby said into the phone. "It's like putting a handmade Christmas present in a garage sale. And your father-in-law didn't give Rose Park to the city to sell."

"I said almost the same thing to Hubert. He...he wasn't interested in helping us."

Abby's stomach hardened. Exactly what she'd been afraid of. Even though Rose Park was Hubert's heritage too, he wouldn't help. She couldn't tell Doris that—even though Hubert was driven by grief—he was being selfish and immature.

"I...I'm not really sure what to do." Doris's words grew wobbly, as if she was about to cry. "Oh—" Muffled sounds came through the line. "Quentin's at the door,

41

dear. I'll have to call you back." She hung up.

Abby frowned at the phone in her hand. Hubert was impossible. Even if he didn't care a bit about his family history, he should help his mother.

"I could hear some of what she said." Kristen pointed to the phone. "Hubert won't help?"

"No. And this idea of selling Rose Park is ridiculous." No help from Hubert. No help from Terrence. Quentin Waller? No, Abby couldn't see Doris's neighbor fighting for the park either, no matter how much he seemed to like Doris.

That left...

Abby herself.

She stared down at her own reflection in the now-black screen of her phone, at the worry lines forming between her eyebrows. That was not the face of someone experienced with politics. And she was busy. What with running her shop, taking care of Emma, helping out at church, taking that next photography class... Did she really want to do this?

But how could she not? The park meant so much to Doris, and Doris had always been there for Abby. When Hubert told Eric not to marry her, Doris had said he was wrong. When Hubert lashed out at Abby at Eric's funeral, Doris had stopped him. Oh, Abby's own parents had been wonderful, but Doris's support had offset the pain of Hubert's attacks.

And the park was close to Abby's heart as well. How could she bear it if she had to live in this town without being able to visit the place where Eric proposed?

She set her phone on the table and looked at Kristen.

"Doris and I will put a stop to this. The town can't just forget about Rose and the Kincaid family's legacy."

"Abby, I don't think this is good for you. You need to move forward. It's been more than three years."

Abby crossed her arms over her chest. Kristen didn't understand. Oh, it wasn't like when Abby had been in high school and Kristen, seven years younger, had still been a little kid, but Kristen had never been married, never had a relationship that lasted anywhere near as long as Abby and Eric had been together.

Abby still cried at every anniversary and holiday, wishing Eric could be there with them, still felt a dull ache when she heard his name. Kristen didn't know how much Abby had wanted to spend the rest of her life with him, wanted more children with him, wanted more time with him. "I—I—"

"I don't mean to upset you." Kristen scooted forward to the edge of the couch. "And I do think it's wonderful how much you still love Eric. But you're only thirty-three. If you let go of your past with him, you could fall in love again."

"This isn't only about Eric." Not entirely. "It's also about helping Doris. And about preserving the town's history, history that's important to Emma."

With each tick of the grandfather clock, Kristen's lips pursed tighter into an expression Abby had seen far too many times.

She had missed Kristen, but not this aspect of her sister's personality, not the way she always thought she knew what was best.

Kristen's mouth drew up even tighter, as though she

43

was struggling to keep quiet.

"Doris and I can address the city council together. And I'll get people to sign a petition."

Kristen's breath came out in an explosion. "Abby, this is a mistake."

Abby held out one hand like a police officer trying to stop a speeding semi headed through downtown. "You're not talking me out of it."

Kristen shook her head slowly from side to side, eyes rolled upward.

It didn't matter.

Selling Rose Park was wrong.

Chapter Four

Once, driving had been as natural as breathing for Nate.

Not that long ago, he'd had a Tesla, a car that had been unnecessary, impractical, and exorbitantly expensive to keep in Manhattan. Back then, he didn't care. Owning his dream car had meant, according to the metric he'd learned before he could reach the gas pedal, that he was a success. And what a car it had been. When Nate had been able to get out of the gridlock, he'd driven for the sheer joy of the experience.

Not anymore.

After the accident, he'd been able to avoid driving in New York. In Abundance, that wasn't an option. And, sure, he could pull into his spot behind the florist shop. But he was only home for a few minutes, and, as he was once again a car owner, he needed the parallel-parking practice.

He swallowed and checked the rearview mirror a

third time. No children on the street or sidewalk. No children anywhere that he could see. He strained his ears, trying to pick up any sounds of a child playing. Nothing. At last he gripped the plastic steering wheel and backed up slightly. Then he moved the gearshift into Park and turned off the engine of his new car.

Well, new to him. The three-year-old white sedan had been a sensible choice, but a pale excuse for an automobile compared to the Tesla and not what the salesman had wanted him to buy. He had tried to sell Nate a muscle car, a powerful street machine that some renegade cop might drive while racing through the city to stop a villain from blowing up an orphanage. A car the salesman knew Nate would feel good in, like he, too, was some action hero.

But Nate was no hero. And—because of his very unheroic past—he couldn't afford an action-hero car. And he certainly couldn't afford a Tesla. He'd left New York with twenty grand, enough furniture for his one-bedroom apartment, and a bunch of expensive suits that were probably wasted on the populace of Abundance. One of the judges, Al had explained, wore gym shorts and sports sandals under his robes all summer. This was not a place where top menswear designers would be appreciated or even recognized. A lot like Nate's legal skills.

But maybe Nate could be a hero in a small way—if he helped bring a wonderful new park to the town.

After Al had finished his regular Tuesday afternoon at the courthouse, he drove Nate over to see Rose Park. Located at the far east end of Main Street, near where it met the highway, the park was an embarrassment, even for a town like Abundance. It was located right on Main Street, which was *not* a safe place for children to play. To solve that problem, apparently, the park had been surrounded by an ugly chain-link fence. And the park was small—too small for a ball field—with play equipment that was rusted and outdated. Oh, the town had tried. The dark green benches were freshly painted and the rosebushes were pruned and mulched. But those bushes didn't have very many blossoms for June. And the equipment and paths, Al had pointed out, weren't even accessible for those with disabilities, an issue that now mattered in a very real way to Al.

Yesterday afternoon, Al's daughter, Frankie, and his five-year-old granddaughter, Kira, had moved to town. Kira, whose Achilles tendons were too short, wore leg braces.

Al said her mobility issues were minor and could be resolved over time. But thinking about Kira made Nate see things differently, made him notice obstacles he never had before. Kira might be able to play at sad little Rose Park, but a lot of kids wouldn't.

Nate climbed out of his sensible car. The lingering fragrance of the air freshener that had been liberally applied to the interior still filled his nose, mixing with the aroma of fried food from Cassidy's Diner.

He glanced toward the diner.

A bubble floated through the air and zigzagged across his line of sight.

Then another.

He looked at the porch of the antique shop, expecting

Emma, but no one was there. Just as well. He needed to take Bear out and feed him before the meeting at the hospital.

He dashed up the stairs and soon raced back down, clutching Bear's leash as the big dog galloped toward the grassy lot behind the florist.

Five minutes later, as he and Bear came back past the side ramp that led to Abby's front porch, another bubble appeared. This time Nate heard a muffled giggle.

Bear gave a loud woof and pulled him up the ramp toward the antique shop.

Behind the railing, Emma and Abby were on a pile of pillows on the porch floor. Abby wore shorts and a T-shirt and lay on her stomach, propped up on her elbows. Emma, wearing a different princess dress—one that was yellow—popped her head up above the rail every few seconds to blow more bubbles.

"What are you two up to?" Nate said.

"Shhhh," Emma admonished. She pushed Bear's haunches down.

The dog obligingly flopped onto the porch.

Nate looked at Abby.

"Oh, hi," she said in that same I-hate-lawyers tone. But she gave him a tentative smile, as if she might be trying to overlook his crime of passing the bar. "We're supposed to be quiet. You're also supposed to hide," Abby said as she gave Bear a pat.

Nate sat on the porch swing and sank down as low as possible. "Why?"

"She doesn't want anyone to know where the bubbles come from," Abby said.

"Ah, I see." What he saw, once more, was how wrong he'd been about Abby. After dinner, when many a single parent would have propped her child in front of the TV, Abby was outside with her daughter, humoring her game.

Emma leapt up, blew another stream of bubbles, and turned to Nate. "Friday's my birthday," she said in a voice that was a little too loud for someone who was hiding.

"Oh. How old will you be?"

"Fo-ur." She set the bubble bottle on the porch rail and held up four fingers on each hand.

"That's pretty old," Nate said. "It explains why you're so skilled at blowing bubbles."

Emma nodded. She grabbed her bubble jar, blew another stream of bubbles, then knelt back down to hide.

A couple walking on the sidewalk, wearing matching youth baseball league T-shirts, came closer and, when the bubbles neared, leaned out of the way to avoid popping them. Both the man and woman commented loudly on how odd it was that bubbles appeared from nowhere.

When Emma wasn't looking, Nate waved at the couple. To think that people walking down Main Street would know about Emma's game and play along. This small-town life did have some good features.

"Hey," he whispered to Abby. "Did you hear that Abundance might get a new park? Today's paper has an article asking people to fill out an online survey about what features they'd like."

Abby sat up quickly, her lips thin. "I know all about it."

Whoa. He'd said a new park, not a new strip club.

"And I read that Redmond and Associates is involved," she said. "I was trying to be polite and not bring it up, but I think it's appalling."

Nate stared at her. "Appalling?"

"I love the park they want to sell, Rose Park. I even volunteer there with Eric's grandmother, helping to take care of it, spreading mulch I get for free from a tree trimmer I know, painting benches, trying to save the roses."

Nate leaned forward. She did all that? "Why?"

"That park holds historical importance in this town. It's named in honor of a woman named Rose, a very forward-thinking entrepreneur."

Nate's stomach clenched as if he'd taken a low punch. "I didn't know." Here he'd thought he would impress her.

"I don't blame you personally," Abby said, softening her tone. "I guess you wouldn't have any way of knowing the details about the park, being new to town, but it makes me furious. Why can't people see that we need to cherish the past?"

He pointed a thumb over his shoulder at her shop. "Like antiques?"

"Exactly." She gave a single, deep nod of her head.

Nate shook his head at his own stupidity. He wanted to do something good for Abundance, not make the town hate him. He should have asked more questions. Now that he knew… "I'll bring up the historic importance with my uncle."

Abby's face softened. "You will?"

"Tomorrow morning."

"Well..." Her voice held a note of surprise. "Thanks." She blinked, and then smiled. Not a tentative smile like before, but a smile that spread across her face and made her eyes shine.

Nate's whole body felt lighter. What would it be like to see her eyes shine like that every day?

Bear let out a bark at a passing squirrel and yanked on the leash.

"I'd better get him upstairs and feed him. I need to be at a meeting," Nate said.

Emma flitted over and blocked his path. "Don't forget. About my birthday." This time she correctly held up four fingers, but that might have been because she held a dripping bubble wand in the other hand.

"A very big day," Nate said, as kindly as he could. He needed to go.

"We're having cupcakes with pink frosting. Right, Mommy?"

"That's right." Abby took Emma's hand and gave a small tug. "But you should let Nate past. He needs to feed Bear."

Emma scooted to the side and returned to blowing bubbles.

Nate hurried toward his apartment, the image of Abby's face still in his mind.

The woman deserved a better man in her life than he was.

It didn't stop him from dreaming.

Frankie McNamara walked out of Redmond and Associates on Wednesday morning and blinked in the bright sun. Twelve years since she'd left to go to college, and her little hometown hadn't changed a bit. From Antiques in Abundance to her dad's law office, to Cassidy's Diner and Porter's Hardware, and on down past the bank and the post office and city hall—it all looked the same. And felt the same.

Summer in Missouri was practically as hot and humid as Houston, but here in Abundance, everything seemed timeless. If the cars on the street were swapped out with older models, everything else would fit in twenty years ago.

The trapped-in-time aura made her feel young again—as if she might run over to the diner and find her best friends in the back booth—and at the same time made her feel ancient—knowing that those friends had long ago moved away.

But moving back here from Texas was the best choice. After the divorce had been finalized, Garrett moved to St. Louis. When her best friend's husband got transferred and they moved away, Frankie realized how alone she was. Kira needed a real family, more than just a mom. For that, Frankie had given up a higher salary in Houston, a more impressive title, and a bigger office. And given up the comforting feeling of knowing that her ex-husband was hundreds of miles away. Being back here in Missouri, with Garrett in St. Louis, and her now living an hour from Mizzou, where they'd met, was unsettling.

She checked her phone. No texts from Mom, but still, it was time to go pick up Kira.

Frankie spun back around, ready to head to her car, and—

Almost ran into some guy.

He caught her arm, as if she'd stumbled—which she hadn't—but... Whoa. Tall, dark, handsome, and...vaguely familiar.

"Frankie?"

At the sound of his voice, her pulse kicked up a notch, and recognition raced in. She pulled her arm away from him. "Cooper?"

"What are you doing here?"

"Uh, I stopped in to say hi to my dad after I went to the bank."

"Your dad?" Cooper's brow furrowed, and he halfway lifted a finger to point to her dad's law office.

"Yeah, my dad, Al Redmond," she said, irritation working its way into her words. If he'd quit interrogating her, she could ask the real question, what he was doing in her hometown.

"Your last name is McNamara. Or it was." He sounded confused—and uncomfortable.

Not as much as she was. "It is again." She really didn't want to discuss her divorce with Cooper Sullivan, of all people. "Al's actually my step-dad, but he and my mom married when I was a month old."

Cooper's eyes widened. "Oh."

"And what about you?"

"Huh?"

"What are *you* doing here?" She didn't have time to waste with Cooper. She needed to get over to her parents', pick up Kira, and enroll her in preschool.

But it was too weird, running into him in Abundance and seeing what had changed about him.

And what hadn't.

Instead of a ripped fraternity T-shirt, he wore a gray polo. His dark hair was longer than it had been in college and brushed his collar, but just like all those years ago, he had that presence, that something that made him the one person you noticed in a room.

Unless of course, you were already dating his best friend, Garrett Parks, when you met him. Then, of course, you didn't notice Cooper.

Cooper pointed at her and tilted his head to one side. "I thought your hair was brown."

"Haven't you ever heard of a salon?" The auburn shade wasn't that different from the medium-brown her hair had been in college. But it was different enough. After what she'd been through with Garrett, she'd needed a change.

Not that Cooper would understand. He'd been on Garrett's side. She could still remember how much his words had hurt that day she and Garrett ran into him in the pizza place. She'd had a weird yearning that with some comment he might have shown her husband that she was beautiful, smart, funny, wonderful…valuable.

But Cooper hadn't said anything like that.

She smoothed a hand over her khaki shorts. Sadly, things like responsibility and fidelity weren't any bigger concerns for Cooper Sullivan than they were for Garrett Parks. The two were nothing but party boys—lean, dark-haired Cooper and her ex, Garrett, the original good-time guy, with bigger muscles, blonder hair, and the ability to drink anyone, even Cooper, under the table.

For the thousandth time, she wondered why she had ever imagined that Garrett would grow up. Why had she ignored her friends when they told her he'd never change? Why had she needed to learn it in the most painful way possible? When he failed not only her, but Kira too.

"This color..." Cooper's voice held an odd, mesmerized note, and he reached out to touch the ends of her hair. "It looks good on you." His hand brushed her shoulder.

Her nerves rippled, and she moved back. "You still haven't told me what you're doing in Abundance."

"I'm here to meet with your dad about a shopping center we're going to build."

Frankie's laugh slipped out. Even after years of working in public relations, she couldn't stop it. She gave a halfway apologetic shake of her head. "Sorry, Cooper, but that's one deal I'll advise Dad to think twice about. Did you pass any business classes before you flunked out?"

"Frankie." His voice deepened. "That was ages ago. I've grown up. Gotten my degree."

Pathetic. "Right." She offered him a quick wave and walked toward her car. No way did Cooper Sullivan know what he was doing in the business world.

But if he was going to be hanging around Abundance long enough to build a shopping center, he'd be reminding her of exactly what she wanted to forget—her ex, who didn't think enough of their marriage or of her to stick around.

She'd thought moving to Abundance was the answer,

the way to give Kira a family. Instead, with Cooper around, Abundance was just a place where Frankie would be reminded of the very family Kira had lost.

Chapter Five

Cooper studied Al and Nate Redmond across the large cherry conference table and tried to keep his expression neutral. His mind still reeled from meeting Frankie outside five minutes ago and learning she was related to the Redmonds.

Sure, he'd known she was from Abundance. When a girl was as gorgeous as Frankie, with those big brown eyes and long legs, a guy didn't forget anything about her, ever.

But it had been a long time since he'd seen Frankie, and he'd had no idea she was related to Al Redmond.

At least he had the chance to talk to Al and Nate—who must be her cousin—before Frankie could say anything bad about him.

Because Cooper needed Redmond and Associates to move this project along, to use its local influence to get this development approved by the city government.

Mom had said that Dad's heart operation was not optional, that every day he waited, every appointment he canceled, made the time bomb in his chest tick faster. Which meant Cooper had to convince Dad that he could handle things in his absence. He couldn't mess things up by losing this project. Somehow, during this meeting, he was going to have to impress the Redmonds so much that—no matter what Frankie might say later—they would know their decision to take on Sullivan Enterprises as a client had been a good one.

"Thanks for coming in to talk with us, Cooper," Al said.

"Glad to be here." Cooper rested his hands on the smooth edge of the conference table. Might as well get it over with. He turned to Al. "I just met your daughter outside. We knew each other in college."

Nate looked up from his legal pad.

The guy was way too polished for a town where someone couldn't even rent an excavator. His suit fit as if it was made for him, and the knot in his tie had a perfectly centered dimple, something Cooper achieved about every third Sunday. The casualness of his own navy chinos and new gray polo suddenly seemed wrong.

"Ah." Al's voice was full of pride and he leaned back with his eyes shining. "You know Frankie."

"I have to admit, sir, that when I knew her at Mizzou I had a lot of growing up to do, so much so that I ended up getting my degree elsewhere." Cooper shifted his weight in the uncomfortable wooden chair. Hopefully this meeting wouldn't be over before it began. "But I did know her my freshman year."

Nate's eyes narrowed.

The older man's eyes, though, remained friendly. "Many of us have mistakes in our youth. I'm interested in what you have to say today."

"Thank you, sir." Cooper fumbled with the files in his messenger bag. "I've got the surveyor's report for Rose Park right here." He handed a copy to each of them. "And a projected timeline." There, that sounded confident and professional. He'd show them that—no matter what Frankie might later tell them about his days at Mizzou, how he ditched classes and took exams while still drunk from the night before—he was now a man who did his homework.

Nate gave the papers a quick once-over. The guarded expression in his eyes didn't change a bit.

Al glanced sideways at Nate.

Who was in charge here? Cooper was beginning to think it wasn't Al.

"I'd like to back up and talk about the parties involved," Nate said. "And the framework of this deal."

"Certainly," Al said, then looked across at Cooper. "I've discussed the situation briefly with Nate, but he's only been here a few days. He's been doing corporate work in Manhattan."

No wonder Al seemed eager to hear what his nephew thought. "Manhattan, huh? I imagine with that background, this deal's a piece of cake."

Nate tipped his head to one side in acknowledgment. An emotion that Cooper couldn't read flickered through his eyes.

This Nate guy made Cooper feel, once again, like a

failure. If he had to guess, he'd say Nate went to some Ivy League school back east. Definitely not to a community college. But no matter what, Cooper needed to make this deal work. He squared his shoulders and plunged in. "Abundance owns a park, Rose Park, at the very eastern edge of downtown, on Main Street."

"I drove him over there," Al put in.

"Well, as you may have noticed, it's in pretty bad shape. None of the walkways or play equipment is handicap accessible, and the rosebushes are struggling."

"Apparently they don't get enough light," Al added. "Either the parks department would have to do major pruning to nearby trees or the roses would all have to be replaced with newer varieties that require less light."

"Sullivan Enterprises would like to buy the park for $1 million and develop it as retail space. We already have interested tenants."

"As I understand it, that property was given to the community. Is that correct?" Nate leaned back in his chair, his gaze never leaving Cooper.

"Yes." Al nodded. "The city attorney and I already worked things out with a representative of the family that donated the land." Al cleared his throat. "With the one million, the city plans to build a new park, four times the size of Rose Park, right near one of the elementary schools. There's a property at the far western edge of town, one street south of Main, on Pine Street, that's well outside the business district. The new land can be bought for one hundred thousand, leaving nine hundred thousand for equipment and a ball field, all handicap accessible."

"The city received a large grant for park development," Cooper said. "And the tax revenues from the retail space we're planning, The Main Place, could help pay for the upkeep of the new park."

"That all sounds good from a financial perspective," Nate said. "But I've only been in town a few days and I've heard rumblings of opposition. Apparently Rose Park has historical significance."

Cooper's muscles twitched. Dad hadn't said anything about opposition to the deal. Hadn't mentioned it once. Cooper thumbed through the papers in front of him, searching for answers that he knew weren't there.

"There is historical significance, it's true." Al said.

Cooper looked up.

Al's face showed no concern. "But as I said, the family that donated the land is on board with the sale. They're thrilled at the idea of a larger park."

"So you think the family support would deflect any community opposition?" Nate said. "What about the local historical society?"

"We're in luck there," Al said. "The president of the historical society is fully behind the idea of a new park. He's got six grandkids."

"Still, we need to acknowledge the historical importance of this woman, Rose, who the park is named for," Nate said. "Have you considered a plaque, maybe even a statue of her, in the new park?"

"There used to be a plaque in Rose Park, but it got damaged in a storm about five years ago," Al said.

"Then a plaque in her honor at the new park— perhaps something more elaborate than the one destroyed in the storm—would actually be more recognition than she's had for years. That seems like it should be more than adequate." Nate tapped his pen on the pages Cooper had worked up. "This timeline looks good. Altogether an impressive package. I'd like to examine the survey more closely, but I think this will work." He stacked the surveyor's report on top of his legal pad and capped his pen.

"Excellent," Cooper said. He never thought he'd get "impressive" out of the guy from Manhattan.

In spite of Frankie McNamara, he might be able to pull off this deal.

Friday evening, as soon as he'd taken Bear out for a walk and given him dinner, Nate went back downstairs and next door to Abby's shop, carrying a gift bag. The previous evening he'd made a trip to the discount store and ended up in the toy aisle. He'd spotted a little stuffed dog that looked remarkably like Bear and bought it on a whim.

Now he fingered the handles of the bag and studied the room. The antique showroom appeared the same as it had the other day, filled with shining wood, sparkling glass, and the steady, comforting tick of the grandfather clock. Today, though, the scent of lemon furniture polish mingled with an aroma that hinted of just-baked birthday cake.

Abby stood behind the counter, a row of items lined up in front of her. "Hi Nate."

Every time he saw her, something about this woman

called to him. Was it the curve of her neck that was exposed by her ponytail? The way she seemed so relaxed? "Hi, Abby. Uh, what are those things?"

"Vintage costume jewelry. One of the main things, along with milk glass, that my shop is known for. These are all bracelets." She slid one on, and the elastic bands that connected the chunky beads stretched to slide over her hand.

Nate leaned in to see more closely. People bought old plastic bracelets? "Interesting. Where do you find them?"

"Flea markets, household auctions, and people bring them to me because they know I specialize in them, but mostly I have an entire room of costume jewelry on the third floor that came when I bought the shop. I'm gradually listing it all online."

Nate ran a finger over a blue bracelet on the counter. Jessica would kill for a room full of jewelry. Only she wouldn't want it to be plastic. He raised the gift bag. "Emma around?"

"Yes, but you shouldn't have. She wasn't really hinting, just excited."

"Well, since I'm already here..." He did feel a little odd bringing Emma a gift. He'd met her less than a week ago. She had mentioned her birthday quite a few times though. "It's nothing big. I saw it and thought of her."

Abby walked toward the base of the stairs.

Nate caught a whiff of Abby's perfume as she passed. Roses. Old fashioned, like her.

She leaned over the stair rail and called to Emma.

A second later thundering steps came above him that seemed far too heavy for a child as little as Emma.

But it was her. He could tell by the way Abby's face lit up, making her even prettier. Was there a possibility he might have a chance with her?

Of course, there was the lawyer thing. Surely he could overcome that, convince Abby that not all lawyers were bad. And as soon as he told her about the city's plans to honor the town heritage, the park issue shouldn't be a problem.

He had a good job. He was helping the community get a park. He might even find a place to volunteer, something like Habitat for Humanity, if there were jobs for someone who knew more about cars than drywall. He was making a new life for himself here in Abundance. There was no reason he shouldn't ask Abby out.

Emma bounded down the stairs, rounded the newel post, and came to a stop in front of her mom.

"Emma, Nate brought you a present."

"For my birthday?" Emma squealed.

"Unless you know someone else around here who's turning four." He glanced slowly toward Abby.

"No!" Emma shouted. "She's thirty-three."

Abby's cheeks turned the palest of pinks. "Emma." She shook her head indulgently.

"I guess this is for you, then." Nate held the bag toward Emma.

She took it, yanked out the tissue paper, and brought out the toy. "It's Bear!"

Abby tapped her on the shoulder. "What do we say?"

"Thank you, Nate! I love him!" Emma wrapped her arms around Nate's legs and squeezed.

Warmth grew in Nate's heart, and he patted the top of her curls.

Emma stepped back, ran a hand over the toy dog's fur, and rubbed his ears, just like she might a real dog's. "Can I take him upstairs? To introduce him to my other animals? And can Nate come to my party?"

"Yes, you can take him upstairs. I'll talk to Nate about the party, but he may have other plans."

Emma hugged Nate again and carried the toy dog up the stairs in the crook of her arm, talking to it the whole way.

"Thank you," Abby said. "That was very kind of you. And we would love to have you join us tonight for cake at seven. It's just my parents, the rest of my family, a few of Emma's friends, Eric's grandmother, and maybe his dad."

"Was Eric your—"

"My husband." Abby's jaw tensed as if talking about her loss still required a gathering of strength. "He was killed when Emma was a baby."

"I'm so sorry." What had happened? A car wreck? Nate certainly wasn't going to ask. He'd think of something else to say and—

"Eric had been in the Army," Abby said. "He had just gotten out after serving in the Middle East and receiving a Bronze Star. He went to Kansas City, stopped for gas at a convenience store, and some kid high on drugs tried to rob the place and…and shot him."

Nate felt as if he were the one who'd been shot—in the gut. He edged back. "That's horrible."

"And then some lawyer got the kid off on a technicality. He never served a day."

"Oh." Nate's stomach felt even worse. No wonder

65

she didn't like lawyers. She'd lost her husband to senseless violence and been denied justice. The ultimate slap in the face after her pain.

"Even though I sometimes have a knee-jerk reaction," she said in a forced tone. "I do know that the lawyer was doing his job. I can't hold your being a lawyer against you."

Nate's mouth went dry. "Thank you," he managed to say. "And, uh, thanks for the invitation to the party." Suddenly, telling her about the plaque in the park didn't seem important anymore. It seemed…useless. He glanced at the door. "But I'm supposed to have dinner with my aunt and uncle and cousin and her daughter tonight."

"Well, thanks again for the gift. It was really sweet of you."

"You're welcome." Nate hurried out of the shop.

Good thing he learned the facts before asking Abby out on a date.

Her husband had been a decorated war veteran, a real hero.

Nate was no hero.

One day, yeah, she might be able to look past the fact that he was a lawyer.

But he didn't see any way she would look past the fact that he was a recovering drug addict.

Chapter Six

Two days later, early on Sunday afternoon, Nate dropped the pizza box on the coffee table and sank back onto his couch, waiting for the dizziness to subside.

This didn't feel like a cold. It felt like the flu. A strain that had been genetically engineered as a biological weapon.

Outside the door to his apartment, the delivery boy clomped back down the stairs.

Nate opened the box. He couldn't smell the pizza, but it looked like plain cheese, exactly what he'd ordered. No pepperoni or spicy sausage or onions, so it would be easy to digest.

Maybe.

He let the lid drop. This situation stunk. He'd told Al that he wouldn't be at church, but said he didn't need anything. Al and Vivian were busy, helping Frankie and Kira get settled. He didn't want to bother them. He was a grown man, after all.

But he felt so awful. He stripped off his hoodie and threw aside the blanket he'd had wrapped around his shoulders. His bones felt like rods of fire.

And he missed everything about New York, even Jessica. So much so that he was tempted to get in his car, drive back, and beg Spillman for his old job.

If he could drive.

Or walk down the stairs to his car.

He'd barely made it to the living room from his bed.

But really, no matter how bad things got here in Abundance, he couldn't go back to New York.

He could just picture himself returning to his old support group there.

"You said moving to Abundance was what you needed, a way to reorganize your life to fit your values," Josh, the leader, would say, sounding bewildered. "Why would you put yourself right back in the middle of the world where you got addicted to amphetamines?"

Nate would have to explain that he had been unable to survive in a small town, a place that had only two restaurants that delivered, both pizza places. He'd even called the pharmacy to ask if they would deliver some aspirin. No, deliveries were only for prescriptions and usually for the elderly, he'd been told.

The young were apparently left to die.

What he wouldn't give to be back in a city where for a fee, couriers would deliver anything. Where Mortimer's Deli was right around the block, ready to bring food over anytime between 6 a.m. and midnight. Mort's vanilla pudding. No, it wasn't orange juice or chicken noodle soup, but it was what Nate ate when he was sick.

He pulled his hoodie back on. Now he was freezing.

His whole body ached.

He was going to have to call Al.

As soon as he had the strength to get off the couch again, he'd try to walk to the bedroom to get his phone.

Abby knocked on Nate's apartment door.

Bear gave a woof from inside, but the door remained shut.

She'd seen Nate's car in his spot in back of the florist from her bedroom window, so she knocked again.

Another bark, but no Nate.

"I don't think he's home, Emma."

Emma let out a dramatic sigh and looked at the picture she'd colored for him, then started back down the stairs.

Abby turned to follow her, but heard footsteps. "Wait, maybe he is here."

"Good!" Emma scrambled back up to the landing. Delivering her picture as a thank-you for Nate's gift was a high-priority mission.

Abby was glad that Emma wanted to thank Nate for the toy dog, but she had a sneaking suspicion that her daughter also hoped they would stay a while, so she could play with a real dog. An extended visit was not what Abby had in mind.

It wasn't the lawyer thing though…

Abby just didn't want to spend much time around her new neighbor. Not after she'd found herself daydreaming about Nate at Emma's birthday party Friday night. While awkwardly standing in silence in the same room with Eric's dad, who—in spite of his feelings for Abby—always did his best to treat Emma with love.

Abby wasn't ready for a relationship. No matter how many times Becky had tried to set her up. Each time, Abby had come up with an excuse.

Besides, even if Nate was attractive, even if he had been really sweet playing along with Emma's princess game, Abby had to think about her daughter. Emma might become attached to Nate and get hurt if things didn't work out. So Abby had no intention of hanging around his apartment to let Emma play with Bear.

The door swung open.

Bear nosed his way past Nate and onto the landing beside Emma, who immediately began to pet him.

"Abby." Nate spoke as if each syllable was a struggle, and he backed away. "I'm...sick."

That was obvious. It was about eighty-five degrees outside. His apartment was even warmer, and he was wearing sweatpants and an unzipped hoodie over a T-shirt. His cheeks were flushed and his hair smashed down on one side as if he'd just gotten up off the couch.

"You do seem miserable," she said. "Do you have a fever?"

"I don't know. I think so."

"Here. Let me check." She raised one wrist and beckoned him closer with the other hand as she would Emma. All-out mom mode had kicked in before she could stop it.

Nate didn't object. He hung his head down to her wrist.

She laid it against his forehead and quickly pulled it back.

"You're burning up." If she had to guess, she'd say his temperature was close to 102. "How long have you been sick? And what have you taken?"

His face fell.

Had he been thinking he wasn't that sick? And was that pizza on the table?

"I woke up feeling miserable in the middle of the night Friday." He turned, coughed violently, and then faced her again. "I haven't taken much of anything."

"Nothing to reduce that fever?"

"I found one aspirin in the bottom of a bottle yesterday morning, but I don't think it did any good." He stared at the floor.

At least he realized he was being an idiot.

"And you're eating pizza?"

"It's all that delivers. Kind of hard to believe. There was this incredible deli a block from my apartment in New York that delivered soup and mac and cheese and pudding. It was perfect when you were sick." His scratchy voice was laced with longing.

Abby rested her hands on her hips. They weren't in New York. Here in the harsh, uncivilized world of rural Missouri, a man was supposed to know enough to keep some canned soup on hand and something for a fever. But now wasn't the time to mention that.

She handed him the coloring page, which she had labeled "Thank you, Love, Emma."

He looked a bit confused.

"For the toy dog," Abby said.

Nate studied picture and smiled weakly at Emma. "The butterflies are very pretty."

"Thank you," Emma said. She took a step closer.

Abby caught her by the shoulder and pulled her back onto the landing. "Emma, Nate's sick. You don't want to catch his cold."

Emma retreated slightly and returned to petting Bear.

Abby turned back to Nate. "Give me a minute and I'll bring you some of the things I keep on hand for when Emma or I get sick. Some acetaminophen, juice, noodle soup mix..."

His eyes widened as if she had offered to donate a kidney for him. "That would be great. I was thinking I might need to call my aunt and uncle and ask them to bring me some juice and something for the fever. I'll repay you, I promise."

"Don't worry about it." She started down the stairs. "I'll be right back."

"There was something I wanted to..." He scratched his lopsided hair. "Oh, yeah. The whole park history thing. I took care of it."

Abby's heart leapt. "You did?"

"No need to give it another thought. People simply needed to be reminded of the historic importance of the park."

"Really? I can't believe it."

He frowned. "Well, I don't mean to sound like an arrogant jerk, but compared to things I handled in New York, this was...small potatoes." He shrugged as if he felt uncomfortable with the conversation. "Not even potatoes. Grains of rice, maybe."

"Oh." She hadn't thought of it like that. Neva did say he'd been a high-powered lawyer in Manhattan. Getting people to agree to preserve Rose Park probably was a pretty minor thing for him. It was a little insulting, the way he worded it, but... Hold on. What mattered was that the park was saved. "Thank you."

Tension she hadn't even acknowledged eased in Abby's shoulders as what he'd done finally sunk in. All her worry and effort collecting signatures and the only thing she'd needed to do was talk to Nate.

Who was now even paler.

He swayed slightly and mumbled something.

"You'd better lie down," she told him. "C'mon Bear, you probably need to go out."

The big black dog led the way down the stairs.

Abby followed, holding Emma's hand. Rose Park was saved. Doris would be so pleased. It could remain exactly as it had been, a place where people could remember Rose, where Doris could remember her husband. Where Abby could remember Eric.

It was important to remember people after they were gone.

And stay loyal to that memory.

She was incredibly grateful to Nate for his help. But bringing a guy a few cans of soup did not—by any stretch of the imagination—mean she was interested in him.

She was simply being a good neighbor.

Nate jerked awake, sat up, and looked around.

Oh. Someone was knocking at the door.

Abby. With Bear, apparently, from the snuffling about and the jingle of dog tags.

Nate heaved himself off the couch.

Too fast. The room tipped, then righted itself.

"Nate? Are you okay?" Abby called through the door.

Not really. *Okay* didn't mean feeling like he might topple over or like his body could be used as a space heater. He wiped a hand over his brow, pulled off his hoodie, and stumbled toward the door.

"Hi." He peered out, impressed that he'd been able to walk—and speak. Two accomplishments stacked on top of each other. Pretty amazing, considering how he felt.

"Hi." Abby held out a small glass bowl and had a large basket propped on one hip. Emma stood beside her, petting Bear.

Nate reached for the bowl. "Is this—?"

"Vanilla pudding. It's Emma's favorite. I made some last night, and it was leftover in the fridge."

Nate's heart grew light. Vanilla pudding. The very thing he'd been dreaming of, though he didn't quite understand the concept of leftover pudding. If there was pudding available, he ate it. All of it. "It looks delicious." He carried it to the kitchen counter and gently set it down. Buoyed by the thought of pudding, he made it back to the door.

Abby shifted the basket off her hip and held it out with both hands. "I brought two cans of tomato soup and chicken noodle soup mix and those zinc lozenges and a half gallon of apple juice—sorry I didn't have any orange, but it's got vitamin C—and acetaminophen and a box of tissues. Oh, and a bottle of Gatorade I had in my fridge."

Her words tumbled out, nervous.

Was she afraid he'd reject her care package?

Not a chance.

Nate took the basket like a drowning man offered a life vest and carefully set it on the coffee table. "Thank you. I can't tell you how much I appreciate this." He pulled out the Gatorade and held it against his forehead. Blessedly cool.

Her eyelashes fluttered and her cheeks turned slightly pink. "You're welcome."

In spite of the fever, in spite of his dizziness, he noticed that blush, noticed how sweet and pretty she looked.

And he was practically a biohazard. He took a step back. "Uh, I better let you go. I don't want you or Emma to get sick."

"Emma, you need to let go of Bear," Abby said.

Emma gave the dog a final hug, and Nate called him inside.

For a second, Bear appeared torn, then he ambled in and flopped down beside the couch.

"Thanks again," Nate said.

"Bye," Abby called. She and Emma disappeared down the stairs.

Nate shut the door, got the acetaminophen out of the basket, and washed down three with some Gatorade. Then he grabbed a spoon and snagged the pudding.

He took a big bite. In spite of his congested nose, he could taste the vanilla flavor. He savored it as long as possible before he let it slide down his throat, cool and soothing. Already he felt better.

Maybe living in Abundance wasn't so bad. Not with someone like Abby stopping by.

What more could a guy want in a neighbor?

He propped his back against the arm of the couch, stretched his legs out on the cushions, and stared toward the front door with the pudding bowl on his lap, the question still in his mind.

What more could a guy want?

Not much, of course.

Except all of her.

A life with her.

A home with her.

Chapter Seven

"We've been waiting until you got here to start revising this nurse-recruitment brochure." Harris Flaherty, Frankie's new boss, turned down a hallway on the first floor of the hospital, his shoes squeaking on the gleaming tiles. "The director of nursing has been chomping at the bit, but I wanted your input. I think we need a more current design."

"I agree," Frankie said. The brochure could have used updating ten years ago, but she didn't want to tell her boss that, especially since Harris could use a bit of updating himself. In his early fifties, sporting a graying comb-over, he was chubby and wore a suit with too much sheen to it. Harris, a former reporter, must allocate his money for clothes with the same frugality he'd needed when he worked at the local newspaper. As public relations manager, though, he had a solid reputation for dealing straight with the media and staying calm in a crisis. If he needed her to bring a bit of style to the office and to the hospital's publications, she was ready.

She wanted everything here at her new job to go well, wanted a good start for her and Kira in Abundance. After two days of orientation from human resources, and then a marathon weekend of unpacking until midnight each night while trying to make their little house into a real home, Monday had arrived. Frankie had spent the morning and early afternoon talking with Harris and meeting more people. At last she was getting to work on a public-relations project.

In spite of the presence of Cooper Sullivan in town, this move was going to be a good thing.

Frankie and Harris entered a hallway that smelled of popcorn left in the microwave too long. Another corner and at last they came to the office of the director of nursing.

"Remember what I said earlier," Harris said under his breath.

The head of nursing was, in Harris's words, so tough she could make a Marine whimper. There was a good chance that the woman had to be tough. All the rest of the hospital administrators were male, and most of the physicians. But, since it was only Frankie's third day on the job, she kept quiet about that point as well.

She merely nodded, switched her notebook and phone to her other arm, and smoothed her bright-green sheath over her hips. The hospital here in Abundance wasn't an academic medical center, like the hospital where she'd worked in Houston. She wouldn't be doing brochures on bypass surgery and neuro-ophthalmology.

In fact, the little town's hospital was more of an outpost. Nurse recruitment probably was one the biggest projects of the year, and from what Frankie had heard, the trickiest.

Harris reached a hand toward the door, and Frankie's phone rang. One of the new numbers she'd programmed in so she could recognize them showed on the screen, the Abundance Community Center. She backed away from the door. "I need to take this. It's my daughter's childcare."

Harris's mouth became a thin, horizontal line. "I'll get things started." He walked into the outer office, toward a secretary.

The door shut behind him with a sharp click, and Frankie answered the call.

"Mrs. McNamara? I'm so glad we reached you. Kira's got a fever of 102.3. We think it's that virus that's going around. You'll have to come get her immediately."

"A hundred and two?" Yikes. The poor thing. But talk about bad timing. The community center had made it clear that their childcare did not have a sickroom and that—unlike the facility Kira had attended back in Houston—parents were expected to be there within a half hour if their child became ill. It wouldn't make a good impression, her third day on the job, but as a woman on her own, Frankie would need to go in and make her excuses and—

But she wasn't on her own. Here in Abundance, she had help—not like her Houston friends who worked full-time—but from her mom, who didn't.

Frankie assured the childcare director that someone

would pick up Kira immediately and dialed her parent's house.

"Mom, Kira's got a fever. Could you pick her up from the community center and stay with her for a couple of hours until I get home from work?"

"Oh, Frankie, I wish I could," Mom said in a weak voice. "I can't drive right now."

"Why not?" Had she come down with the virus too?

"The doctor thinks it's best."

A quiver ran through Frankie's stomach. Mom wouldn't go the doctor for a virus. "The doctor thinks it's best because…"

"Well, um, I had a seizure a couple of weeks ago. I can watch Kira at the house though."

Frankie nearly dropped the phone. "A seizure? Are you all right? And why…why didn't you tell me?"

"Your father and I didn't want to worry you. The doctor says it's just a precaution. That he's almost certain I'm fine."

Mom didn't sound worried, and she wasn't one to miss an opportunity to fret, so she probably was all right. But still… Frankie found a spot in the hallway that wasn't near anyone's office door. "I'm your daughter. Don't you think you should have told me?"

"You were so far away." Mom's words held that note that always made Frankie feel guilty, even when she hadn't done anything wrong. "Now that you're here, well, it will be nice if you can drive me to my appointments for all these tests the doctor's running. Days like today, when your father's in court, it's hard to get around."

Frankie hadn't even thought of that. Could barely keep up with the information that Mom was revealing. And she had to find a solution for Kira. "We'll have to talk about that later. You said Dad's in court. What about Nate? Do you think he might be able to get her?" He'd been sick and missed church yesterday, but maybe it was just a twenty-four-hour thing. Even if Kira didn't know him well, he was her cousin and she'd been around him a couple of times in the past week.

"Dad said Nate called in sick this morning because he could barely get off the couch."

Tension crept up Frankie's throat, and she started back toward her meeting. No Mom, no Dad, no Nate. She was going to have to make her excuses to Harris and the director of nursing. Not the way to start a new PR project, or a new job, especially not the job that had to work out to make this move successful. But somehow, some way, she would fix things at work. She couldn't fail her little girl. "I need to go get Kira, Mom, but we'll talk later. I want to hear more about what's going on with your health."

"Give Kira a hug for me. You're lucky you have a job where you can leave anytime, unlike your father's. He just can't leave the courtroom."

"Uh...yeah. Bye, Mom." Frankie hung up. With a less accommodating childcare facility and her parents viewing her move to Abundance as a way she could help them, not the other way around, things were going to be difficult.

Oh, she wouldn't get charged with contempt of court, but she'd bet her next paycheck that Harris would not see her leaving the office "anytime" as fine.

Thursday morning Nate walked out of his office with Thornton Miller.

"Thanks, buddy." Thornton shook Nate's hand.

"Don't worry. I'll discuss this with Al, but I'm sure taking you on as a client will be fine. We'll get things straightened out." Nate led the way into the lobby.

"I appreciate it," Thornton said. His easy grin, which had been absent when he appeared at the law office earlier, was back, peeking out from under his thick mustache. Whether a client was a good ol' boy plumber like Thornton or a slick, high-powered executive from Manhattan, they usually needed reassurance when criminal charges were involved.

Luckily Nate had been in. He'd struggled to the office on Tuesday, despite his illness, and only today felt normal.

Al stood by Jewel's desk, searching through a stack of folders. "Morning, Thornton," He called through the little sliding window of her office.

"Morning, Al." Thornton pulled on his Abundance Feed Store ball cap and left the office, letting in a wave of heat from outside.

"Aha!" Al extracted a folder from the pile and held it high. "Found it." Al, on his first day back after having the bug, still looked rather ashen.

"We're both floundering a bit with Jewel out sick, aren't we?" Nate said.

"This is the first day she's missed in two years."

Which was possibly Nate's fault. Maybe he should have stayed home Tuesday.

Al walked into the lobby and angled his head toward the front door. "You're considering representing Thornton?"

"I guess you heard about what happened?"

"Word does tend to get around when a man cleaning his gun in his apartment accidentally sends a bullet through his ceiling, into the fish tank of his upstairs neighbor."

Nate gave a half shrug. Despite the fact that Thornton had probably made himself the laughingstock of Abundance, Nate liked the guy.

"He's very fortunate that no one was injured." Al stepped into his office, then returned without the folder. "I've got no problem with you representing him, but"— he tipped his head to one side, and deep creases formed on his forehead—"how do you know him?"

"Uh…" Nate smoothed a lump out of the corner of the lobby's Oriental rug with one foot. A good question. A reasonable question. But a question he couldn't answer. Replies that had worked in these situations back in New York—a mutual friend or membership in the same organization—weren't good options. He couldn't think of a thing to say that was honest, and he couldn't spell out that he'd met Thornton at a support group meeting. That information was confidential.

"Ah-hh." The deeper lines eased in Al's forehead as if he somehow knew. "That reminds me. I've got to run over to the courthouse, but there's something I've been meaning to tell you." He dug into his pants pocket and then held his hand toward Nate, palm up.

A large bronze coin with the Roman numeral four in the center.

Nate picked up the AA chip and studied it. It was heavy for its size.

Maybe that was because it held so much meaning.

And he hadn't had a clue. No wonder Al had been so gracious in offering Nate a job. "How... How long?" Nate stammered.

"I've been a recovering alcoholic for twenty years," Al said. "It's been almost five years since my last drink." He pulled an index card from the pocket of his suit jacket. "You seem like you've been doing well so far, but I want you to remember two things. First, you need to read these." He handed the card to Nate.

In Al's neat, almost straight-up-and-down script, Nate read:

1 John 1:9

Isaiah 41:10

"Those will help you remember"—Al coughed—"that God loves you and offers you strength." He barely managed to get the words out before a coughing spasm overtook him.

Nate tried to look grateful for the card. He knew a lot of people found great comfort in the Bible. So far, he hadn't. The little bit he'd read of it recently only brought him guilt, and he had enough guilt every time he thought about the accident and how Ashley had been injured. He waited until Al stopped coughing, then looked back at him. "And the other thing you want me to remember?"

"That Vivian and I believe in you," Al said. His voice,

though scratchy, rang with solid support. He clapped Nate on the shoulder and headed out the office door.

Nate felt as though a tropical ocean wave had gently washed over him. He let out a long breath, headed to his office, and typed first one Scripture reference into the search bar on his computer, then the other.

If we confess our sins, he who is faithful and just will forgive us our sins and cleanse us from all unrighteousness. 1 John 1:9 (NRSV)

Do not fear, for I am with you, do not be afraid, for I am your God; I will strengthen you, I will help you, I will uphold you with my victorious right hand.
Isaiah 41:10 (NRSV)

Nate closed the website. Those verses sounded nice, but they didn't matter when it came to someone like him. He even vaguely remembered from Sunday school when he was a kid that God forgave. But Nate was pretty sure God had a limit to what he could forgive, a limit Nate had far exceeded.

God didn't have any great love for him.

But he had Al and Vivian, support he hadn't been expecting.

And he hadn't accidentally shot up somebody's fish tank.

The big slice of peach pie with ice cream on top was the perfect reward.

Cooper scooped up the last bite, tipped the plate to catch some melted vanilla ice cream, and slid the spoonful into his mouth. The piecrust was flaky, the peaches tasted like they had ripened on the tree, and the ice cream had real, old-fashioned flavor—not like that cheap kind that came in a giant plastic tub.

Cassidy's Diner was authentic, in every sense. The gray counter with a wide silver ledge, the little glass salt and pepper shakers, the booths, which—except two that were brown vinyl instead of red—looked original. And his meal tasted right out of 1962. Mashed potatoes made with real butter, fried chicken, and—best of all—homemade pie. No wonder the place was packed. Cooper held onto the flavor of the pie until it was only a memory and glanced over toward Grace, the owner of the diner.

"Another slice?" she said.

"No thanks," he said, "but it was excellent." He didn't have pie every single time he came in, but almost.

Today he had definitely earned it.

Dad himself couldn't have handled Cooper's morning meetings better. Two local businesses, a barber shop and a nail salon, were both eager to lease space in The Main Place. This summer, Cooper had been scrambling so hard to impress Dad that he hadn't even made it into St. Louis to see a Cardinals game. Maybe it was finally paying off.

He tapped the email on his phone. Had Dad read his email about the meeting yet? No, but there was a message from Nate Redmond.

Cooper skimmed it. The farther he read, the lower he sank into the red vinyl booth.

Question after question after question.

Each one seemed to add to the heat building in his chest. Maybe Nate was simply far more experienced than most of the people Cooper dealt with. More likely, Nate had talked to his cousin Frankie and was now suspicious of every detail in the proposal.

Couldn't Cooper ever make a good impression on her?

Memories of the last time he'd seen Frankie and Garrett together, maybe a year before he heard they got divorced, played in Cooper's head like a movie.

He'd been working construction in Columbia, a job Dad had conveniently gotten him so that he could get "more real-world experience" and "fully understand real estate." The fact that the summer was the hottest on record and the grueling job was on the Mizzou campus, where he should have earned his degree, was in no way coincidental.

Cooper had stopped on his way home for a carryout pizza. He'd been coated in sweat and grime, but lured in by a coupon and so exhausted that he was certain if he went home to shower first, he'd never make it out the door to find food. Right inside the restaurant door, he'd found Garrett and Frankie in a booth near the cash register, in town for some alumni event.

As usual, being around Frankie had made it hard to think straight. She'd been wearing a green sundress and high-heeled green sandals. How sad was it when a man could remember a woman's shoes? He'd awkwardly laughed and joked with them, acting like he and Garrett chatted all the time on social media. Which they didn't. Because Cooper was working ten hour days. By the time a shift ended, every bit of his body, including his thumbs, was tired. Tapping out messages on his phone held no appeal.

At last his pizza had been ready and he'd stopped at their table to say goodbye. Awkwardly, he'd tried to hide his feeling for Frankie, to come up with something that sounded like he was sincerely happy they were married. He'd whacked Garrett on the back and said, "Frankie, you are so lucky to have this guy."

She'd paled. He could still remember it. Probably because of how bad he smelled. He'd hurried out, driven home, and showered, then eaten the whole pizza and thought about the woman his friend had married. The woman he'd always dreamed of.

The woman who was now being a real pain.

Cooper walked to the diner register, racking his brain for a solution. More than any other deal, this one mattered. He had to convince his dad, once and for all, that he could handle the company.

Maybe what he needed was information. He paid his bill, left a sizable tip on the table, and stepped outside to send a text message to Mimi, a mutual friend from freshman year who he still kept in touch with. Did she have a moment to talk?

By the time he'd gone two blocks, she'd replied. If he called right now, she was free.

Cooper climbed in his truck. He should have left a window open. He lowered the windows, turned the engine off, and dialed, careful not to touch the steering wheel, which was hot enough to leave singe marks.

"Hey, it's Cooper."

"Cooper! How's life in the high-powered world of real estate development?"

"Not very high powered, but going okay. How's life as a professor?"

"Assistant professor, which means it's stressful. But I do have a paper coming out next month that might help me get tenure."

Mimi taught in the same business school where Cooper had flunked out. He tried to appreciate the irony and failed. "Congrats," he said.

"Thanks. What can I do for you?"

He explained about his run-in with Frankie, emphasizing how good the development would be for the little town, how he needed to win her over.

"I don't know how to help you, Cooper. I haven't seen her in years. Last thing I heard was that she and Garrett got divorced."

"Yeah. I knew that."

"I don't know if this is true, but I heard Garrett cheated on Frankie. Apparently she tried for two years to get him to quit and to work things out, but he wasn't interested."

Cooper's stomach drew up in a knot. He punched at the volume on his phone, but it was already all the way up. Even so, maybe he'd heard wrong. "For two years before the divorce?"

"That's what I was told."

He hadn't heard wrong. The more he thought about it, the tighter the knot grew in his stomach. "I had no idea," he mumbled. No idea he had been so dumb. No idea that Garrett had been cheating on her when he ran into them in Columbia. And no idea that Frankie had known.

Honestly, Cooper thought he might throw up. Because what had he said? He'd told Frankie she was lucky to have Garrett.

She hadn't paled because he'd needed a shower. She'd paled because he said she was lucky to be married to a guy who was cheating on her.

No wonder she hated him.

"Hey, I've got a class starting in ten minutes," Mimi said. "I'd better organize my notes."

Cooper thanked her, told her they'd get together one day soon, and hung up.

He dropped his elbows onto the steering wheel and sank his head into his hands. After a moment, the heat of the steering wheel registered in his brain, and he moved his arms back. Mostly though, what registered was the fact that he was an idiot. Not only did he need to get on Frankie's good side to ensure the development went through and convince Dad to have the surgery.

He needed to ask for her forgiveness.

Chapter Eight

Either having Nate babysit Kira would go well, or it would be a disaster.

Frankie parked in front of the florist shop and opened Kira's car door. This evening would be fine. She shouldn't worry so much.

She'd tried to find a nice teenage girl to babysit, but all the girls Mom had suggested had been busy. And Kira and Nate were both over their illnesses. But Nate didn't seem like a guy who'd spent many Friday nights with little kids. Then there was his dog. Nate said it was friendly, but would it be friendly to a five-year-old girl?

"Frankie? Is that you?"

The woman walking toward her looked like someone she should know, but—"Abby Hamlin?"

"Well, I'm Abby Kincaid now," she said in a soft voice.

"Oh, sorry," Frankie said. Of course, Abby had

married Eric, who Mom had said had been killed. Should Frankie bring that up today, years later? Probably not, unless Abby mentioned it. Instead, Frankie put a hand on Kira's shoulder, about to introduce her.

Abby, though, had already knelt down to Kira's level. "Hi, I'm Mrs. Kincaid. What's your name?"

Kira answered.

A prickly feeling filled Frankie's chest. Would Abby see Kira's big brown eyes, two dark braids, and dimples? Would she see that Kira was a sweetheart who was one of the smartest kids in her preschool class? Or would she only see Kira's leg braces?

Abby gave no indication that she even noticed the braces. "I have a little girl who's about your age. She's four."

"I'm five," Kira said.

Abby tipped her head in acknowledgment. "What do you think?" she said to Kira, in a grownup-to-grownup tone. "Would you be too old to play with someone who just turned four?"

"No," Kira said with certainty. "We'd have fun."

"Wonderful! Emma ran in to get a drink of water, but she'll be right back." Abby stood, then looked again at Kira. "Frankie, your daughter is beautiful." Sincerity rang in her words, and she pulled Frankie into a hug. "And it's so good to see you."

This—this was what Frankie had come back to Abundance for. This kindness. This welcome. This comfort that felt as warm as pajamas right out of the dryer. From people who didn't care that Kira had been born with Achilles tendons that were too short and that she had to wear braces on her legs. Frankie squeezed Abby tightly. "It's good to see you too."

A little girl with strawberry-blonde curls bounded off the porch of the antique shop and ran toward them. Abby proudly introduced her as Emma.

After asking her mother's permission, Emma led Kira down the sidewalk to show her the picture she'd drawn with sidewalk chalk. By the time they'd gone twenty feet, the two of them looked inseparable.

Abby angled her head toward the antique store. "My shop is the only one in town supporting the arts by providing drawings on the sidewalk."

"Your shop?"

"I bought it from Royce Danner right before he died. Well, if you can call it that. He sold it to me for five dollars. Said he didn't have any family. I still can't get over how generous he was. I don't know what I would have done otherwise, after Eric was gone."

Frankie laid a hand on her arm. "I heard about that. I'm so sorry."

"Thank you." Abby's eyes seemed to focus on something far away, then return. "I figured you knew, even though you moved away. The small-town thing. And I heard you're single now."

"Yeah. Sure to remain that way since I've moved to Abundance. It's not exactly overflowing with eligible men."

"True, but you never know. You might find just the right person."

"With the way my marriage ended, I don't even want to." Frankie let out a soft chuckle. "We should get together sometime. I've got a special event at the hospital tonight, though. My cousin's babysitting." She turned and called toward the antique shop. "Kira, come on. I need to drop you off upstairs with Nate."

"I'll save you the trip," Nate said from the top of the stairs. When he was halfway down, an enormous black dog squeezed around him and let out a woof. Seconds later the dog wriggled his way between Frankie and Abby, wagging his shaggy tail.

Frankie gave the dog a small pat on the head. "He...she..." She pointed to the dog.

"He," Abby said.

"He seems friendly." Frankie brushed some long black dog hair off her white skirt.

"He is," Abby said. "No need to worry about that. And gentle. He's been around Emma a lot."

Nate joined them on the sidewalk just as Kira and Emma returned.

"Are you okay on the stairs?" he asked Kira.

The prickles returned to Frankie's chest. Surely Nate wasn't going to make Kira feel like some breakable ornament because of her braces. She wanted to be treated like any other kid.

"Or should I carry you like this?" He grabbed Kira under the arms, zigzagged her back and forth a bit, weaving her toward the sky, then turned her upside-down over his shoulder. Breakable didn't seem to have entered Nate's mind.

Kira burst out giggling.

"Me next!" Emma cried.

Frankie's chest eased. This was going to work. "I

94

think my daughter and cousin will get along fine, don't you?" she said to Abby.

Abby didn't seem to notice. Her gaze was fixed on Nate. The same Nate who had told Frankie in no uncertain terms that his last relationship back in New York was over, who was now standing much closer to Abby than to her.

Frankie studied the two of them. She might not find "just the right person" in Abundance.

But Nate might.

Nate turned Kira right-side up and whispered something in her ear.

She squealed so loudly that he recoiled and made a face.

Abby couldn't hold in her laughter. What a goofball. He'd be a great baby-sitter for Kira. Though in the future, with the way the girls seemed to be hitting it off, she'd be happy to help Frankie out herself.

Kira giggled and turned toward Emma. "Nate bought Play-Doh. Eight colors. And a Fun Factory! Ask your mom if you can come over."

"Nate, you shouldn't buy Kira stuff. You'll spoil her," Frankie's words came straight out of the mom handbook, but a grin spread over her face.

"It's not hers," Nate said. "I'm keeping it. I will, however, let Kira and"—he raised his eyebrows at Emma—"her friends play with it when they come over."

Abby glanced over at Nate. Wasn't that kind of him, including her girl, Emma? Really, he didn't have to.

Emma's soft little hand slid into Abby's and gave a gentle tug. "Pleeease, Mommy? Can I go play with Kira?"

"Are you sure you don't mind if we join you for a bit?" Abby said. She didn't want to impose.

"Not at all," Nate said. Once again, he looked like he belonged in a magazine ad. Maybe for toothpaste. A brand whose target market was women who were attracted to men with classic good looks and dark-blue eyes.

Abby let her gaze linger on him for a moment, and nerves jumped in her stomach. That had to be a pretty big target market. Nate was—

Stop it. So what if he was handsome. Really handsome. She wasn't interested. She was going over for Emma's sake, nothing more. "We'll stop by for a little while, but it's almost time for dinner, Emma. It's Friday, remember? Pizza."

Nate put Kira down. "The Play-Doh is in a bag on my kitchen table."

The girls and Bear headed up the stairs, Bear's tags jingling and Emma slowing a little to match Kira's pace. Abby would have to remember to tell her how nice that was later on.

"You all have fun." Frankie said. "I'll be back before eight-thirty. I'll have my phone on if you need me, Nate. And thank you. You really are a blessing."

"Me? Hardly," Nate called to Frankie. "But I do feel like the fun uncle. I always wanted a fun uncle." He stopped and shot a look at Frankie. "Not that Al, uh…"

Frankie chuckled. "I know. Dad's more the kind of

uncle who gives you a nice graduation check."

"And a job," Nate said in an overly loud voice. "A job I'm extremely grateful to have."

Frankie waved away his comment, gave Abby a wink, and walked toward her car.

Abby took a half-step back. What was that wink for?

"Was it too obvious?" Nate asked. "That I was trying to get my foot out of my mouth with that last bit?"

"Oh, no," Abby lied. "I'm sure Frankie didn't think that." It had only been obvious to anyone over the age of five.

"Well, I doubt Al will fire me tomorrow," Nate said. "You should see the stack of cases he dropped on my desk the other day. Abundance must have had a town-wide Make-a-Will Day."

Abby followed him up the stairs and into his apartment.

She'd paid little attention when Nate had been sick, had barely stepped in the door. But now she could see that Neva Cartwright hadn't exactly gone all out when she'd redone the place, especially not the kitchen. The fridge wasn't dorm-sized, but it was about a foot shorter than Abby's. The stove had two burners and an oven that might fit a bread pan if it went in lengthwise, and the floor was made of rubber tiles with interlocking tabs along the sides, circa 1959 if she had to guess. The girls sat smack-dab in the middle of that kitchen floor, ripping open cans of Play-Doh. The minute Nate walked in, though, Kira got up.

"Nate," she said, pointing to a candy jar. "What are those?"

"Sour-cherry hard candies. My favorite."

Within seconds, both girls had decided the candies were their favorites as well. They returned to the Play-Doh, and Nate led Abby into the living room.

A couch and a chair in black leather and shiny metal sat near a glass-topped coffee table. No pictures on the white walls, no pillows or—

"It's a little stark, I know. I have paintings to hang, but I haven't, what with being sick."

"It's very nice." She sank into one end of the black leather couch. Not her taste. Far too modern, to be sure, but the upholstery was very soft, very upscale.

"Speaking of being sick," Nate said, "I can't thank you enough for the supplies you brought over. I went to the store last night and replaced them." He sat in the chair across from her and angled his head toward her basket on the floor by the TV. Inside, two plastic bags bulged with supplies.

"I was happy to help." She studied the bag of cold supplies more closely.

Zinc lozenges and a bottle of apple juice peeked out. As did a big purple plastic bottle that proudly proclaimed *Includes Super Bubble Wand.*

Her heart gave a lurch, as if it were sliding over some obstruction in her chest. An obstruction that she'd been able to keep in place when Nate bought Play-Doh for his cousin. But that bottle of bubbles for Emma, which probably cost sixty-nine cents, did her in. She couldn't lie to herself any more. She wanted to be here.

And not just for Emma.

"Uh, now that you're feeling better, what are you

thinking about Abundance?" she asked, keeping her voice light. "Are you liking it here?" She gestured to the window and immediately jerked her hand back. She must look like a flight attendant, pointing out the exits. She smoothed her hand over the hem of her jean shorts, then tucked it under her thigh.

His gaze met hers, but he gave no indication that he had noticed her making a fool of herself. "I am liking it here," he said, sounding a little surprised at his own words. "I wasn't sure how I'd adjust to a small town, but I'm coming to appreciate the connectedness, like seeing people at the discount store and recognizing them from the diner. And people are so nice. You, with the soup and the pudding and the medicine, and people I've never even met. I forgot my wallet the other day when I went to Whole Hog Barbecue. They told me to pay the next time I was in."

"You do realize that folks know who you are? And they certainly know where you work, and probably even where you live."

"It was still nice. And, well, this may seem odd, but I drove out to the north edge of town yesterday, out to where Sixth Street becomes some county road, and I just stared across the cornfields, at the open expanse of the horizon with no buildings." He glanced at the floor. "It was kind of...freeing."

An odd tingle ran through Abby's chest. "Yeah," she said slowly. "I know that spot, and I know what you mean."

Outside, thunder rumbled, hinting at a storm. Inside, the tingle in Abby's chest grew.

Hold on. She needed to get over herself. The odd feeling in her chest was from the electricity of the coming storm. The fact that they both liked the same view was simply a coincidence. Probably lots of people liked it and just didn't mention it.

"So, tell me about your work with antiques." Nate leaned toward her, elbows on his knees. "Have you been interested in them for a long time?"

Yes. This was much better. She could talk about antiques all night. "I started working at Antiques in Abundance when I was in high school."

"What attracted you? Finding hidden treasures?"

"Not exactly." Everyone always thought that, and it was part of it, but not the main thing, not for her. "I'd say the design and the history. I was an art history major."

"I took some art history classes. It makes you appreciate things more, doesn't it?"

"Yeah." Her voice came out weird. But he got it. Like Royce. Nobody else in her world seemed to. Except her cousin Jack, but despite being a wildlife artist, he wasn't one to chat about art. Until he'd married Tess, he hadn't been one to chat, period.

Eric had never understood. He'd been an accounting major. Yes, she'd gotten a double major in business, at his urging and that of her parents and Royce, and yes, she did use that knowledge almost every day. Those classes, though, and that part of the job, never brought her joy.

"I went to a great lecture about a year ago," Nate said. "About the Turkish elements in Vermeer's work."

Excitement bubbled in Abby's chest, taking up all the space and leaving no room for the unsettled feelings that had seemed to swamp her. She hadn't been around anyone who cared about an artist like Vermeer since Royce died, and oh, how she had missed talking about art. "Tell me about it." She slid off her sandals and tucked her feet under her on the couch, knees angled to one side.

"So, the lecturer was a guy from England," Nate began. And, even though months had passed, he told her all about the lecture, as if the whole evening was there in his brain, point by point.

Before long she was telling him about the photography classes she'd taken, and Nate was saying how he missed the restaurants and the view from his apartment and the feeling of importance that had been part of every day in New York.

And then suddenly, the girls shrieked with laughter.

Bear jerked his head up and barked.

Abby looked over.

Bear had laid his head back on his paws. Everything seemed fine.

Nate, though, moved to the other end of the couch, facing the kitchen, and he gave the dog a warning stare.

Bear settled back down to sleep.

But now Nate was much closer than he'd been in the chair with the coffee table between them, and the unsettled tingle had returned Abby's chest. She let out a slow breath and tried to act calm.

Nate turned to her and repositioned himself on the couch, a couple of inches closer.

She caught a whiff of his cologne, fresh and light and outdoorsy.

He looked over at her. There was something in his

eyes she couldn't read. Something that seemed to pull at her. Something—

"Mommy?" Emma appeared at Abby's side. "I'm hungry."

Abby jumped up. The microwave on the kitchen counter said it was almost seven. She'd gotten so caught up talking that she hadn't even realized.

Emma tapped her on the thigh. "Can Kira and Nate come over for pizza?"

Abby turned toward Nate. "Um..." Talking was one thing, but having him over—she couldn't. It wouldn't be right. It would be disloyal to Eric. It would be—

"Would you and Kira like to join us?"

Abby swallowed. That had been her voice.

"We'd love to," Nate said.

What had she done?

Chapter Nine

The pizza delivery had been too fast.

The meal had been eaten too quickly.

The time with Abby was ending too soon.

Nate sat at one end of the wooden kitchen table, with Emma on one side, Kira on the other, and Abby at the other end, in a room that, in spite of the modern appliances, felt as if it had fallen back in time. The old-fashioned sink. The checkered place mats. The wall calendar from the feed store.

Would it be rude to have another cookie? Abby had taken the oatmeal-raisin cookies out of a cookie jar shaped like a big white clock and placed them on a flowered china plate. They were definitely homemade. Definitely delicious. He took his fourth cookie and inhaled its sweet scent. Butter, cinnamon, and something else he couldn't identify. Molasses maybe. If he ate slowly, it might prolong the evening.

All too soon, the cookie was gone. And, judging by the clock on the stove, all too soon Abby's grandfather clock would strike eight, making it even harder to extend the evening.

"May I be excused?" With one sentence, Emma ended the meal.

"Yes, you may." Abby rose and took Kira and Emma's plates to the sink.

"Let me help you," Nate jumped up and brought over his own dishes.

"Thank you for dinner," Kira said.

Frankie would be proud of her daughter's good manners, but Nate wished the girl hadn't been taught so well. The comment sounded too final, like he and Kira should leave. And he wanted to stay. Wanted more time for talking with Abby. Wanted more time to see her beautiful face, to appreciate how green her hazel eyes looked with the shirt she was wearing. And he wanted more of the way she made him feel like everything he said was important.

Which was insane. Just because she was beautiful and kind and sweet and right next door did not mean she'd want to get involved with him. If she did, he'd have to tell her the truth, and that would end everything. How could he stand it if he somehow earned the love of a woman like Abby and then lost it when she learned about his past?

But she seemed like she'd come to accept his profession, in spite of what happened with her husband. She'd been upset about Rose Park, but the city was going to put up a plaque at the new park, so that was taken care of.

Was there anyway she could forgive his addiction? Any way she could understand the pressure he'd been under in New York, the shame and regret he felt for what he'd done? Any way she could see that he wanted to be a new person and have a new life—one where he could date a woman like her?

No.

The guy who'd killed her husband had been an addict.

Like he had been.

Like he could be again.

"Emma, why don't you bring down the jewelry case?" Abby took the place mats off the table and wiped up the crumbs. "I bet Kira would love to sit here with you and play princess and see all the royal jewels."

"You have jewelry?" Kira's eyes sparkled.

"Tons of it," Emma said. "It's not really real, but my mom saves all the best princess stuff for me."

"Cool." Kira's voice held awe and she looked at Abby with big eyes.

"I'm Princess Aurora," Emma said. "You can be Princess…"

"Chloe," Kira said immediately.

Nate looked at her. Clearly, this princess stuff was way more important than he'd realized when his sisters played it as kids. Legos he could see getting excited about, but a bunch of fake rings?

"I'll go get the jewelry," Emma said, as she raced from the room.

Abby called after her. "Remember your royal—"

The racing steps slowed, then went up the stairs.

Abby put the leftover pizza in her fridge. "I can deal with the dishes later, Nate." She pointed to a door that led off the kitchen. "Would you like to go on the screened-in porch while the girls play in here?"

Alone with Abby. On the screened-in porch. He needed to say no. He was setting himself up for pain.

But it had been almost a year. He felt more grounded. More like himself with the park and the pro bono case he'd been working on. More like the man he wanted to be.

"It's so nice for Emma to have a friend over," Abby said. "She and Kira really seem to be hitting it off."

See? It would be cruel to separate the girls. "Sitting on the porch would be great." He opened the door for Abby.

The porch was small and appeared to have been added onto the house by a previous homeowner, a do-it-yourselfer who could have used professional advice. The floor slanted and one of the boards between the screened sections was slightly angled.

"I love to sit out here in the evenings." Abby flipped on the ceiling fan, making the air, which still held some of the humidity of the day, the perfect temperature.

"I can see why." Despite the off-kilter carpentry, he could. Earlier, it had seemed like it might rain, but the storm must have blown past. Now the setting sun made the sky a mix of orange streaks and the rich blue of twilight. A row of evergreens blocked the view of the house that sat back-to-back with the antique shop. A little vase of sweet-smelling white flowers sat on a small table, and a couch and a wicker rocker held blankets and pillows and the promise of relaxation. The whole room made him think of a time when phones were heavy and black and sat on tables, when life ran at a rhythm instead of 24/7, when no one had ever heard of people pushing themselves so hard that they got addicted to drugs.

He sank down onto the couch. Sure, there was a part of him that missed New York. Another part of him wanted this.

Inside, Emma returned to the kitchen and Kira exclaimed over the jewelry.

Abby moved to the rocker and started to sit down. "Oh." She stood and then sat at the other end of the couch. "I forgot. Emma spilled water all over the rocker cushion."

Nate did not cheer. It would be wrong. But Emma was such a great kid. Now Abby was only a foot away, close enough that he could smell the rose perfume he'd noticed the other day.

This was a bad idea.

He didn't care.

"So, we talked about me," Abby said. "What made you become a lawyer?"

"Al." Nate paused a moment, unsure of how much to tell her. One glance at her face and the words fell out. "My own dad and I had a rather rocky relationship. As a little kid, I was always the shortest in my class, the guy that got beat up. Dad was a mechanic, had been a Marine. I think he was mortified."

Abby's eyes grew tender with a look Nate hoped was compassion, not pity.

"For a long time, I believed physical strength was the only thing that mattered. And I didn't have it."

Abby's mouth thinned. Not her kind of parenting, he'd imagine.

"But one summer Mom and I were visiting here, and Al defended this woman who was accused of stealing some rare coins. Marjorie Pullman."

"I remember that," Abby said. "Her daughter was in my class."

"She was barely getting by, and got hired as a cleaner for someone wealthy here in town."

"The Hughes family."

"Yeah." That was the name. "Then you know how Al proved that some so-called friend of theirs actually stole the coins."

"It was like a movie, right here in Abundance."

"It was. And it made a big impression on me. I decided that I wanted to be a lawyer and defend the helpless."

Abby's forehead crinkled. "I thought you worked in corporate law."

"I did." He looked away, then back at her. "I let a few comments from my dad equating money with power play too significant a role in my decisions in law school. But the partner who hired me did talk about pro bono cases. I thought with the clout of the firm behind me, I could make a difference."

Her face eased. "I bet you did make a difference."

"I almost never got the chance. That was only a line they used to sound good in interviews. When I tried to make time for pro bono work—" What was he doing? He couldn't tell her the rest. "Well," he said, speaking faster. "You can only go without sleep for so long. Anyway, I moved here to try to align my life closer to my original goals."

"That had to be difficult, leaving the city to come to Abundance."

"Yeah." Difficult didn't begin to describe it, and he'd conveniently omitted the fact that it had taken a thunderbolt crashing into his world to make him realize he needed to make changes. It was too soon to tell her that.

"I hope moving here works out for you. That you can be the person you want to be."

"Thanks. You've, uh, you've made moving here a lot...better."

She glanced down. He couldn't tell for sure in the fading light, but a flush of pink may have risen on her cheeks.

Had he said the wrong thing? She *had* made his move to Abundance better, made him feel like he had a friend. Oh, he could see that a friend was probably all she wanted. He could accept that. He—

Suddenly, she raised her head. Her eyes met his, and she held his gaze.

Electricity rippled between them.

Deeper and deeper he sank into her eyes, and all thoughts of friendship evaporated from his mind. He slid one hand up her arm until it rested on her shoulder.

Would she move away?

No. She exhaled, and her lips parted slightly.

He ran his thumb back and forth over her upper arm. Her skin was so soft, so silky.

Inch by inch, she scooted closer.

Electricity shot through every cell in his body. He leaned in and—

"Hey, guys." The door from the kitchen banged open.

Nate jerked his head toward the door, and Abby leapt back from him as if she'd been shocked.

"Aren't you cozy?" Frankie stuck her head out and gave a knowing smirk. "Kira let me in."

Abby's cheeks were bright pink. She pulled a small pillow in front of her chest.

He was going to kill his cousin.

The next afternoon Abby leaned against the counter in her shop, fingers tightening on the edges of an envelope. The name on the return address was the man who shot Eric. What on earth could he be sending her?

She held the envelope up toward the light from the window. The contents looked like a single sheet of paper with a few lines, handwritten. Her stomach twisted and an urge came over her to wash her hands—in bleach.

The absolute gall. There was nothing he could say that she would possibly want to read. Oh, she knew forgiving was the Christian thing to do. She was Emma's Sunday school teacher, after all. She knew that her unforgiving attitude affected her relationship with God. But forgiving felt disloyal. No amount of prayer and no urging from Kristen was going to change that. Abby slid her hands toward the center of the envelope, ready to rip it in half, tear it into shreds, and—

The cowbell rang and someone walked in.

Abby froze, then threw the envelope on the desk and

turned to greet her customer.

Only it wasn't a customer. It was Neva Cartwright from the flower shop next door, holding a bouquet of six yellow rosebuds tightly clustered in a glass vase.

"I wanted to make this delivery myself," Neva said. "Just so I could see your face."

"Oh." Abby came out from behind the counter.

"Seems like you've made quite an impression on my tenant," Neva said with a note of teasing as she handed her the bouquet. "Almost overnight." She thrust her hands on her hips and chuckled. Every part of her jiggled except her big, dark hair, teased and lacquered into place in 1982.

"I, um..." Abby's cheeks grew warm, and she turned to set the vase on the counter. Maybe if she stared at the flowers, Neva would hurry off for some other delivery.

Instead, Neva pulled her into a hug that smelled like carnations. "Don't you be embarrassed, sweetie. If I was twenty years younger, I'd be chasing him myself. Though it seems he's the one chasing you."

Abby's cheeks grew hot. What if Neva passed along this opinion to every person she saw the rest of the day? Asking her to keep quiet was out of the question. That would only make her talk more.

Neva gave her a pat on the shoulder and left the store with the cowbell clanging loudly.

Abby ran a finger over one of the six yellow roses. So beautiful. So sweet of Nate to send them.

She freed the tiny card and pulled it out of its envelope. There in handwriting that had to be Nate's —it was too masculine to be Neva's—it read:

Would you be free to go to the Nelson with me after church on Sunday?

Abby's shoulders tightened and her heart fluttered in her chest.

The Nelson-Atkins Museum of Art in Kansas City. One of her favorite places in the whole world.

But the roses made it clear. It would be a date.

An actual date.

Was she ready to date again?

Nate was easy to be around and easy to talk with. He was sweet with Emma and a nice friend and—okay, fine, who was she kidding?

He wasn't a friend. A woman didn't spend hours lying in bed after a friend went home, as she had last night, thinking about the line of his jaw, the muscles in his arms, and how much she had wanted him to kiss her.

But…was she ready to forget about Eric?

She shoved the card back in the tiny envelope. No, she couldn't do that. It was disloyal. Eric was the love of her life. The man she had been meant to be with.

But it had been almost four years.

She held the tiny envelope by two opposite corners, twisted it ninety degrees, replaced her hands in their original spots, and twisted the envelope another ninety degrees, as if it was a tiny gear that she was turning, notch by notch.

She loved Eric. Could never imagine not loving him. Would give anything to have him walk in right now, as whole and healthy and handsome as he had been that last time she'd kissed him goodbye.

But Eric was dead.

She was here alone.

Except for Nate.

Nate, who made her heart race every time she was around him.

Abby twisted the envelope the other direction, faster and faster and faster.

How was it possible that she wanted Eric back and wanted to go out with Nate at the same time? Surely that had to be a sign of insanity.

Or was it a sign that she was ready to date again?

Would that be wrong?

Would it be okay?

Maybe…

Maybe…

Maybe she could try just one date.

"The winners!" The guy who'd come up with the answer to the final trivia question leapt to his feet and began dancing and strutting beside each table of losers at Whole Hog Barbecue with obnoxious glee. "Hah!" he shouted as he made his way past Nate and Thornton.

Thornton gave the guy a light shove, sending him toward the next table.

The man's trivia-quiz partner—his wife, Stacey, according to Thornton—hid her face with one hand and dredged a French fry though the ketchup on her plate with the other. How'd a joker like that ever get a woman like her?

Nate tipped his head toward the man, who was now doing the limbo under the joined hands of people from nearby tables. "I know there's no beer or wine on the menu, but do you think he was drinking before he came here tonight?"

"No." Thornton laughed and his round belly jiggled. "Earl Ray doesn't need alcohol. That's just the way he is. And he and Stacey haven't won Trivia Night in a while."

"The name of that eighties heavy metal band was right on the tip of my tongue," Nate said. "If I'd been a little faster, we could have won."

He'd always been good with trivia. When Thornton had insisted that Nate join him at the barbecue place for the weekly trivia game, Nate had been intrigued. A night out would be good for him, and most people, he'd reasoned, probably thought he knew Thornton because he was his lawyer in the now-infamous fish tank incident. Even if people knew about Thornton's past addiction, they wouldn't connect it with Nate.

He had, though, expected to do better in the competition.

Thornton wiped buffalo sauce off his mustache and rocked back in his chair. "You did real well. I mean, you were at a disadvantage tonight with one of the categories being 'Local Livestock.'"

That was an understatement. Nate had expected categories like music and sports, and he'd done fairly well with questions from those areas. But the few answers their two-man team had gotten right about livestock and "Abundance High School Faculty, Past and Present" had been Thornton's doing.

And the guy had also come up with a lot of the answers in Current Events. Nate wouldn't admit it out loud, and he wasn't pleased with what it said about his tendency to judge others, but Thornton's answers had surprised him.

Of course, shooting a neighbor's fish tank wasn't the smartest thing a man could do. But Nate, more than anyone, should remember that intelligence didn't prevent a person from doing stupid things.

All in all, it had been a fun evening. Thornton was good company, they'd been tied for the win until the very last question, and the barbecue was delicious. It was getting late, though. Nate checked his watch.

"Yeah," Thornton said. "We'd better get going." He stood.

They settled their bills and walked out to the large white pickup truck with a logo of a smiling toilet on each door. As the engine started, the radio clicked on to what sounded like a minister. Nate glanced over. There hadn't been preaching on the way over. Thornton must have accidentally hit the tuning button and ended up here. He'd turn it off any second.

Instead, he turned it up. "I hope you don't mind. This guy's one of my favorites. I listen to his podcasts and everything."

Nate gave an awkward shrug. Before he moved to Abundance, he hadn't been to church in years. Even when he was a kid, his family hadn't attended church every Sunday. Once a month, at best. Here, he had to attend church every Sunday because of Al. And now he was getting more preaching on the ride home. He really was in the Bible Belt.

The radio minister started talking about hope, hope

for everyone. After a few minutes he launched into a reading from the Bible. Luke 7, he said.

Nate ignored it as best he could, but when the minister told a funny story about his lack of athletic prowess, Nate got sucked in. Before he knew it, he was listening to a sermon about Jesus and a prostitute and perfume. Which didn't make sense, maybe because he didn't hear all of it. But he didn't think Jesus loved everyone. Not prostitutes.

Not former drug addicts.

Still, hope and forgiveness were appealing.

Thornton pulled his truck up in front of the florist shop, into the spot right below Nate's apartment. After the diner closed, all the downtown parking spots were empty, which still amazed Nate every time he saw the empty street. "We'll have to do it again some time," Thornton said.

"Thanks," Nate pushed open the door and climbed out. "I'd like that."

Thornton waved and pulled away, the metallic letters of *Miller's Plumbing* on the back of his truck reflecting in the streetlights.

Nate waved back. He actually would like to go to Trivia Night again.

Imagine that.

Part of him wanted to call Jessica, tell her he was fitting in, and shout "Hah," like that guy Earl Ray. The smarter, happier part of Nate thought about the fact that Abby had said yes to going to Kansas City with him. No way he was calling Jessica. Still, he was proud that he was adapting to life in Abundance, slowing down and seeing things besides success as important.

Who knew? He didn't own a Bible, but maybe he'd read that part from Luke on the Internet. Or, if his apartment seemed too quiet later, maybe he'd listen to five minutes of one of those podcasts. That minister was pretty good with jokes.

And maybe he'd talk more about hope.

Chapter Ten

Monday afternoon, as soon as he finished meeting with potential merchants for The Main Place, Cooper stopped at Porter's Hardware to pick up some drywall screws.

Abundance was such a great town. He couldn't believe there was a real, old-fashioned hardware store right in the middle of downtown, next door to the diner.

Porter's Hardware sold the latest power tools and the most advanced paints and stains, but it also had a high ceiling with softly whirring fans, a counter that had to be original, and shelves behind it that looked like they had once held penny candy and fabric for farmers' wives to sew into dresses. Not to mention the store offered personal service that put the big boxes to shame. The sales guy, Hank Hamlin, came over the minute Cooper walked in and showed him to the aisle with the screws. Then he left him alone. No annoying chatting. The perfect customer service.

Cooper found the package he needed. He could stop by Mom and Dad's after he got home to Fayette and put up that shelf. He even had his toolbox and cordless drill in his truck. Dad had lots of tools, but they weren't exactly organized, and he often got irritated trying to find the one he wanted. No need to raise his blood pressure. Mom said he was already less than enthused at the thought of another shelf. Not surprising. Probably why she'd asked Cooper to put it up. With luck, he could put up the shelf, make his mom happy, and stay out of any discussions between her and Dad about how many knickknacks she had.

He pulled his phone out of his pocket and checked the screen. Still no reply from Frankie. He'd gotten her number from Nate and called, asking if they could meet for coffee. He wanted to apologize in person and—

Wait. The woman who'd gone around the end of the next aisle was her.

He clicked off his phone and hurried over.

Frankie stood in front of a display of towel hooks with her eyes narrowed and her reddish-brown hair piled loosely on her head, looking drop-dead gorgeous in a blue-and-green shirt, a black skirt, and high heels. She stared at the writing on the side of a package as if it was in a foreign language.

"Hey," he said as he drew nearer. "You need some help?"

"I'll talk to Hank." Her heels made a *click, click, click* sound as she moved toward the center aisle, leaving behind a hint of spicy perfume.

Just then Hank came down the aisle with an older

woman. "I'd be happy to mix up a shade of paint for you, ma'am," he said. "If it's not right, we can adjust it."

Frankie spun on one heel and returned to the towel hooks, completely ignoring Cooper.

He wasn't giving up. This was his chance. "Really, Frankie, let me help you. I know all about this stuff. I worked in construction."

Still facing the display, she glanced over at him. "You did?"

"After Mizzou, Dad decided I needed to learn the value of hard work. Remember how filthy I was when I saw you in Columbia?"

At the word *Columbia*, she looked away.

Talk about the wrong thing to say. "Wait."

She glared at him. He'd guess he had about ten seconds before her gaze incinerated him or she spun on her heel and left.

"That day at the pizza place in Columbia—" he said, talking fast. "I know it sounded like Garrett and I were close, but I didn't know what he'd been doing." Even now, disgust rolled in Cooper's stomach at the thought of it. "Garrett should have been shot for the way he treated you."

Motionless, Frankie studied him. Then, little by little, her face softened. "Shooting him is one of the kinder possibilities I've considered," she said in a dry voice. "But I was afraid I'd be arrested."

Cooper laughed. In spite of how she'd been hurt, she still had spunk. Red hair fit her. And she was talking to him, definitely a step in the right direction. He pointed at the bathroom fixtures. "What exactly are you trying to do?"

121

"Put up a towel hook for my daughter. She's too short to reach the ones we have."

"I can do that right now if you'd like," he said. "I even have my toolbox and cordless drill in my truck."

"Really?"

"I was going to stop by my folks' house once I got back to Fayette and put up a shelf for my mom, but she's not expecting me tonight. I can help her out tomorrow."

"I can't ask you to—"

"It's no big deal, and I'd like to help you." Not simply as an apology. Or because he wanted her support on The Main Place project. Or even because she was gorgeous. The urge seemed to well up from inside him to take care of her, to make her life easier. More than anything, he wanted to put up that towel hook. He grabbed a big, sturdy one with a silver finish and held it toward her.

"Well..." She turned toward the display, one hand hovering over the towel hooks. After a second she plucked out a more delicate fixture, one in a bronze finish. "Okay."

Yes! He threaded the package of the silver fixture back on the display hook, took the other package from her hands, and examined it. "Is there tile where you want to mount this?"

"Yes." She faced him. "Is that a problem?"

"Uh, no." The only problem was how hard it was to think while looking at those big brown eyes. "It just means I need to use a different drill bit." He forced himself to focus and mentally inventoried the supplies in his toolbox. "We're good. This is all we need."

A few minutes later, after Hank had checked them

out, Frankie and Cooper went out to the street.

She patted the side of a silver SUV. "This is me. I have to pick up Kira. It may be half an hour before I'm home."

"If you'll give me your house key and tell me the address, I'll start unloading my tools and finding the studs."

She wriggled a key off her keyring and told him a street address. "There's only one bathroom. I'm hoping you can mount this below the other towel hook, about this high." She put a hand at her waist. "And Cooper..."

His heart sped. "Yeah?"

"I know you said taking care of this was no big deal," she said in a low voice. "But it is to me."

It was to him as well. It was a chance to make up for his comment at the pizza place.

A chance to show Frankie that he wasn't the idiot she'd known at Mizzou.

And a chance to be near her.

"Mr. Sullivan, I'm going to learn how to waterski," Kira announced from where she sat at the kitchen table, coloring.

Frankie drew in a deep breath. Not this again. From behind her daughter, Frankie caught Cooper's eye as he came down the hall. She gave a tiny shake of her head and slid the chicken casserole into the oven.

"Cool," Cooper said.

Good. A nice, short answer. One that said let's talk about something else.

Kira had seen kids skiing on TV last week and had become obsessed. Frankie had hoped she would forget about it, but it hadn't happened yet. If Kira tried skiing, she couldn't wear her braces. Without them, she'd stand on her tiptoes. Wouldn't that make her more likely to get hurt? There were other logistical issues as well, like the fact that they didn't own skis. Or a boat. Too much to think about. Frankie had all she could handle, getting unpacked and settled in at her new job.

"Kira, why don't you tell Mr. Sullivan about the kitten you're getting tomorrow?"

"It's a little boy kitten. He's gray and has white feet," Kira said. "Have you ever water-skied, Mr. Sullivan?"

Frankie tossed her oven mitts on the counter. Her daughter was nothing if not stubborn. And Frankie knew all too well that the trait had been inherited from her. Hopefully Cooper would ask more about the kitten.

He stopped near the kitchen table, drill case in one hand, toolbox in the other. "I have," he said in a matter-of-fact tone. "It's fun. You'd like it."

No, no, no, Cooper. Not the thing to say.

Kira's eyes gleamed. She'd found an ally. "See, Mom."

"My dad wouldn't let me ski when I was five though," Cooper said. "I had to be older, and I had to put my head all the way under at the swimming pool."

"Oh," Kira said flatly.

That was the exact right thing to say, Cooper. Mentally pumping her fist in victory, Frankie tried to appear mildly interested in the conversation but calm.

He gave her a long look, then his gaze seemed to drift

to her favorite black high heels.

The nerves in her stomach twitched.

Not only was he handsome, not only had he put up the towel hook and ignored the piles of boxes she still had to unpack, he offered logical reasons not to think about water-skiing this summer. She and Kira could focus on something more doable, like swimming lessons. All big points in his favor.

But gratitude couldn't outweigh the little voice that said she needed to get him to leave before he decided to ask her out. She could feel the question hovering in the air. Despite how nice he'd been, despite how good he looked holding a power drill in that white dress shirt with the sleeves rolled up, dating Cooper Sullivan would be a bad idea.

He'd been so kind, though. Good manners demanded she be polite.

"Would you like to stay for supper?" she said in her most welcoming voice. *Say no. Say no. Say no.*

"I need to get back home to Fayette."

She let out a silent breath. "I understand," she said, trying to sound sincerely sorry he couldn't join them.

His jaw tensed, as if her sincerity had failed, as if he'd noticed her relief. He turned with a jerk and walked toward the front door.

She hurried over.

"Let me get the door." She hadn't meant to be rude. He'd been so sweet, really gone out of his way. She followed him out, across the shady yard, to where he'd parked on the street.

He put his drill on the passenger seat of his truck and

landed his toolbox next to it with a thump, causing things inside to clank against each other.

"Cooper, really, I can't thank you enough." One of her heels sunk into the grass.

He closed the door of the truck with a bang—not exactly slamming it, but using enough force that she was now certain she'd insulted him. He turned to face her. "I'll get out of your hair," he said brusquely. "But I am sorry about what I said at that pizza place back in Columbia. I wanted to help you today to make up for that, even though I know you told your dad how I'd flunked out of Mizzou."

"I never said a word to my dad," she cut in. "Not one word."

"Oh." His face grew less rigid. "I thought you were going to."

She shifted her weight, searching for a solid spot in the grass, a place where her heels wouldn't sink in. All he'd tried to do was help her, and she'd been rude with her less-than-heartfelt invitation to dinner. The least she could do was be honest. But how honest? "I…"

She glanced up at him.

His gaze searched hers. She'd seen that expression so many times before. Seen that same questioning look in his eyes. Always, always, whatever she'd told him in college, he had been understanding. Even though he'd only been at Mizzou one year, even though it had been more than a decade ago, memories of that understanding came flooding back.

All right then. She squared her shoulders and looked him in the eye. "I did intend to talk to my dad. The only reason I didn't is that most of the time I'm around my parents I spend biting my tongue because Mom keeps telling me how she hopes Garrett and I can patch things up."

"Why would she want that?" Cooper's voice rose in disbelief.

Frankie repositioned a foot and her heel sank all the way in. She reached down, yanked off her pumps, and held them in one hand, standing in the grass in her bare feet. "Probably because I never told her and Dad about the other women or how rude Garrett was about no longer wanting to be a part of our lives."

Cooper tilted his head to one side. "Why not?"

Even with Cooper, exposing this section of her soul felt raw. But she wasn't blowing him off, wasn't lying to him again. "Because I'm too embarrassed about how he treated me and how he wasn't there for Kira when she needed him." She studied her toes.

"Not even when you were married?"

Frankie raised her head. The disgust in his words sounded so good, so validating, as though he really understood what a jerk Garrett had been. "Not even when we were married," she said in a low voice.

How many times had Garrett ignored her calls and texts? Come home late when Kira wanted to see him so desperately? Come home late after he'd promised he'd be there for a family dinner and Frankie had made a special effort to cook a great meal? Come home late after she had put Kira in bed and mindlessly watched TV, picking at the fringe on a throw pillow, until she was exhausted enough to go to sleep alone without crying?

Her chest ached even thinking of those nights. Maybe that was why she never told her parents. Too much pain. "I...I always made up excuses for Garrett." Excuses to tell Mom and Dad. Excuses to tell Kira.

Her own anguish seemed to be reflected in Cooper's eyes, mixed with disbelief.

"They put Kira's legs in a series of casts to try to lengthen her Achilles tendons. Whenever they removed a cast, she hated that cast saw." Frankie swallowed. She'd assured Kira it was safe, she'd kept up her best brave-mom face, but she'd hated that saw too, hated it because it scared her little girl.

"Garrett was supposed to be there with us, every time, and most of the time he never showed and, and—"

Cooper put a hand on her arm.

She was losing it. Totally losing it. Her chest was tight and her voice was shaking and she should be saying goodbye and instead she was telling him all this.

Before she could think, before she could stop him, Cooper pulled her close, surrounding her in warmth and strength and support. His voice, deep and furious, rumbled in her ear. "I cannot imagine letting down that sweet little girl."

Frankie's brain stuttered, as if she'd walked into a door. In less than a second, though, the confusion melted away. Cooper was on her side. It felt so right, being here in his arms.

Why had she been in such a hurry to get him to leave?

Would it have been so awful if he had asked her out?

No, that was crazy. No matter how much better Cooper made her feel about Garrett, she didn't want to get involved with a man.

She edged backward and switched her shoes to the other hand.

Cooper held her gently, his fingertips brushing her arms.

She needed to take another step back, needed distance.

Instead, she looked up at his dark hair, his gray eyes. Her heart raced.

The message in those eyes was unmistakable. If she stayed this close to him, if she didn't give some sign that he should stop, he was going to kiss her.

Did she want that? Should she want that? Should she…?

Her brain faltered. One by one, she uncurled her fingers. One shoe, then the other, fell into the grass.

And he drew her toward him and brought his lips to hers.

Her heart raced. She ran her hands past his rolled-up sleeves and over the muscles of his arms, and threaded her fingers into his hair. How could she ever have wondered if she wanted this kiss? She wanted this kiss and the next kiss and the next kiss.

He slid a hand down her back and drew her closer.

She melted into him, all thought gone, until at last he leaned back against his truck, blinking.

She let out a ragged breath. "Wow."

His Adam's apple rose and lowered. "Wow is right. How could Garrett have ever wanted to spend time with another woman?"

Frankie's cheeks grew warm.

Cooper took her hand. "Can I call you? Take you out? I'd like to get to know you again."

Somewhere, deep in her brain, the little voice was back, telling her that this was a bad idea. She shouldn't get involved with any man. It would only lead to pain.

But the little voice couldn't compete with her heart, pounding in her ears. "That would be great," she said.

Half an hour later, Cooper climbed back in his truck, carry-out dinner in hand. The mom-and-pop burger joint wasn't a chain, didn't even have a drive-thru, but he often stopped there on the way back to Fayette from different job sites because of the awesome bacon cheeseburgers.

Sure, he would have rather stayed at Frankie's and had that chicken dish he'd seen her fixing, even eaten a frilly salad if she'd put it before him, but this dinner would definitely do. He unwrapped the burger, inhaled the aroma of beef and bacon, and balanced the wrapper on his leg. With classic rock cranked up on FM, he got back on the highway and took an enormous bite, careful not to drip on his shirt. A great burger, topped with the tang of sharp cheddar and three strips of crispy bacon, along with lettuce, a slice of dark red tomato, onions, mustard, and ketchup. A solid F-150 truck to drive. And a beautiful woman who'd agreed to go out with him.

Life was good.

And that kiss back in Frankie's driveway…

If a guy was going to wait more than ten years to kiss the girl of his dreams, that was the kiss he wanted.

A kiss worth every day of the wait.

A kiss that would probably replay in Cooper's mind and in his dreams for years to come.

He turned the air conditioning down a notch and took a long, cold swig of his Dr. Pepper. Probably best not to think too much about that kiss while driving.

There was only one problem with the idea of a date with Frankie—the danger that it might mean everything to him and not much to her, the danger that he was setting himself up to get hurt.

He took another bite of his burger, barely catching a blob of mustard before it landed on his shirt, and he gazed at the horizon.

Maybe, with one date, he'd see that she wasn't everything he made her out to be, that a lot of what he felt was because of the way he'd built her up in his mind.

Or…maybe she'd see that she'd dated the wrong guy all those years ago at Mizzou, that all along she should have been with him.

One date. Dinner out, maybe down in Columbia at some nice restaurant? Or some cultural thing? They had decent shows on campus at Mizzou, and he'd be more than happy to plunk down some big bucks for good seats.

He started to take another bite, then sat up with a jerk.

Mustard, ketchup, and a small piece of onion spurted onto his shirt.

He scrambled for a napkin, tried to blot the mess but smeared it, making it worse.

He didn't care.

He'd thought of the perfect date to take Frankie on.

Sunday afternoon Abby sank down onto a cushioned bench in front of a small Impressionist work by an unfamiliar painter. She'd read the information card and even made a few notes in her phone so she could look him up later. Gazing at the work, a pastoral scene of rolling hills and pervasive light, filled her heart with joy. She could, quite willingly, sit here in the museum and stare at it for hours.

But Nate might get bored.

She glanced over at him, reading the card beside a large painting on the wall to her left. No. He didn't seem bored. Not...

An ache exploded in her chest.

Not. Like. Eric.

Why should the fact that Eric had found art museums boring make her miss him? Nate liked art museums. That should make it easy to think about him, not Eric. It didn't. Could she be any more confused?

Should she even be here?

It had been more than a week since Nate had asked her out. Which was more than enough time to make arrangements for Emma and time for Abby to debate this date with herself again and again. She'd almost called Kristen to talk about it, but didn't. Kristen would be so excited that it would make Abby more nervous. She had been about to cancel, more than once, but whenever she'd get ready to, she'd run into Nate on the street outside her shop. He'd make her laugh or look so cute with Bear that she would talk herself into the date again. And Thursday night, as she had prepared her Sunday school lesson to teach the three- and four-year-olds, even the curriculum seemed to push her toward Nate. The tale of Joseph in Egypt struck her as a story of someone who moved on. Oh, there was more to it of course, but to her it seemed like an example of someone who let go of past pain. Maybe she, too, could do that.

She was here, wasn't she? She smoothed the skirt of her dress and tried to act calm.

After a few minutes, Nate sat beside her on the bench. He didn't say anything, didn't ask her how long she might be, simply sat there and enjoyed the painting.

Then he moved his arm behind her on the bench, supporting her lower back.

The warmth of his skin radiated through her dress and thin sweater, and she could smell the outdoorsy scent of his cologne.

The ache grew in her chest, as if her memories of Eric were a physical force, pushing out thoughts of Nate, warning her away from him. She sat forward, moving a fraction of an inch away from his arm.

Which made her feel even more awkward.

"I love the Impressionists, especially Monet," she said, a little too fast. "I know art history majors are supposed to have more obscure favorite painters. I don't care."

"Monet's famous for a reason. I don't think anyone will hold it against you if you appreciate his work."

Maybe she should address the issue. Maybe that would be better. She drew in a deep breath and turned to face him. "Nate, I wasn't sure about today. I haven't dated anyone since Eric died."

"I know. You still wear—" He glanced toward her hand.

She clasped her right hand over her ring. "I meant to, I mean, I was going to take it off. I got all flustered trying to decide what to wear and then it was time for church and—"

"Abby," he said in a don't-beat-yourself-up tone. "How long were you married?"

"Five years. And before that we dated for three years."

"That's a lot of your life. I don't expect you to forget about it. And Eric was Emma's dad. That's where she got the red hair?"

"And the blue eyes."

"He served in the Army?"

"Yeah. He had just gotten out before he was killed. That week we had when Emma was tiny—it was the only time he got to see her. We were so happy. And then…"

Nate wrapped an arm around her shoulders. "This doesn't have to be a date, you know. Today can be a trip as friends." He squeezed her shoulders and moved his arm away.

The moment it was gone, her stomach grew rigid. The truth welled up from deep inside her, warring with the ache in her chest. Yes, she would always love Eric, but she felt a connection with Nate.

Like a road dividing before her, she had to make a choice. She could cling to the past, stay in the past, and make her whole world in the past. Or she could take a step toward the future. But she had to choose.

Her heart beat to an off-kilter rhythm. She always would love Eric.

But…

She swallowed. "I...want it to be a date."

"Are you sure?"

"Yes," she tried to sound decisive, but her voice came out shaky.

"Then you might want to let go of the bench."

She looked down. Her fingers were clutching the upholstered bench so tightly that her knuckles were white. "Oh." The air left her lungs in a whoosh, and she deliberately loosened her hands.

Was there any way to make Nate understand? She wanted to move on, at least wanted to try, but so far this first step wasn't easy. "You planned this fabulous day, even arranged for Frankie to watch Emma. I really do want this to be a date, but I feel a bit like I'm unravelling."

He caught her gaze and hesitated for a long moment, as though deciding what to believe. "Come on," he said at last. "I think it's time to see the mummies."

"Why?"

"Don't you get it? Mummies? Unraveling?"

She groaned. She got it.

His joke was horrible, but bit by bit the tension inside her began to fade.

She could do this. Really. She turned one palm face up and stretched her fingers toward his.

He gave her an encouraging smile and took her hand.

Chapter Eleven

After she took his hand, Abby had relaxed.

A little.

Even as they left the art gallery, she'd twisted her wedding band again and again.

Once they'd reached the restaurant, though, she seemed more at ease. And delighted with the ambience, especially the original tin ceiling. She had exclaimed repeatedly about how nice it was to eat in a place that had linen tablecloths and crystal water goblets, an experience in short supply in Abundance. And the food, in Nate's opinion, had been excellent.

Now, with dinner over, she seemed to be having fun, seemed to be truly happy. More than anything, Nate wanted her to be happy tonight.

But what about tomorrow and the next day? His past hung over him like the smell of subway urine. Sooner or later Abby would learn the truth. She certainly wouldn't be happy then, and neither would he. He had read that section of Luke from the Bible online, even gotten signed up for an email that came each day with a few paragraphs about a Bible verse. "Walking toward Peace," it was called. The ideas in those emails seemed to line up with what he knew, deep inside, like how it was the right thing to do was to tell Abby the whole truth. That he'd taken only one pill at first, hoping for the energy to stay up and finish a pro bono case. But that one pill led to another the following week. And then another. Before he knew it, he was relying on them.

But the day had already been emotional for her. From what he could tell, simply being out on a date brought back memories of Eric. He couldn't bring up drugs and make her relive Eric's death. Not tonight. Maybe, though, he could tell her part of his past. That alone might end things between them. She'd never have to hear the whole story, never have to go back through her own painful memories because of him.

"Oh, Nate. What a beautiful courtyard." Abby's face lit up and she wandered through the gate of a wrought-iron fence that surrounded a tiny garden.

Water gurgled in the courtyard fountain, covering the noise of the street, and two butterflies danced between the pink and white flowers. A single bench sat in the shade of the building and faced the fountain. And though there were storm clouds on the horizon, they were a ways off.

Nate followed her in. When they had arrived at the restaurant, they'd parked on the other side of the lot in the back. When they walked in, they had missed the courtyard and instead seen a wooden fence that most likely hid a Dumpster. This was a far better side to go past. There should be a sign in the back parking lot.

"What a great spot," he said.

Abby sat down on the bench with a sigh. "This whole trip has been great, better than I could have imagined," she said. "I guess you could tell I was a little nervous." She reached for his hand and angled her head toward the spot beside her. "You planned such a lovely day, and you were so understanding."

The way she talked, he was practically perfect. Far from it.

"Abby..." He didn't want to do this, but he felt like a liar. She deserved better. "I've really enjoyed spending time with you today." He sat beside her.

Her hair was down, not in her usual ponytail. She'd worn a white sweater in the restaurant, but it now sat on the bench beside her. Her pale blue sleeveless dress fit loosely and offered no hint of cleavage, no short skirt, pretty much the opposite of anything Jessica would have worn. Abby didn't need any of that to be attractive. The goodness shone out of her. "And you look beautiful tonight."

She gave him a modest smile.

"But I do want to explain more about why I left New York."

Her face grew serious and she leaned closer.

He stopped for a second, searching for the right way to put things. "My life had become a bit of a disaster. I wasn't handling things well, not well at all, and I"— Did he have to say this? Could he make some joke and never tell her anything?

No.

"About a year ago, I caused a wreck that seriously injured a little girl. Her name is Ashley, and she's better now. I wasn't charged—a cop saw the whole thing and said it wasn't my fault—but I know in my heart it was. I wasn't paying attention the way I should have been." He watched Abby's face.

Her eyes clouded, but otherwise her expression didn't change and she didn't say a word. She glanced at him, then looked out past the fountain.

Pain stabbed into his heart. She'd looked away, as if she wished he weren't there. He'd been stupid to ask her out. Stupid to tell her anything.

And much, much more stupid to get hooked on amphetamines.

Like a fool, he'd tried to quit cold turkey. Three days later, on a Monday when he'd been so tired and foggy that he'd called in sick, he'd gotten a call from the garage where he kept his car. Somehow he'd missed the emails saying they were having the garage repaved and he had to find another parking spot for a week.

And then...Ashley.

Oh, the cop, a guy who said he'd been on the force for thirty years, had told him three times that no one could have stopped in time. "Absolutely impossible," the guy had said.

But that cop didn't know that two blocks before Nate had almost fallen asleep at the wheel.

In his head, when Nate thought about the laws of physics, he believed the cop.

In his heart he felt that somehow, some way, if he'd

been more alert, he could have avoided hitting that little girl.

And he always would.

Suddenly Abby turned back to face him, eyes shining, and she laid her other hand on top of his.

His throat grew thick with emotion. She wasn't rejecting him. She wasn't condemning him. She still cared. In spite of what he'd told her.

He let out a ragged breath and more of the story poured out of him. "That's why I left New York. It took a while for me to...figure things out, but I realized I needed to make some major changes, needed to get a fresh start. The way I was living was all wrong. Al overlooked what I had done, even the way I injured that poor girl, and gave me a job." He wasn't ready to tell her about the drugs, but everything else he wanted to tell, wanted her to understand, wanted her to accept.

"Nate," she said, her voice full of compassion. "If it was an accident, you have to forgive yourself. I see how kind you are with Kira and Emma. There's no way you would ever have wanted to hurt a child."

"No, I never would have, but I think part of the reason I value Kira and Emma is because of what I've done. I'm not that great a guy. A screaming kid on the subway or on a plane... I used to just wish they would shut up. Now I think about kids differently."

"Lots of people who haven't spent time around kids find them annoying. You're judging yourself too harshly." She squeezed his hands.

No, he wasn't. She didn't know the whole story. But if she could forgive this much, though, maybe one day she could forgive the rest as well. "Thank you," he said. "You're..."

Incredible. Kind. Gorgeous.

Kissable.

Very kissable.

Gently he slid one hand up her arm until it rested on her shoulder.

She turned slightly, shifting her body closer. The sweet fragrance of roses from her perfume blended with the scent of the flowers around them, and the Missouri evening grew warmer.

His heart faltered, unsure, wanting to believe, wanting...

He gazed into her eyes, into nervousness and hesitancy and what looked like longing.

Slowly, ever so slowly, he brought his lips to hers.

And she kissed him back.

His heart beat faster and faster and faster. Sunshine and lush grassy fields and blue, blue skies. The smack of a baseball when he hit a homerun as a kid. The biggest court victory he'd ever had. None of it compared to her kiss.

Time dissolved as he drew her closer and deepened the kiss. This moment, this place, this woman was all he knew, all that mattered, all he needed.

At last he sat back. "Abby, I—"

He couldn't go on. He didn't have words for the way she touched his heart. Not words a guy used on a first date. "I—"

A raindrop hit her nose.

Nate took her hand and pulled her to her feet. "I'd

better drive you back to Abundance. You're getting wet, and Emma might miss you if I keep you here all night, kissing you." Which was exactly what he wanted to do.

Abby's cheeks turned pink. "Thank you. For making my first date in a long time so special."

"My pleasure." Despite the sprinkles, he pulled her into his arms and held her close.

Then the rain picked up and he took her hand as they raced toward the car.

Once he'd shut her car door, he glanced back at the restaurant, at the tiny courtyard, savoring one last second of their time in Kansas City. If there was any way he could make it happen, his future would include a lot more time with Abby.

"What is that amazing smell?" Frankie inhaled deeply and raised her eyes toward the roof over Abby's front porch as if she were gazing at heaven.

"Well, I did invite you here for Brownie Fest when I picked up Emma last night, didn't I?" Abby waved Frankie inside. The rich aroma of chocolate was indeed amazing, filling the whole house. Tess's brownie recipe really should be declared a national treasure. Which was why, more than a month ago, Abby had decided she and her friends needed Brownie Fest.

"This place is gorgeous," Frankie said. "I mean, I remember it being nice when Mr. Danner owned it, but not like this."

"Thanks. I didn't change that much, simply updated things a bit." Abby turned to Kira. "Emma is delighted you could come tonight."

"Me too," Kira said.

Frankie touched Kira's arm. "Remember what I said about breakables."

"I will."

Abby let out a silent sigh. A five-year-old like Kira, who'd been taught good manners, was a wonderful playmate for Emma to have over. There'd been that one boy from preschool that just hadn't been ready for an antique store. Emma had fun at his house, playing in the sprinkler. When he came over to play with Emma, though, and Abby got distracted—for less than a minute by a phone call—he'd broken almost $700 worth of Depression glass. Of course, Abby hadn't told his mom, but any future playdates with him would be at the park.

Kira, on the other hand, seemed like she was being very careful.

She and Emma wandered over to a corner of the showroom where an antique teddy bear sat in a small rocker. Emma introduced him as "Fuzzy."

"Come on in and meet everybody," Abby said to Frankie. "You're right on time, but I think some of us were a little eager for chocolate. Everybody's already here but Kristen."

It was only a matter of luck that the chocolate, in the form of brownies, wasn't a disaster. Abby had been so distracted when she was baking. How was she supposed to focus on flour and melted chocolate and butter when all she could think about was yesterday in Kansas City?

Eric had taken her on some lovely dates. She wouldn't want to compare. But the day Nate had planned had been so sweet, so thoughtful—the art museum and a fabulous dinner at The Cartwright House. Even when she'd been...well, downright weird, he'd been kind. She hadn't realized, until it happened, that being on a date with him would bring back memories of Eric and make her miss him all over again.

Later, though, when Nate had kissed her in that courtyard, she hadn't thought about Eric's red hair or pale blue eyes or the bravery that had been so much a part of him. She'd only thought about Nate. His strong arms around her, his deep-blue eyes, his lips on hers. She—

"It's so kind of you to invite us over," Frankie said. "When I picked Kira up after work, as soon as I told her we were going to see Emma again, and that it was called 'Brownie Fest,' well, she was so excited that I could barely get her to eat dinner."

"I'm glad you all could join us," Abby said. If they enjoyed tonight, she'd invite them every month. It had to be hard moving back to Abundance after a divorce, and she'd already mentioned to her other friends that Brownie Fest needed to be a regular event.

Abby led Frankie into the kitchen. "Hey, everybody. Do you all remember Frankie from high school?"

Tess, Becky, and Stacey turned from the kitchen counter, where they were assembling their sundaes.

"Well, not me, since I went to high school in St. Louis." Tess pushed her long blonde braid over her shoulder, stepped closer, and introduced herself.

"You married Abby's cousin Jack, right?" Frankie said.

"I did. We've got a little girl, Lettie, and I'm a pastry

chef down in Columbia."

Frankie pointed at Tess's brownie. "That explains why your bowl looks so perfect."

Banana slices were arranged on one side of Tess's brownie with perfectly formed dollops of whipped cream, and caramel sauce drizzled in a neat zigzag over the whole plate.

"Occupational hazard," Tess said.

"Not for me." Becky held out her bowl, where she'd heaped strawberries haphazardly on top of her brownie. "You'd better remember me." Her rich-brown hair was twisted up on top of her head and her dark eyes sparkled. "After we sang together in the high school choir."

"Becky!" Frankie hugged her. "Of course I remember you. I heard you got married."

"I did. Right before Christmas. To the new high school principal. Did you know Stacey Gilcroft?" Becky pointed to Stacey, who was squirting whipped cream over a bowl that held a brownie with a spoonful of every topping on the table—ice cream, strawberries, bananas, fudge sauce, caramel sauce, and sprinkles. "She married my older brother."

Frankie's brow crinkled. "I don't…"

"I doubt you'd remember me from school." Stacey set down the whipped cream and walked over. "I'm ancient."

"You are not," Becky said.

Stacey rolled her eyes.

"I think I saw your face on a billboard," Frankie said. "Are you in real estate?"

Stacey nodded and her brown hair bounced.

"And you married Earl Ray?"

Stacey's eyes twinkled and she held up two fingers, her manicure gleaming. "Twice."

"Now that's a story I need to hear," Frankie said.

Kira and Emma burst into the kitchen, and Emma grabbed Abby's hand. "Kira got one of Mr. Waller's kittens! Please, please can I have one?"

"Sorry, pumpkin. Remember my allergies."

Emma dropped her hand to her side, and she studied the floor. "You're not being nice."

"Probably not," Abby said. She gave Emma a firm gaze, hoping she made it clear that this was not the time for a scene.

"Emma, you can come play with Kira's kitten anytime you want to," Frankie said. "And girls," she added in a bright voice, "Look at all these brownie toppings. Abby, it reminds me of when you trained Shelly Dwyer and me to work at that frozen yogurt stand at Mizzou."

Kira and Emma turned toward the counter. "Ooooh," Kira said. Emma snuck a sprinkle from a bowl, and she turned back toward her mom, face brighter.

Abby glanced over at Frankie. "Thank you," she mouthed. Kitten crisis averted. And now that she thought about it, the brownie toppings were arranged exactly in the order she would have put them in back at the yogurt stand. She hadn't even noticed.

That part-time job had been a long time ago. Before she'd married Eric. Before Frankie had married and divorced Garrett. Before Shelly had gotten her big break and landed the TV news job in Kansas City.

"Girls, let's get your sundaes fixed and then you can take your bowls up to Emma's room," Abby said. The counter was too high for either girl to reach, so she handed Frankie a bowl.

"Come on Kira," Frankie said. "Tell me what toppings you want."

The desire for her own kitten apparently forgotten, Emma moved to the counter behind Kira and, while Abby fixed her sundae, described the stuffed animals she wanted Kira to meet, including the toy dog from Nate. After both girls promised to eat at Emma's play table, which had a plastic cloth under it, they went upstairs.

A few seconds later, Kristen burst in. "Check it out," she said, turning to show off a new haircut.

"I know you," Frankie said. "From youth group. You were—"

"Four years behind you," Kristen said.

"Kristen recently moved back to town," Abby said to Frankie. "Like you."

"There's something about Abundance," Stacey said. "Once you've lived here or even just visited, you want to come back."

Soon everyone had a sundae and a place at the table. Abby took a bite of her dessert. She may have gotten the brownies a bit too chewy around the edges, but what a recipe! Was there any better flavor than rich, sweet chocolate?

"I've got news," Becky sang out, and she looked from side to side to make sure she had everyone's attention. "I've found the perfect guy to set Abby up with."

Abby swallowed her bite, no longer interested in

chocolate. "Becky, you don't need to do this."

"I'm not taking no for an answer," Becky said.

"You've rejected the last three guys she suggested without even meeting them," Kristen said.

"This guy is great," Becky said, as she scooped up some of her brownie.

Abby's chest grew tight. "Um…" You'd think, in this town, everyone would've heard about her trip to Kansas City. Sometimes in Abundance, literally every single person knew your business. Sometimes, something big skated right under the radar. Not that she wanted all her friends to have heard. She was barely getting used to the idea of her date with Nate. No way did she want it analyzed.

Becky waved her spoon as though she was scolding Abby. "It's time for you to date again, and Bryce is wonderful."

Frankie raised her eyebrows at Abby.

Abby shot her a quick glance, pleading with her to keep quiet. "I have no interest," she said to the group, "in dating some guy named Bryce." She turned to Tess, desperately searching for a new topic. "Have you thought about what you're bringing to the community picnic?"

Kristen leaned in. "What's wrong with a guy named Bryce?"

Abby didn't answer. Somehow she had to get Kristen—the world's most stubborn sister—to drop this issue.

"I have a pretty good idea what's wrong with Bryce," Frankie said with a note of delight in her voice.

Nerves tensed in Abby's chest. What had she been

thinking, including Frankie? She fit in far too well with this crowd. Abby opened her mouth to say something, but no words came out.

"I think Abby's much more interested in someone named Nate," Frankie said.

Like four puppets whose strings were pulled at the same time, Becky, Tess, Kristen, and Stacey twisted their heads toward Frankie.

Abby shrank down in her chair.

Becky scooted closer to Frankie. "Nate Redmond, your cousin?"

"Yep," Frankie said.

"Ohhh," Stacey said. "I saw him the other night at trivia. He's way cuter than Bryce."

"This is excellent." Tess said. "How can we get them on a date?"

Frankie's eyes sparkled. "They went to Kansas City yesterday."

The other women drew in a collective breath.

Becky elbowed Abby. "You went on a date and didn't tell me?"

"Or me?" Kristen sounded indignant.

"It wasn't, I mean, it was, but—" Abby bunched up her napkin. "I don't even know if he'll ever ask me out again." He'd been really sweet when he said goodnight, but she'd been so nervous, acted downright neurotic, and—

"I saw you two when you picked up Emma at my house last night." Frankie gave Abby a who-are-you-kidding face. "He'll ask you out again, I guarantee it."

Warmth encircled Abby's heart, as sweet and

delightful as hot fudge sauce. Nonchalant—she needed to act nonchalant or they'd grill her mercilessly.

It was no use. She could feel her smile spread from ear to ear.

Chapter Twelve

"Are you sick of that little town yet?"

That was Jessica. No *hello*, no *how are you*.

"No. Not sick of it. Uh, hold on a minute." Nate set the phone on his kitchen counter, ran water in the skillet he'd been scrubbing, and left it to soak. All those great New York restaurants with delivery service had let him avoid disasters like the burned-on mess he'd created in the skillet a few hours ago with his dinner. Man, he missed those restaurants.

Otherwise, he didn't miss the city as much as he'd thought he would. Maybe with this conversation he could get that point across to Jessica. With a glance at the Play-Doh tubs and the Fun Factory on the kitchen table, he took the phone to the couch. He liked living here, liked being around Kira and Emma and Al and Vivian and Frankie.

And he liked being around Abby. Their time together

yesterday in Kansas City had been great. She made him feel like he mattered. Like he was important. Like he was strong enough with her on his side to handle anything, even his addiction.

"Nate? Are you there?

"Yeah. I was in the middle of doing dishes."

"You? I thought your idea of doing dishes was throwing away the carry-out plastic."

"I'm adapting."

"Right." Jessica over-enunciated the word. "You're not going to adapt to the lifestyle there or to the legal work. Tell me what you did last week. Drew up three simple wills and counted the cows?"

Actually, one day he had done four wills. Four basic, boring wills. "I've been working on a new development."

"What are they getting, a feed store?"

"Jessica, there's more to Abundance than agriculture." There had to be. He just didn't know what it was yet. And he didn't know what someone with his legal experience was going to find that would be challenging. Was he going to be bored out of his mind?

Bear shuffled over, rubbed his head against Nate's leg, and lay down at his feet.

Nate scratched the big dog's ears. Despite the fact that he'd already brushed Bear today, long black hairs stuck to his fingers. He wiped his hands on his jeans, and the dog hairs fell to the floor, joining others. Jessica would hate that.

"I talked to Spillman," she said. "He's willing to take you back. The salary would be a little lower, and you have to expect a longer wait for partner, but—"

Nate jerked upright. "I don't want you talking to Spillman." She'd gone way past the line. Her own denial was one thing, but she had no right to actively interfere in his life. They were over. This time he was going to get her to understand that. "You need to accept this—I'm not coming back to New York. I wouldn't even have a place to stay. My apartment is rented."

"Well, I wouldn't be opposed to sharing."

"Not happening."

"You could always rent a new place. Or, with as much money as you saved over the past years, you could probably buy a place."

"Even if I wanted to—and I don't," he added firmly, "my savings are gone."

"Gone?" Jessica's voice grew higher. "Tell me you didn't buy a place there already."

"No. I put it in...a long-term investment."

"Nate, this is ridiculous." Her tone held desperation. "That guy from California moved into your office, and the partners are talking about hiring."

With Jessica, what he wanted didn't matter. It was all about her. "One more time," he said. "Let me spell it out for you. I'm. Not. Coming. Back."

Jessica replied with an angry sniff.

He could imagine her tossing her shiny, dark hair over her shoulder.

But she wasn't worth going back for. Sure, she was beautiful and smart, but getting involved with her had been a mistake. There was no softness, except what she offered in a calculated gesture. There was no warmth, except what she pretended when it suited her purposes.

And he could never in a million years picture her playing dress up with a daughter.

After rehab, he'd known he had to end things.

At first, she'd seemed to accept it. She'd moved on and dated someone else. After they broke up though, she'd shown up at Nate's house one night, drunk, and said she wanted to get back together. Sure, he knew that dating him, working just down the hall, was convenient for her. He understood her workload. He fit into her plans. She wanted to keep it that way.

"Nate, are you listening?" she said over the phone.

"Yeah." Now he was.

"I can be patient. Eventually, you'll realize your future's in New York. But if you want that future to be with Spillman, you'd better come to your senses soon."

"Jessica, I don't want—"

She'd hung up. He threw his phone onto the couch cushion. She still didn't get it. To her, his plans didn't matter.

Nate stomped into the kitchen and attacked the dirty skillet with renewed vigor. Jessica's call had had an effect, but not the effect she wanted. More than ever, he could see that his future was not in New York. It was right here in Abundance. It might even include Abby.

Which meant he needed to be honest with her and tell her the whole truth about why he moved here. He couldn't build a relationship with her on a lie.

Aunt Vivian had mentioned a big Fourth of July picnic that the whole town attended. Nate would see if Abby wanted to go with him, and some time over the course of the evening he'd find an opportunity to tell her everything about his past.

Including the drugs.

"Thanks for speaking with me, Mr. Turner," Nate said into the phone as he made a note to call Cooper. "I appreciate your willingness to discuss the tax benefits of donating your land on Pine Street for the new park. The people of this town are lucky to have such civic-minded business leaders."

Nate held the phone in place with his shoulder, dug into the drawer for a bigger binder clip, and listened to Archie Turner expound on the criminal amount of tax that he paid each year. Some choruses were the same whether a person lived in the big city or a small town.

"Yes," Nate said. "Definitely discuss this with your CPA. As I mentioned, if you do decide to donate the land, the city council would need to vote to accept the donation, but I think they would leap at the opportunity."

A few minutes later, Nate hung up and stretched out a kink in his neck. A good conversation. He'd done his best to be convincing. All he could do at this point was let the ideas sink in, but he thought, he really thought, it might work.

He leaned back against the lumbar support in his chair and looked around his new office with approval. The room was still small. The carpet was still cheap. The desk was still simply functional.

None of that mattered. What mattered was the stack of files on the corner of the desk that Al said Nate needed to deal with before the end of the day, when the Fourth of

July weekend started.

One stack.

One three-inch-high stack that was about seven hours of work. That was all. He gave it a little pat. He'd be done and clear for the week if he stayed until five thirty. He could actually have a long weekend, starting tomorrow, Friday, where he wouldn't do a single bit of legal work. He'd take Abby to the picnic, eat hot dogs, watch fireworks, and relax. He hadn't had a relaxing Fourth of July holiday since he finished law school. No doubt about it, there were serious advantages to moving to Abundance, like a life outside the office and the pro bono case that was in that stack of files.

Top of the list of the best things about Abundance, of course, was Abby. The more he thought about the conversation he planned to have with her this weekend, the more he believed she would understand about his drug issues. Once they worked things out, life in Abundance could be better than ever.

He turned on his computer. A large rectangle appeared, asking if he wanted to update the system.

Definitely not.

He wasn't wasting the whole afternoon waiting for updates from the laptop manufacturer to load. He was going to get his work done and have a weekend.

He clicked the box that said *Remind Me Later*.

Fifteen minutes later, Jewel's voice rang out. "Yoo hoo. I'm back with doughnuts."

Nate hurried to the kitchenette. Last week there had only been two jelly-filled doughnuts. By the time he reached the box, both had been on Al's plate. This week, when Jewel had moved doughnut day to Thursday on account of the holiday, he was getting there early.

Jewel stood at the counter, opening the box of donuts. "I saw that look on your face last week, Nate. I think you're going to like what's in here."

Nate looked in the box. Six of the twelve doughnuts were jelly-filled. "Jewel, I bet you've heard this before, but, well, you really are a jewel."

"Awwww." She waved off the compliment with an airy gesture.

"Nate." Al strode into the kitchenette and loaded a plate with three jelly doughnuts—probably not the nutrients Vivian would recommend for someone who'd been ill. "Help yourself to some doughnuts and come in my office. Archie just called me."

Nate's pulse picked up speed.

He added a healthy serving of two jelly doughnuts to his own plate and grabbed a napkin between sticky fingers. He hurriedly followed Al into his office and sat down, facing him.

Al took a giant bite of doughnut and chewed rapidly. "Years ago, Archie Turner was the star of the Abundance High baseball team. After he heard your tax ideas, he got right on the phone to his accountant. He'd much rather make a contribution to the community that will benefit baseball players than give money to the government. He's ready to donate the land."

A tingle of excitement spread through Nate's chest, and he set his plate on the edge of Al's desk. "Then all the proceeds from the sale of the current park can go to equipment and landscaping?"

"Every penny."

"Which means that large climbing structure the mayor wants is well within the budget."

"Precisely. Selling Rose Park is going to be the best thing Abundance has ever done."

Nate settled back in his chair. He'd done it. Oh, Archie had donated the land, and the city had gotten the grant, but in his small way, he'd helped.

Nate bit into one of his doughnuts. Delicious. Life in Abundance kept getting better and better. The community was going to have a beautiful park with all the amenities—including a brand-new ball field, the big climbing structure, and the historical plaque—and he was part of making it happen.

He couldn't wait to tell Abby.

Abby and Emma stopped, halfway in Doris's front door, as Hubert's red pickup truck pulled up in the driveway behind Abby's minivan.

Her stomach tightened. What if Hubert had heard about her date with Nate? She really, really didn't want a scene this morning.

"I'll only be a minute," Hubert called as he climbed out and slammed the truck door with a bang. He gave no indication that he'd heard of Abby's date, simply headed across the yard.

"Hi, Grandpa!" Emma said. She waved, wiggling her whole body like an excited puppy wagging its tail.

"Hello, Emma darlin'," he said in a hollow tone. He smiled at her, but judging by his eyes, the action caused him physical pain. He walked past the house toward Doris's shed.

Emma looked up at Abby, confused.

Abby patted her shoulder. How could she explain Hubert? Couldn't he try a little harder for Emma?

Apparently not.

Best to distract her. Abby pulled the door open a bit wider. "We're here," she called out. She had phoned earlier about the churn, and Doris had said to come on in.

"In the kitchen," came a reply.

They went in the house and were immediately surrounded by the smell of strawberries.

Emma stopped in the living room to play with the golf tee and pegboard game that Doris had bought at Cracker Barrel when she visited Branson last fall, but Abby went back into the kitchen, where the strawberry smell was even stronger. "Hubert's here."

Doris leaned over the counter, ladling hot, red jam into glass jars. "He's getting the lawn mower to take it in for a tune-up. Something he said he couldn't fix."

"He still mows your lawn?" Abby hadn't seen him at Doris's house in more than a year.

"Yes," Doris said with a mix of pride and resignation. "He still does all the chores Zane asked him to do around here when he first got sick. But the boy barely talks to me." She looked back down at the pot of jam, suddenly focused on scraping out the last ruby-colored drop.

The "boy" was a fifty-five-year-old man who should see how much he was hurting his mother. Abby didn't say that. It wouldn't help. Until Hubert let go of his pain and anger, she didn't think anything would help. Time to change the subject. "Thank you so much for letting me borrow your ice cream churn."

"Are you sure you want to go to all that trouble?" Doris wiped up a drip from the top of a jar.

"I'm sure. I want to make Rose McFee Kincaid's famous chocolate cherry cordial frozen custard. It will be perfect to take to the Fourth of July picnic tomorrow, to celebrate the fact that the town is appreciating its history and saving Rose Park."

"And you're certain this Mr. Redmond is right? That Abundance agreed not to sell the park?" Doris said. "Because I haven't heard anyone else say so."

"He told me that he took care of it."

"Maybe it's still hush-hush," Doris said.

"I bet you're right," Abby said. "I'll ask him more about it this weekend." When they were enjoying the ice cream.

The recipe was exactly the type of thing Nate would enjoy. That man had a sweet tooth. The night he and Kira came over for pizza, he'd eaten four of Abby's homemade oatmeal cookies. And his favorite candy was cherry.

He—

Hold on. What was she doing? Going to all this trouble, making homemade ice cream? It wasn't as if she'd fallen in love with the guy.

Had she?

Abby's breath caught and she backed up until she ran into the kitchen counter.

Sure, she'd taken a big step in going out with Nate.

Falling in love would be a much bigger step, a giant

step, a step she hadn't even thought about.

But her heart *had* raced when Nate kissed her in the courtyard behind the restaurant. And when he squeezed her hand when he walked her and Emma to the door. And when he waved at her from the sidewalk Monday night when she was getting things ready for Brownie Fest.

And when she was with him—even when he texted Wednesday night to ask how her week was going—she felt all happy and bubbly and alive.

She did think about him.

A lot.

An awful lot.

And—

She took a shaky breath. She had. She'd fallen in love with Nate Redmond.

"Abby?" Doris tapped her on the shoulder. "I said I can't help you look for the churn right now, but it's down in the basement somewhere."

"Oh," Abby mumbled. "Okay. I'll find it."

Emma came in, carrying the pegboard.

Doris's eyes lit up. "I'll keep working and Emma can keep me company." She angled her head toward the table. "Emma, why don't you take that chair over there away from the stove."

Emma sat down and happily began putting the golf tees in the holes.

Abby opened the door to the basement. She'd fallen in love. Her—the woman who had barely been able to sit on a bench beside Nate when they went to the art museum. She didn't even know when it had happened.

And it didn't make a bit of sense.

But, from what she knew about love, it didn't have to. She couldn't change the way she felt about Nate any more than she could change the type of art she liked. She'd just have to try to get used to the idea.

At the bottom of the stairs, she scanned the shelves. What a mess! Doris was so excited about trying to win a prize for the best watermelon at the county fair. If there was a prize for the basement that smelled the mustiest, felt the clammiest, and had the biggest collection of spider webs, she'd win that one, hands down.

There. The churn was up on that shelf, and on the far side of the basement, a ladder conveniently was stored against the wall. Well, somewhat conveniently. The ladder was incredibly heavy. Abby tugged it across the floor and wrangled it into position.

A little wobbly. The concrete floor in this basement wasn't exactly flat, especially by the drain, but she'd made a special trip out here before she opened the antique shop. She wasn't going to deviate from her plan now.

Abby squared her shoulders and climbed onto the first rung of the ladder. Whoever had put the churn away had been taller than her. She was pretty sure she was going to have to climb higher than she wanted to in order to reach that top shelf.

"Abby," Doris said as she came down the stairs. "Quentin came over and took Emma to see the kittens."

Abby climbed up another rung and brushed away the cobwebs overhead.

Doris moved to the base of the ladder. "And then Hubert came in."

There was a note of unease in Doris's voice. Had

Hubert said something thoughtless to his mom? "And...?"

"He said Archie Turner has decided to donate land to the city, which...which means all the money from the sale of Rose Park can go to developing the new park."

"Sale of Rose Park?" Abby jerked her head to look down at Doris.

The ladder wobbled, and Abby grabbed one of the shelves to steady herself.

"That's what Hubert said. And that the new park would have ball fields and climbing equipment and bathroom facilities with flush toilets, and that it would be real nice." But Doris didn't sound like she thought it would be nice. She sounded sad.

Abby climbed up another rung, caught the churn between her fingertips, and pulled it toward her.

How had this happened? Whatever Nate had tried to do must have fallen through.

In theory, the new park would be nice. Emma would love a big climbing structure and might be willing to use the bathroom at the park if it wasn't one of those disgusting pit toilets. But why couldn't they put some of those things in at Rose Park? Why did they have to sell it? That simply wasn't happening. Somehow, someway, she was going to stop it.

"Apparently Archie got the idea to donate the land from Al Redmond's nephew."

"Al Redmond's nephew?" Abby heard her voice shoot up into a range she rarely reached. "Nate?"

"I thought you said he was helping us," Doris said.

Abby's whole body felt numb. "I—I thought he was."

How could Nate do this— after he'd said that Rose Park was protected because of its history? After he'd taken her on a date and kissed her? After she'd figured out she was in love with him?

She'd trusted him and stopped collecting signatures.

All along he'd been helping the developers build a new park. All along he'd been lying.

She handed the churn to Doris and carefully climbed down the ladder.

She was still going to make ice cream. Emma was all excited about it.

But Nate Redmond certainly wouldn't be eating any.

Chapter Thirteen

Cooper pulled his family's ski boat into his favorite shady cove and slowed the engine. Most lakes would be crowded today with every cove filled with skiers. After all, it was Friday, July 3, the official holiday this year, and the weather was perfect. The sky was a bright blue, the temperature right around ninety. Luckily Thompson Lake was fairly small and mostly used by people like his family, who had owned a cabin here for years. There were other boaters on the lake, but not too many.

Frankie, in the captain's chair beside his, looked gorgeous in shorts and a bright-blue one-piece, her short ponytail threaded through a ball cap. She laid a finger over her lips and angled her head toward the bow.

Kira lay stretched out on one of the seat cushions, fast asleep, one life vest securely strapped on, another piled under her head as a pillow, with her braids spread out to either side. The sun, the big lunch of bologna-and-cheese sandwiches he'd packed, the slow country song on the radio, the gentle rocking of the waves, and the time they'd spent in the water—with Kira in a life jacket and he or Frankie right by her every minute—had taken their toll.

With the throttle low, he steered the boat until Kira was completely in the shade of the trees along the shore.

"She's having such an amazing day." Frankie's words were quiet but rich with emotion. "We both are. I don't know how to thank you."

Cooper pulled an icy root beer from the cooler, dried the can on a towel, and offered it to her. "It's no big deal. My folks aren't coming to the lake this year." Bringing Frankie and Kira here had seemed like the perfect date.

Frankie popped open the root beer, letting out a hiss of carbonation. "You with the 'no big deal' again. Like helping me with the towel hook. This *is* a big deal. Not only have you motivated Kira to give swim lessons another try, but she's had so much fun."

"I'm glad." He paused, watching a teenage boy drive a speedboat past the entrance to the cove. "Can you believe that idiot? He's too young to drive a boat, and he's getting way too close to the shore. If I'd done that when I was a kid, Dad would have read me the riot act." He tipped his head to one side. "Actually, I'm surprised he didn't give me his safety lecture before I brought the boat out today."

"You mean the same safety lecture you gave Kira and me before you let us come aboard?"

"Yeah," Cooper said. "That one. You wouldn't be willing to tell my dad that I know it by heart, would you?"

She laughed.

"It might help," he said. "I'm still trying to get him to see he can trust me with the business."

"Still?" Frankie leaned closer.

He caught the faint scent of her perfume, spicy and sweet, mixing with the fragrance of the waterproof sunscreen he'd brought.

"Yeah, still. He needs to take time off to have bypass surgery. That's why I want that development in Abundance to go well. Maybe then he'll see that I can handle things."

Frankie toyed with the hem of her shorts. "I think you'd handle things great. I shouldn't have been so hard on you when we first met again. I assumed you'd stayed the same, like Garrett did, but you've changed since we were in college."

"Thanks. It means a lot that you'd say that."

"I shouldn't have judged you by Garrett. But he wasn't always horrible. We did have some good times together when Kira was little."

Thinking back to when he'd known Garrett in college, Cooper could picture that. The guy had been hilarious. It didn't change Cooper's opinion of him today. "Maybe, but after what you told me the other day, I still want to punch him."

"I know the feeling. I..." Frankie ran her fingers over the hem of her shorts once more. "You know and I know that getting a cast removed isn't dangerous, but I could never get her to see that, and every time, she wanted her dad so much. I—" She looked over at Kira.

Still fast asleep.

An odd expression passed through Frankie's eyes—defiance edged with guilt. "I didn't punch him, but I did make his life miserable for a while after the divorce."

"What did you do?"

"Well," she whispered. "I started a…what you might call a self-help-of-the-month club for him."

"A what?"

"For a few months there, I signed him up for brochures that come in the mail, sometimes coupons for sample prescriptions, each month for a different condition."

Cooper felt the corners of his mouth twitch. "Condition?"

"Yeah. The first month was narcissistic personality disorder."

Cooper couldn't hold back the grin any longer. Narcissistic fit Garrett all too well.

"I sent him self-diagnosis brochures," Frankie said. "Plus a book I ordered and mailed with no return address. And I signed him up for a bunch of stuff online. You know how if you shop for something, after that advertisements for it seem to be everywhere on the Internet?"

"Yeah," Cooper said.

"It's the same if you search for a medical condition."

Cooper bit his lip to keep from laughing out loud. He didn't want to wake Kira, and he had to hear more. Granted, this wasn't exactly the kindest side of Frankie's personality, but if anybody had deserved it, it was Garrett. "What about the next month?"

"Excessive flatulence."

Not a problem he'd ever noticed around Garrett, but something about the way she said it, with her voice perfectly calm and not even a snicker, made it hard to keep from snorting.

"And the month after that?"

"Let's just say there are several treatment options for a health condition some older men have..." Her eyes twinkled.

Talk about hitting below the belt.

Cooper shook his head. How far gone was he on Frankie if he even found her sneaky revenge tactics attractive? Which, he had to admit, he did. They showed her grit. Nobody was going to keep Frankie McNamara down, certainly not a loser like Garrett.

"Did I mention that I made sure to use his work address and his work email so he got all this helpful information at the office?" she added. "Really, if a man's going to cheat on his wife, he shouldn't make his passwords so accessible."

Cooper burst out laughing, then clamped a hand over his mouth.

Kira stirred and rolled to face the back of the seat.

"Frankie, remind me to stay on your good side," he said.

A flash of pain crossed her eyes. "I know it wasn't very Christian of me, and I did stop. I mean, after that I started thinking about moving back home and got involved trying to find a job here."

"What did you do in Houston?"

"Pretty much the same thing as here. Publications for a hospital, but the hospital there was a lot bigger, and I got paid about twice as much." She gave a rueful smile.

"That's quite a sacrifice." Even given the difference in the cost of living.

"I hope it was the right decision. I wanted Kira to be around more family, and after Garrett moved, I knew her family in Houston would always just be me."

There wasn't a drop of uncertainty in her tone, as if she was sure that she would always be single, sure that no man would ever want her. That scumbag Garrett had no clue how much he'd hurt her.

At the opening to the inlet, a bigger boat passed. The wake rolled toward them.

Their boat bobbed and turned until the sun shone on Frankie's shoulders. Skin that had seemed golden in the shadows looked pink in the brighter light. The second coating of sunscreen that Frankie had asked Kira to put on her half an hour ago had been too late.

"Hey, we've drifted, and you're getting burned." Cooper stripped off his T-shirt and held it toward her. "It's soggy, but sunscreen can only do so much."

She glanced at his chest, and her eyes widened.

A jolt of awareness shot through him.

"Thanks." She pressed two fingers into the skin on her shoulder and frowned at the redness, then took off her ball cap and pulled the T-shirt over her head. In the process, her arm brushed against his.

His heart made an uneven bounce, like a skier crossing the wake, and every nerve in his body came alive.

Between the way she looked in that blue swimsuit, the sacrifices she'd made for Kira, and the backbone that kept her standing despite that loser Garrett, Cooper didn't stand a chance.

He might be setting himself up for disappointment, but at least he knew the truth—one date with Frankie would never be enough.

Ten years ago, she'd been everything he ever wanted in a girl.

Now she was everything he ever wanted in a woman.

Frankie tugged the hem of the damp T-shirt away from her stomach.

It didn't help. The fabric immediately plastered itself back against her swimsuit.

Seconds ago, that T-shirt had been against Cooper's skin, and thinking about his skin made her feel...well, it made her feel too much. Things she hadn't felt in years—a flutter in her stomach, an awareness of how close he sat, a realization that the ninety-degree-day was suddenly a hundred and ten, right here in the shady cove.

Sitting here a foot away from him, with their captain's chairs angled toward each other, was way, way too close.

Today was nice. Fun. A treat for Kira.

That's all it was supposed to be. Frankie even had a long talk with herself after that kiss in the driveway. Made sure to mention the word "friends" aloud a couple of times when Cooper called and invited them to the lake. Because getting involved with anyone, even a nice guy like Cooper, was a mistake.

A mistake she was not making.

But he'd been really nice to invite them today. And

thoughtful texting her last night to make sure they liked bologna. And kind making sure Kira was in the shade.

She glanced back over at him.

His smoky-gray eyes caught hers.

Friend. He's a friend.

He leaned back and took a long drink of root beer. The muscles in his chest rippled as he moved his arm.

She rubbed one big toe across a small puddle on the deck of the boat. Her heart should not be racing like this.

"Frankie." Cooper's voice sounded deeper than normal. "There's something you need to know."

She looked up at him.

"When I kissed you the other day in your driveway, it wasn't just some spur of the moment thing."

"It wasn't?"

"I mean, I didn't offer to help you fix that towel hook because I wanted to kiss you, but I've wanted to kiss you for years, pretty much since the first day I met you."

Her heart gave an awkward lurch. "Oh." She stared out at the sunlight sparkling on the water, shifting and changing every second. And just as quickly, the meaning of events that happened back when they were freshman changed in her mind. The hours he'd spent talking to her, even when she thought he'd had a class to go to. The times he'd hung around her and Garrett. The nights he'd been there to make sure she got home safely when Garrett was too drunk to drive.

She'd thought Cooper was simply being a gentleman. Now she saw things differently.

And she saw him differently as well. Maybe—maybe—he was someone who might really care, who might think she was valuable, who might have thought so all along. Was this day on the lake possibly the beginning of something—?

No. She couldn't get involved with Cooper, couldn't handle the rejection that was almost certain to come sooner or later. Couldn't do this to Kira.

Frankie jerked her head around and looked at her daughter.

Kira's eyes were sweetly closed, her eyelashes fanned out across the top of her cheeks. This conversation wasn't affecting her a bit. And truly, Kira was a kid who—with the exception of her nervousness about having casts removed—rolled with the punches. If Frankie dated Cooper for a month and he dumped her, Kira wouldn't think about it for more than a day.

But Frankie would. She edged ever-so-slightly back in her seat.

Cooper placed one hand on her arm.

Goosebumps raced over her skin like dragonflies dancing on the water of the cove, and she felt her chest fall with a shaky exhalation.

With one finger he traced the edge of her jaw and the outline of her lower lip.

As if pulled, she scooted toward him and splayed her fingers over his bare shoulders.

His gray eyes grew darker, and he leaned closer.

Fear and delight swirled together inside her as he lowered his lips to hers.

Tiny kisses. Gentle kisses. Undemanding kisses that melted her fear away in the lap of the waves against the boat and the coconut smell of sunscreen and dreams as light as fluffy, white clouds.

Maybe, this once, it was okay to take a chance.

Chapter Fourteen

Up and down Main Street, merchants had decorated for the Fourth of July. American flags hung from each light post. Helium-filled balloons in red and white and blue floated above benches and fire hydrants, attached by ribbons that shimmered in the hot Friday-afternoon sun. And bunting was draped at precisely the right angle across every storefront.

Nothing original, nothing elaborate.

Still, Nate wanted to see the decorations. Specifically, the ones in front of Abby's store.

Bear had other ideas.

Nate tugged on the leash. "C'mon, boy. Don't you want to see Emma?"

Apparently not. The squirrel in the maple tree half a block in the other direction was more intriguing.

"Bear?"

The leash strained.

"Bear, heel!"

The big dog gave the squirrel a warning woof and turned toward Abby's.

Nate patted his back.

Tomorrow he'd be celebrating with Abby and Emma. They'd watch the fireworks from the roof of the hardware store, where Abby said her cousin Hank worked. Earlier in the evening, they'd attend the picnic. Abby had promised Nate a large bowl of the chocolate cherry ice cream that she was making today in one of those hand-cranked churns.

The considerate thing to do was to stop by and offer to help crank. Nate had never made ice cream, but he'd seen it done in a movie. If he remembered right, the handle got hard to turn when the ice cream was almost ready. Abby might need help. Besides, stopping by would be the perfect opportunity to tell her the news about the park and how it could now have the big climbing structure the city wanted. Emma would love it.

He and Bear stepped onto the porch of the antique shop.

A car rolled by and a kid gazed out the window at the bunting along Abby's porch rail and at the balloons tied to the bench in front of her shop and in bunches on either side of the porch steps.

The sign on the door said *Open*.

Nate stuck his head inside. "Abby?"

No answer.

He couldn't take Bear inside. One sweep of that big, black tail and a china pitcher or a glass candy dish would shatter on the floor. He tied Bear's leash to the porch rail.

"Wait out here a while, boy. I'll be right back."

He walked inside, into the welcome air conditioning, and his eyes gradually adjusted to the lower light. He peeked into the rooms on both sides of the entry hall. No Abby, but a clank came from the kitchen. He headed toward it.

The door to the kitchen burst open.

Abby rushed out and came to an abrupt halt. A drip of melted chocolate was smeared across her T-shirt. Her ponytail was frizzy and stuck off to one side. Her cheeks were pink and her mouth was pinched up. Making ice cream must be even harder than it looked in the movie.

"Could you use some help?" Nate moved closer.

Abby's scowl deepened, and her hazel eyes turned almost gray.

"Is everything all right?"

"No, everything is not all right," she said, every syllable sharp. "And I'm not interested in your help."

"Not interested?" A trickle of alarm spread through him. Had she found out about his past somehow? "What's going on, Abby?"

She planted both hands on her hips. "You said you were protecting the history of Rose Park, but you're actually destroying it."

He gave her a reassuring smile. She was all upset and it was simply a case of small-town gossip getting the facts wrong. "I don't know what you've heard, but the history is going to be commemorated, far more effectively than a name on the entrance to the park. The developers are going to put up a sizeable plaque in the new park, telling all about the woman Rose Park was named for." He waited for Abby to smile back.

She didn't. "The reason Rose Park is important," she said in a tone that implied he was stupid, "is because that's where Rose and her husband, Simon Kincaid, had their hotel. Simon Kincaid—as in Eric's great-grandfather, the man who donated the land. That park was very important to Eric. And to me." Her eyes burned into Nate as if he'd done bodily harm to her daughter. "Not to mention the fact that Eric proposed to me in Rose Park. By one of the rosebushes. Not by some tacky strip-mall store."

"Oh." How was he supposed to have known all that? "I thought you'd be excited about the new park. Archie Turner is donating the land, which means the city will be able to afford a top-of-the-line climbing structure."

"I've heard all about it. Archie's going to get some great tax deduction that you recommended." Abby tossed her head. "I can't believe you've been working to destroy Emma's heritage and my memories of Eric."

What? "I ensured that the historical importance of this woman would be acknowledged, which is what I thought you wanted." What she'd *said* she wanted. "Redmond and Associates was hired to help this deal go through. I was doing my job."

"Oh, yeah. Your job. As a lawyer. Where handling things here in Abundance is small potatoes." Sarcasm dripped from her words. "No, wait—not small potatoes," she said, rolling her eyes. "Grains of rice."

Heat poured through Nate's chest, and he drew himself up to his full height. "Abby, I'm new to Abundance and didn't know all the intricacies of the area's history. Your expectations were unreasonable. I had no idea you had a family connection or a personal connection to that specific piece of land. Besides, I thought you were interested in a future with me. Not just a past that's dead and buried."

She recoiled and her face went white.

The words he'd spoken replayed in his brain, and, in a fraction of a second, his throat closed and his mouth went dry. No. He couldn't have said that. He'd intended— "Oh Abby, I meant Rose, not Eric."

Her chest jerked in uneven breaths.

What to do now? He'd totally ruined things, first by not doing more research, and then by speaking without thinking—exactly what a lawyer knew never to do. The woman seemed to fry out the synapses in his brain.

"Abby, I had no idea about the hotel. It was never my intention to destroy something that was important to you."

She raised her head slightly. Every muscle in her face was taut.

"Really," he said. "It wasn't."

"You said everything was taken care of to protect the history," she said angrily. "I stopped collecting signatures on my petition and—"

"I thought everything *was* taken care of. I thought the new commemorative plaque would be great, and I even thought I told you about it. Didn't I mention it when I was sick?" Or had he been so excited about the pudding…?

She looked up and off to one side. "I remember you mumbling something but I don't know what you said—"

"I should have done more than mumble." Should he mention that he'd had a fever and barely been able to stand up? No, he wasn't making excuses. "We should have discussed it in Kansas City." Anybody with his experience should have expected there to be more to this deal than appeared on the surface, but all he'd thought about was how beautiful she was, how much he wanted her to have a great time, how much he wanted to kiss her.

"Just for today," he said, leaning toward her. "Could we ignore this? And Monday I'll figure out a solution."

She stepped back, out of his reach, and crossed both arms over her chest.

"Please, give me a chance to salvage things after the holiday."

"You really think you can save Rose Park?"

"I do," he said as emphatically as he could.

She looked at him for a long moment, her gaze tightly focused on his.

"Really, I can fix this." There was no question in his mind. One way or another, he would find an answer. "And I'll crank the ice cream."

At last her face relaxed. "Okay," she said. "If you really think you can fix it Monday. Because we both should have communicated better." She tipped her head slightly to one side. "And I could use some help. That churn was meant to be cranked by a family of twelve taking turns, not by one person."

"Let's forget about this—just for now—and have a real holiday weekend."

"All right," she said, all anger gone from her voice. "That sounds nice."

Tension eased from his chest. Abby was one in a million. A woman who could forgive mistakes. A woman who gave second chances. A woman he could see himself with long term.

He'd worked multi-million-dollar deals in Manhattan. Surely he could referee a battle over a ball field in Abundance.

Time to taste history.

Abby wiped the salt and condensation from around the top of the metal churn and eased off the lid. She'd tasted the custard mixture before she poured it in the churn, but this was the real moment of truth. In spite of all that had happened with Rose Park, she wanted Nate to think the ice cream was amazing, wanted him to think she was amazing. Because when she'd explained things better and he said he'd fix things, she believed him. They'd had a misunderstanding, but Nate was really someone she could trust.

Carefully, she pulled out the paddle and put it on a platter. With Emma and Nate watching, she scraped off a taste with her finger and licked it clean.

The flavor exploded on her tongue. Chocolate every bit as rich as Tess's brownie recipe, but cool and creamy with a velvety texture and a sweet hint of cherries. Rose's recipe for chocolate cherry cordial frozen custard was even better than Abby remembered from when Doris made it five years ago.

Her delight must have been evident.

Emma ran to the silverware drawer, then scraped a

spoon along the paddle. She licked up a taste. "Do we really have to wait until the picnic to eat it?"

"Well," Abby stretched the word out and grinned at Nate. "How about you let Nate have a couple of spoonfuls so he can taste it, and then you can have all that's left on the paddle."

Emma bounced up and down. "Yaaaaay!"

Abby handed Nate a spoon. "This recipe is Rose McFee Kincaid's. She served this in her hotel."

He scooped up a bite and set the platter on the kitchen table for Emma. "This same recipe?"

"Yes. According to Eric's grandmother, Rose made all kinds of special desserts. That's one of the reasons people liked staying at her hotel."

Nate popped the spoon into his mouth, and his eyes widened. "This is incredible. It's so creamy."

Delight danced in Abby's chest. "That's because it's made from custard. I couldn't even guess how many calories are in it. My mind refuses to go there."

"Ignorance is bliss." Nate scraped another spoonful off the paddle.

Abby replaced the lid of the churn. "I'll take this downstairs and put it in my deep freeze, so it can firm up before we go to the picnic tomorrow."

"Let me do that." Nate took the churn from her arms. "It might be heavy." He angled his head toward the door to the basement, and Abby nodded. He headed down the stairs.

The churn wasn't that heavy. It only held two gallons, but Abby wasn't complaining one bit about Nate carrying it. When he'd been home, Eric had done things like that.

Footsteps came back up from the basement, and Nate reappeared. "You know, I've been thinking about the situation with Rose Park. Don't give up hope. I've got some ideas."

She let out a happy sigh.

On the counter behind her, her phone rang.

She turned and grabbed it. "Hello?"

"Abby? How are you?"

The voice seemed familiar, but it wavered from one syllable to the next.

Abby moved to the back of the kitchen, where the reception was usually better. "Doris?"

"I'm at the hospital, dear. I fell." There was a rustling sound and then she came back on the line. "They've given me a pain killer and stabilized my hip, but as soon as the surgeon gets here, he'll be operating."

At the word "operating," Abby's chest grew hollow. "Doris, I'm so sorry! Are you there all by yourself?"

"No. Hubert's here. He was mowing when it happened. He was supposed to call you..."

He probably had, but Abby had been outside helping crank the ice cream. Well, sort of helping. Nate had done 90 percent of the work. And Doris had needed her. Doris, who seemed so frail after being ill.

Once, while waiting in the doctor's office, Abby had read an article about hip fractures in the elderly. Sometimes they even led to people dy—

No. She wouldn't let her mind go there. She'd focus on what she could do to help. "I'll be right over."

"Nonsense," Doris said. "I'm going to be out of it for hours. Just come see me when the operation is over. In case I'm not thinking straight for a while though, I wanted you to know…about Matilda."

Abby sank into a chair at the kitchen table. "Mattie?" What did Eric's younger cousin have to do with Doris falling?

"I was talking with Terrence, and he's very upset now at the idea of the city government selling Rose Park. Mattie did a project for school where she researched her ancestors. She and Terrence are coming in a couple of weeks to take pictures of the park."

"Oh."

"It's more important than ever that we save Rose Park," Doris said. "You don't mind going to talk to the council alone, do you? To convince them to save it?"

"Of course I'll go," Abby said in her most soothing tone. The last thing Doris needed was to be worrying about the park. "I'll take care of it."

"Thank you, dear."

"I'll be there when you wake up from surgery," Abby said. Or maybe before it even started.

Doris had already hung up.

For a second, Abby just stood there. She really, really hoped Nate could find a way to save Rose Park. If not, she'd have to revive her petition.

And get ready to speak to the city council.

Chapter Fifteen

Cooper punched a button on his truck radio, filling the cab with Garth Brooks' voice.

An amazing start for a Monday. Dad had been scheduled for an appointment with his cardiologist. Then Dad's Thursday meeting over in Moberly had called and wanted to reschedule to this morning. Though Cooper could barely believe it, he'd convinced Dad to let him handle the meeting. He was on his way across mid-Missouri to Moberly, and Dad was sitting in the cardiologist's waiting room. At long last, he was winning his father's trust.

Yesterday, when he and his folks grilled out, Dad had actually seemed impressed when Cooper told him that he'd enforced Dad's boating safety rules when he took Frankie and Kira out on the lake.

"Can't believe those rules actually sunk in," Dad had said, but he'd been smiling.

Cooper didn't tell him that he hadn't done it for him, but because he wanted to keep Frankie and Kira safe.

He scratched the back of his neck. Apparently he'd been so busy reminding Kira to make sure she was well coated with sunscreen that he'd missed a spot on himself. That one little spot was peeling. He didn't care.

The day at the lake with Frankie and Kira had been awesome.

He took a sip of his Dr. Pepper.

His phone rang, and he wedged the pop bottle into the console and punched the button on the steering wheel to connect the call.

"Cooper? Nate Redmond here. Could you meet Wednesday at ten in our office? We've got an issue we need to address."

"What's going on?"

"Over the weekend I learned that some members of the family that donated Rose Park oppose its development."

"You're kidding."

"I wish I was," Nate said dryly. "The man Al met with, Hubert Kincaid, is one of two grandsons of Rose McFee Kincaid. He strongly supports the development, but his mother and a brother who lives out of town oppose the sale. Apparently, Rose Park is located on the site of a hotel that Rose ran."

The more Nate explained, the hotter Cooper's chest grew. This couldn't be happening. Dad was going to be furious and would insist on being right back in the middle of this deal.

Even if it meant missing surgery.

"We hired your firm specifically so we could avoid situations like this," Cooper said.

"I understand that and so does Al," Nate said. "From what he tells me, he asked all the right questions. Hubert's answers may have been less than forthcoming."

Cooper blew out a loud breath. "You're saying we've got one family member practically lying to us, trying to get the park built? And all the others were against it?"

"That pretty much sums it up," Nate said with a note of disgust. "I thought I'd left this kind of mess behind in New York. Apparently not. Anyway, I'm getting the principal players together Wednesday morning to brainstorm until we find a solution."

"I'll be there."

"Oh, one more thing, to further complicate this situation," Nate said in a hopeless tone. "Hubert's mother, who opposes the sale? She recently fell and broke her hip. They say surgery went well and she should fully recover, but if the city develops Rose Park against her wishes while she's recovering, it's going to reflect very poorly on all of us involved."

"Perfect." Cooper rubbed his left temple. Talk about a mess.

"I have some background information about the hotel and Rose that I can send you. She was a pretty forward-thinking woman."

"I'd like to read it."

"I'm emailing it as we speak," Nate said. "See you Wednesday."

"I'll be there," Cooper said. He'd read that email, and he'd do everything he could to fix this mess. Before

Dad heard about it.

At last, Wednesday had arrived. Nate settled into his chair in the conference room. With luck, this group could come up with a way to keep this project moving forward.

Nate looked around the table. Al sat at the far end, still a little pale. That virus had really hit him hard. On Nate's left, Cooper scribbled something in the margin of a spreadsheet, and Mayor Hartley grunted and moved as if trying to find a comfortable position in a chair that might be too small for him. On Nate's right sat Archie, a stocky, gray-haired man, and Hubert Kincaid, Abby's somber father-in-law.

"Thank you all for coming today," Nate began. "Al's been under the weather, so he asked me to lead our discussion. Acting on behalf of Sullivan Enterprises, Redmond and Associates wants to ensure that any development brought to the area is fully welcomed."

Al nodded encouragingly.

Nate opened his mouth to continue.

"Exactly what the city wants," the mayor interjected. "Something that will benefit all involved."

"It's been brought to our attention," Nate said. "That some members of your family, Mr. Kincaid, don't agree with the view that the park should be developed. I believe a petition against the sale of Rose Park is even being circulated."

Hubert Kincaid's face grew pinched. "My mother and brother and daughter-in-law aren't too happy with the idea. You'd think they would see that the children of the community are more important than commemorating something from the past."

Several people made sounds of agreement.

"There's one thing that particularly concerns me." Cooper tapped the end of his pen on a notepad. "From what I've learned, Rose McFee Kincaid set a real example with the way she treated both guests and employees without discrimination. Bulldozing a park that commemorates her could be seen as a lack of respect for her ideas about equality."

"We certainly don't want to do anything that will make Abundance appear sexist or racist," the mayor said. "It could hurt any chance we have for attracting industry, and it wouldn't represent the values we hold here in Abundance."

"Our goal today is to brainstorm ideas and come up with a plan that will allow the sale of the park, while at the same time honoring Rose and her values in a way that will make everyone happy, including your family, Mr. Kincaid," Nate said. "We're hoping you can help us see things from their viewpoint, and then we can present our best idea for their thoughts."

"I'll try," Hubert said. The frown lines on his face grew deeper. "My mom and daughter-in-law spend a lot of time taking care of Rose Park. I don't really see how they're going to be happy if it's sold."

"It has to be sold," Archie said. "The grant money alone won't pay for three ball fields."

Nate looked from Al to Cooper to the mayor.

"Three ball fields?" Cooper thumbed through his papers.

"Well, that's what this town needs," Archie said. "Three real ball fields. Good ones, with lights, seating, and scoreboards." He scanned the table for support.

Everyone else remained silent.

Archie's chin jutted out toward the mayor. "When I first talked about selling you the land, I told you that was my intention."

Nate's stomach gave an awkward roll. The current budget had money for one ball field. One. Not three. And Archie hadn't said a thing about three ball fields when he'd agreed to donate the land instead of selling it to the city. Finding money for three ball fields wouldn't mean scaling back the climbing structure, it would mean eliminating it completely. If only Nate had been involved in all of these negotiations from the beginning.

The mayor shifted again in his seat. "I told you then, Archie, that the city is having a survey done and that the park needs to meet the needs of the entire community, not just the youth baseball league. For one thing, we can't just move over the play equipment from Rose Park. We need all new equipment, so we can be in compliance with the Americans with Disabilities Act." He rubbed the back of his neck. "And we sure can't put a tax levy on the ballot for the parks. We've got to pass a tax increase for fire and EMS. One of the city's fire engines has to be replaced. "

"We're not here to talk about fire issues," Archie said. "We're here to talk about ball fields, and as for that ADA stuff for playgrounds…Have you ever seen a normal kid try to play on that weird equipment?"

Nate struggled to keep his mouth from dropping open

and looked down the table at Al.

Al's cheeks were reddish purple. "Archie," he bellowed. "I—I—" Coughing overtook him.

"ADA compliance is legally required," Cooper said quickly. "And more kids than you realize have disability issues, like Al's granddaughter, Kira, who recently moved to town."

"I know the people of Abundance want to do what's right for all the kids," the mayor said firmly. He gave Archie a look that said he was way out of line.

"I don't care," Archie said, his tone petulant. "I run the youth baseball league. I'm giving the city the land. I want it used for ball fields." He landed hard on the end of the word *fields*, emphasizing that it was plural. "I've a good mind to forget the whole deal. If the city wants a new park, it can find a location somewhere else. Maybe if all the league families chipped in, we could use my land to build the ball fields we need."

Nate's chest grew tight. He'd read dozens of emails about the park that had been exchanged before he arrived in town. The single ball field had been mentioned in several of them. Had Archie not read the emails? Or not accepted what they said? Or was this some last-minute power play to force the city to do what he wanted?

This meeting was supposed to solve problems, not multiply them. He leaned toward Archie, both hands on the table. The man was in business. He had to understand money. "I think you'll find construction of those fields requires quite a large outlay." Nate circled the line item for one ball field in the park budget and slid the paper toward Archie. "Not to mention the value of the land you'd be donating. Unless you formed a non-profit, you wouldn't get any type of tax credit."

The mayor leaned toward Archie. "Think about this. We need to work together."

Nate studied Archie's face, waiting for some sign of understanding. Once the man thought about the cost of a single ball field, he'd see their logic. Because, sure, Abby would be happy if the whole deal fell apart, but the kids of Abundance needed a nice park. And—once they got Archie to agree to one ball field—Nate knew they could figure out a way to build the new park and honor Rose McFee Kincaid.

Archie's eyes flickered toward the budget. Stayed.

Nate held his breath, watching. *Yes, study that number. Let it soak in. You don't want to incur three times that expense on your own, Archie. It's not like most families can contribute thousands of dollars for youth baseball. You'd be footing almost all of the cost yourself.*

Archie raised his head, crossed his arms over his chest, and set his jaw, his whole body protesting how he had been wronged.

Al must have known Archie for years. He should know the right thing to say to get him back on board with the deal. Nate looked down the table.

Al's face was still beet red, his expression clear. Whacking Archie over the head with an oar was far more attractive than getting him back on board.

Nate shot a desperate glance at the mayor. "The important thing here is the community," Nate said, scrambling. "Archie, you're an astute businessman. I'm sure you know that a park with facilities for all, including a ball field for your youth league, is going to be invaluable to Abundance, not only for the quality of life of those already living here, but as an incentive to those who might move here. Your role is key. Already I've heard people talking about what an incredibly generous gift you are making by donating the land."

"I know an award for Citizen of the Year has been mentioned," the mayor said.

Archie's posture didn't change a millimeter. Silent, he scanned the faces of those at the table. Then he lurched to his feet. "Unless the new park has three ball fields, three *decent* ball fields, you can forget about any land donation." He stormed out of the room.

Nate's stomach sank. He dropped his head into one hand and looked at the mayor.

The mayor was rubbing his temples, and his eyes were pressed shut, as if he were trying to keep his head from exploding.

Nate shoved his papers back in a pile. So much for this meeting solving problems. The entire negotiation was a disaster. A complete, unmitigated disaster. He'd thought he could handle this deal easily, impress Al, and win over Abby with a brilliant solution. None of that was going to happen.

For all he knew, Al might decide his practice would be better off without his new associate.

Chapter Sixteen

Frankie dashed into Cassidy's Diner and scanned the room. She had forty minutes for lunch with Cooper and didn't want to waste a minute of it.

As usual, the diner was packed with townspeople discussing the latest news and the place smelled amazing. No wonder. The sign behind the counter read: "Today's pies: Lemon Meringue, Glazed Fresh Strawberry, Blackberry."

Fresh-baked blackberry pie—she was almost certain that was what she smelled. But where was…?

From a booth near the back, Cooper stood and waved.

Frankie waved back. Such a handsome man. His dark hair was slightly tousled, and his gray eyes widened appreciatively as she walked closer.

"Hi," she said. "Have you been waiting long?"

He sat back down. "No. I just got here."

She slid into the vinyl booth across from him, scooted

over to avoid a spot where the foam under the vinyl had seen better days, and tugged at the hem of her bright-purple dress. It was a wee bit short. If she wasn't careful to keep it pulled down, the dress gave the wrong impression. But the cut was very flattering, and she did want Cooper to think she looked nice.

A month ago, if anyone had told her she'd be interested in another man—especially Cooper Sullivan, she'd have burst out laughing. Now, well…she was eager to see what happened next.

"This is such a treat," she said. "I haven't had lunch outside the hospital since I started there three weeks ago."

"Seeing you sure makes my day better," he said, then added more quietly, "because I had a disaster of a meeting this morning." He scowled out the window at her dad's office.

"Do you want to talk about it?"

"Let's just enjoy our lunch." He reached out and gave her hand a squeeze.

A tingle ran up her arm, but she pulled her hand back.

Cooper raised one eyebrow.

"I'm not sure I'm ready for all of Abundance to ask me when we're getting married."

Cooper's shoulders stiffened.

"Shh. I'm not suggesting it," she whispered. "But that's what people are going to think if they see us holding hands in Cassidy's. This town doesn't get a lot of excitement, and there are some people around here who aren't above exaggerating things—a lot."

Grace Cassidy stopped at their table and quickly took their order.

As she walked away, Frankie's phone rang. She pulled it from her purse and checked the number. "Sorry. I have to take this. It's Kira's doctor." She answered and said hello.

"Mrs. McNamara? This is the nurse from Dr. Weston's office. I've got Kira's physical therapy appointment all set up on Monday, July thirteenth. They were really nice about working her in soon, so she won't lose any progress, and they fit her in at the end of the day, like you asked, so you won't have to miss as much work."

"Thank you. Where's the office?"

The nurse gave an unfamiliar street address.

"I guess Abundance has grown since I was a kid here," Frankie said. "I don't know where that is."

"Oh," the nurse said briskly, "it's not in Abundance. It's in Columbia. Dr. Weston refers his patients to a clinic there. You'll need to leave an extra fifteen minutes for checking in."

"But Kira has lots of therapy appointments. I can't take her to Columbia every time."

"That's how Dr. Weston handles things. He says his patients get better outcomes with the services offered in Columbia, because they have a pediatric physical therapist."

Frankie's stomach sank, all interest in lunch gone. Dr. Weston was the only pediatrician in town and came very highly recommended.

Back in Houston, she'd had her choice of dozens of PT clinics for Kira, one of them right in the hospital where she worked.

"Kira's appointment is at three thirty," the nurse said.

"Three-thirty? That's the last appointment of the day?"

"For an initial visit. I also made her an appointment with Dr. Barnes, the orthopedic surgeon Dr. Weston refers to. It worked out well. I got that appointment at two thirty the same day. You're lucky they had a cancellation."

"Can't Dr. Weston order her therapy?"

"Only for the first visit. Dr. Barnes oversees it." The click of a computer keyboard came over the line and then stopped. "Do you want me to cancel the appointments?"

Cancel? "No." Kira had to have her physical therapy. "Thank you." Frankie hung up and rolled her eyes toward the ceiling.

"What's wrong?" Cooper said.

"I have to take Kira to Columbia for physical therapy. I never dreamed of such a thing. I feel like such an idiot."

"There's nothing in Abundance?"

"There's one provider, but her pediatrician prefers a clinic in Columbia. I never even thought of this after living in Houston."

"Could your mom take her?" Cooper leaned back to give Grace more room as she placed a burger and onion rings in front of him and a Cobb salad in front of Frankie.

"I would have thought so, until I moved here and learned Mom's had some health issues that she never told me about."

"Is she okay?"

Frankie poured dressing over her salad. "I think so. She doesn't seem that concerned. But she had a seizure and can't drive until they figure out why. I can't believe she hadn't told me about it."

Cooper gave a knowing nod. "The old protecting-you-from-worry routine. My parents tried to pull that on me with my dad's heart trouble. I don't think I would have learned about it if I hadn't found a bottle of pills on the kitchen counter and looked them up online."

Frankie jabbed at her salad, knocked a chunk of tomato off the side of the plate, and sighed. At least someone understood, someone was supportive. No wonder she liked spending time with Cooper.

She liked working at the hospital in Abundance too. Oh, it wasn't perfect, but she could make a difference there, and the people in her department were nice. Her co-workers, though—and her boss—wouldn't be nice if she was asking for an afternoon off every time Kira had a PT appointment.

Frankie took a sip of her iced tea. Her sick leave was going to evaporate. It wasn't only Kira's PT appointments. Mom thought Frankie should be driving her to her appointments as well. And sometimes, though Frankie wouldn't take off work for something like a cold, she'd need to take sick days for herself, like if she got the stomach flu.

She'd thought moving here from Houston was such a good idea. A slower pace, her parents to help her, a real feeling of family for Kira.

In theory, it sounded good.

But all of that required keeping her job.

Which seemed less and less likely.

201

"Can I interest either of you in a slice of pie?" The owner of the diner stepped closer to Cooper and Frankie's table and tucked a wisp of brown hair behind her ear. "That blackberry just came out of the oven about an hour ago."

Cooper could smell it, practically taste it. Ordering pie had been a foregone conclusion the moment he walked in the diner.

Frankie picked up her phone and checked it. "I wish I could, Grace, but I have to run." She tucked her phone into her purse and slid the strap over her shoulder.

Grace turned to Cooper.

"I've been in here often enough," he said, "that you know I always have time for pie. I'd love a slice of blackberry with a big scoop of ice cream."

"Coming right up." Grace went to the next table.

Frankie scooted out of the booth, and a flash of worry crossed her eyes. The same worry he'd seen pass through them again and again, ever since she got that phone call. He could tell that she'd tried to focus on their conversation, but she was too upset.

With good reason. She had enough stress with moving. Now she was worried about her mom, and it seemed she'd been counting on her help with Kira. If he'd been in Frankie's shoes and his mom had been retired, he'd have assumed she'd help.

To be honest, Mom wouldn't have given him much choice in the matter. She'd have helped whether he wanted it or not.

Cooper stood. "Is there anything I can do?"

Frankie shook her head, a fast, tight movement a mere fraction of an inch in either direction. "It's not your concern. If anyone should have known how difficult it is to find the right services for Kira, it was me."

The guilt in Frankie's voice cut into his heart. She was so determined to do what was right for her child in spite of the inconvenience, in spite of her new job. And just this past Sunday the sermon at church had been about going out of one's comfort zone to help others. "Let me know when her next appointment is," he said. "Maybe I can juggle my schedule and take her."

His chest tightened. Wait. Did he really speak those words out loud? He barely knew Kira. He had no idea what was involved in taking her to therapy. And it was way too early in whatever relationship he had with Frankie to make such an offer. She was going to think he was weird. He gulped and tried to think of what he could say to dig himself out of this pit.

"Oh," Frankie said in a breathless voice. "Thank you. I mean, I could never—you wouldn't know the answers to their—" She reached over to rest a hand lightly on his arm. "It's incredibly nice of you to offer, Cooper, but she needs a family member with her."

Cooper's chest eased. The same feeling he might get if he'd accidentally shot off a nail gun aimed at his foot—and realized the gun had jammed. "Okay." He wouldn't be taking Kira to any appointment, and Frankie didn't think he was some weirdo. In fact, she seemed like she'd thought the offer was nice. Good, all good.

But part of him still wished he could help, still wished he was a family member.

If he and Kira were family that meant... What was he thinking? Somewhere, deep in his brain, Frankie's mention of marriage must have resonated.

Frankie pulled out her wallet, but he waved her offer aside.

"Thanks," she said, as she took a half step away from the table. "I'm sorry, but I've got to run." She hurried toward the door, working her way through the crowd near the register, so that he only caught an occasional glimpse of her glossy auburn hair, her short purple dress, and her long legs.

Was it any wonder that thoughts of marriage had stuck in his brain? The woman was so gorgeous and so...brave. Like a warrior, ready to fight on behalf of her child.

Grace returned with a large slice of blackberry pie, heaped with two big scoops of vanilla ice cream. The melting ice cream pooled around the blackberry filling that had oozed out, and the smell was incredible.

Grace picked up his glass. "I'll be right back with a refill."

Cooper spooned up a big bite of pie and ice cream. The flavors filled his mouth—the sweet creamy vanilla, the rich, juicy flavor of the blackberries, and the perfect flaky crust that every pie at Cassidy's shared. For a moment nothing else mattered. Not Frankie's problems. Not even the self-destructing park deal.

Eventually his brain re-engaged. His offer to take Kira to physical therapy had been a bit nuts. He didn't have that kind of relationship with Frankie or with Kira. Not yet.

Maybe he needed to change that.

Because having this woman in his life was amazing.

Ordinarily, after the meeting he'd been in with that Archie Turner idiot, he'd have been totally depressed, but lunch with Frankie had lifted his spirits. After spending time with her, he knew that somehow he could make The Main Place project work. He'd seen meetings like the one this morning before. Things could work out in the end, once all the parties had their say and got some small victories. He'd make sure of it.

Maybe there was even a way he could make Frankie's life a little easier, make things a little better for Kira right here in Abundance. A way to do good, while at the same time start smoothing over some of the ruffled feathers from the meeting this morning.

Kira's issues didn't seem to affect her mobility very much, but someone like Archie probably wouldn't see her as—how had he phrased it?—a "normal" kid.

Cooper hated, absolutely hated, talking to crowds. One-on-one, though, he was a good communicator. If he could show Archie some photos of really well-designed accessible play equipment, maybe mention how all kids liked to play on it, that might help. He'd also mention how a well-constructed playground made it easier for older adults to play with their grandkids.

Granted, it wasn't much, but if even one person greeted Frankie and Kira with less prejudice, it might make their lives easier. And it would get people involved in The Main Place project to think beyond their own interests.

Which was the first step toward making this deal a success.

Abby gave Emma one more hug and turned out her bedroom light. "Sleep well, pumpkin."

"You too, Mommy," Emma said in a dreamy voice. Two minutes, tops, and she'd be asleep. Abby had let her play in the tub longer than normal since it was Friday night. The warm water, along with three bedtime stories, had done the trick.

Abby eased the door shut and let out a long sigh. It would be good to sit down. Even better to get to bed early tonight. It had been quite a week.

Suddenly, her phone rang, blaring through the quiet house.

She sprinted toward her bedroom and grabbed it from her dresser. "Hubert, hello." Abby scurried toward the stairs.

"Mommy?" A sleepy voice came through the door.

"Everything's all right, Emma. You have sweet dreams," Abby called out in a soft voice. Then she whispered into the phone. "Wait a minute. Let me get downstairs."

"I'm sorry to call so late," Hubert said. "I meant to talk to you earlier, but things took longer than I thought with Mom."

On the first floor, away from the stairwell, Abby spoke normally. "Not a problem. Now that I'm downstairs, Emma won't hear me talking. Is Doris all right?"

"She is. I wanted to let you know that she's all settled in at the rehab facility."

Abby sank into a chair at her kitchen table. "Oh, I'm glad to hear that." She'd planned to phone him the next day to check. Frankly, she was a little shocked he'd reached out and called her. "Tomorrow's Saturday, so I won't be able to visit until evening, but Emma and I will be sure to stop by." She didn't want Doris to think she was neglecting her.

"Mom would like that. It meant a lot to her that you all visited her so much at the hospital." Hubert sounded exhausted.

"We'll be there," Abby said. "It's been hard seeing her like this. Are you—are you doing okay?"

"I am. Just a lot of paperwork and things she wanted brought from home. But Abby—" Hubert paused. "About Rose Park and that petition you've been circulating—I've been talking with people the past few days. It really would mean a lot to local kids to have a nice new park."

Abby pressed her lips together. This was why he called. She'd thought he was focused on his mother, but it was really more about the "nice new park." Well, there was no reason the kids couldn't have a nice *old* park. The city could do so much to improve Rose Park. "Now, of all times, we need to support Doris," Abby said, working hard to keep her tone calm.

"There's more to this. You have to think carefully. If the town is going to be able to afford the park the kids need, it has to have the money from the sale of Rose Park."

Heat spread through Abby's chest. The city had received a grant, money specifically for parks. She'd heard all about Archie's plans for three lighted ball fields. Maybe, when Emma was older, Abby would understand why the city could possibly need three ball fields. Right now, it seemed excessive. Greedy, even. Abundance did not need to sell off its historic heritage to cater to one man's obsession with baseball. And Hubert shouldn't be fighting for Archie's plans against his own family.

She drew in a slow, steady breath. Time to get off the phone before she told her father-in-law what she thought of what he was doing. "Goodnight, Hubert. I'll be praying for Doris, and I'll go see her tomorrow evening." Abby clicked off her phone and went up the stairs to get ready for bed. Though, with the way her heart was racing, she didn't see herself falling asleep any time soon.

Chapter Seventeen

What was going on? Nate sat up in bed, struggling to connect with reality instead of his all-too-familiar nightmare.

But those noises weren't from the wreck that he so often relived at night.

They were real and came from outside.

He made his way across the room and found his phone on the dresser. Almost one in the morning. Friday—no, now it was Saturday.

Another thump outside.

He shut off the air conditioner that filled one bedroom window, and shoved the other window open.

The sound of breaking glass came from the direction of Abby's shop.

Adrenaline shot through him. He scooped the jeans and T-shirt he'd worn last night off the floor and yanked them on over the gym shorts he slept in, then slid his bare feet into tennis shoes and pulled the baseball bat from under the bed.

As he ran down the stairs, Bear at his side, he dialed Abby's number.

"Nate!" Her voice shook. "I think someone's breaking into my store. I called the police and the operator is staying on the other line with me, but—"

"I'm on my way." He hung up.

The streetlight illuminated four young men in front of Abby's, one of whom was spray-painting the front of the shop.

No sign of the police, and not another soul in sight on Main Street.

Four against one.

As if sensing Nate's thoughts, Bear edged closer.

Correction. Four against two.

Nate ran a hand over the big dog's shoulders. "C'mon, Bear," he said. He tightened his grip on the baseball bat and ran toward the antique shop. "What do you think you're doing?" he yelled.

The spray painter stopped and turned in Nate's direction. Another of the punks shoved one of Abby's planters over.

It landed with a loud crack.

Nate raised the baseball bat and ran closer. Bear charged at them, barking at top volume.

The four kids sprinted across the street and down an alley, too far ahead for Nate to catch up. Bear, though, stayed right on their heels.

From down Main Street, a siren wailed.

Nate pulled his cell phone from his jeans pocket and

dialed. "Abby? They're gone. And the cops are almost here. I'll be waiting on your porch."

Hands trembling, Abby crept down the stairs.

In the dim light, she could see that one of the window shades in the showroom was ajar. Below it, on the floor, shards of broken glass encircled a large rock.

For a second, she couldn't breathe. Her shop, her beautiful shop—vandalized. If it hadn't been for the window shades that her cousins Earl Ray and Jack had insisted she needed for privacy, that rock would have hit her big display of milk glass.

How could this have happened? In downtown Abundance?

An icy feeling radiated out from her core, and for an odd moment she thought she should have put on her coat, not shorts and a T-shirt. She shivered, turned on the front porch light, and padded over in her flip-flops to peek out the door.

Nate stood on the porch, a baseball bat in one hand.

She pulled open the door, and tears welled in her eyes. "Oh, Nate! Are you sure they're gone?"

"They're gone. Are you all right?"

"Yes." She rushed toward him.

He let the bat fall to the porch with a *thunk* and drew her into his arms, into safety and warmth and strength. For a moment, the tiniest of moments, she sank into the comfort of having someone take care of her. Sank into the rightness of his embrace. The faint, outdoorsy scent of his cologne. The softness of his T-shirt. The solid muscles

211

beneath it. The gentle scratch of his beard against her cheek. The connection she'd felt, ever since that day in Kansas City.

A car door slammed.

She jerked back.

Two police officers climbed out of their cruiser and came closer.

"Ma'am?" the taller one said.

"I saw the stupid punks that did this." Nate stepped forward. "Four of them, young, male. They ran off that way." He pointed to an alley across Main Street. "My dog ran after them."

The shorter officer dashed across the street.

The other one shone his flashlight over the front of her store, stopping at the broken window. Then he moved the light to the right.

Abby jerked back.

In red spray paint across the soft-yellow wall, uneven letters read *Rose Park Sucks.*

Abby's legs grew weak.

In a haze, she felt Nate cup a hand under her elbow and lead her to the porch swing.

Now she understood what her father-in-law meant on the phone last night when he talked about the community. He hadn't been trying to change her mind because he supported the new park. He'd been concerned about her.

Because the people who wanted Rose Park sold were not just planning to talk to the city council.

They'd taken matters into their own violent hands.

Flashes from the police cruiser's red lights poured in around the edges of the curtains and stained the walls of Abby's second-floor family room.

Nate sat in silence, watching those angry lights. They didn't belong in this room. Not with that afghan that looked as if it had been made by someone's grandmother. Not with the faint hint of Abby's rose perfume in the air. Not with those photos of Emma all along the wall over the couch, photos that he'd bet Abby had taken.

Everything about the room was comforting and cozy except for two things. The triangular wooden case that hung proudly between two windows and held a folded flag. And those red lights.

He should have done a better job of diffusing the tension at the meeting about the park, and he should be outside, shoulder-to-shoulder with Abby, talking with the police. Sure, he was honored that she trusted him enough to ask him to watch Emma, but he felt useless, powerless. Even Bear, who had loped back not long after the police arrived, was there with her.

How could the idiots in this town have vandalized her property? Didn't they realize the pain their action could cause?

And she was out there facing it alone.

He glanced at the flag and swallowed. She'd probably had to face a lot of pain alone.

Not anymore. First thing in the morning, he'd be on the phone with Archie. Oh, Archie hadn't been one of the spray painters. Not a one of them had his stocky build or moved like a man his age. But Archie knew who was involved. One way or another, Nate would get the point

213

across that violence was not the answer and that Archie needed to share that message. If nothing else, Nate could appeal to the man's own motivation. Vandalizing the property of the young widow of a veteran was no way to garner public support, especially not if Archie wanted his three precious ballfields.

And Nate would talk to Cooper. There had to be a solution. No park was worth terrorizing a member of the community.

The bell on Abby's front door clanked.

Nate dashed to the top of the stairs.

Abby stood right inside the door, gripping the newel post. Her T-shirt hung on her shoulders as though her body had shrunk, and her nose was pink from crying. "Is Emma okay?"

"I haven't heard a peep." He moved down the stairs as quickly as he could without making them creak, pulled Abby into his arms, and held her close.

"I still can't believe what they did to my store," she said in a thin voice.

He rubbed one hand across her shoulders. If only he could ease the tension that knotted them. "I'm so sorry, Abby."

She stepped back and fumbled in her pocket, then pulled out a tissue and wiped her nose. "And they're wrong. Rose Park needs some work, but it's"—she blew her nose—"it's a beautiful place. There has to be a way to make folks see its importance to the community. Baseball is important—but so is our town's history."

"You're right. There must be a way to fix this." He drew her back into his arms, back where she belonged, back where he wanted to keep her forever so he could protect her.

She let out a sigh, and the tension left her shoulders.

Gently he kissed the top of her head. No way was he going to let Abby or Emma be frightened or in danger ever again. "I'll figure this out," he said. "One way or another."

Chapter Eighteen

Nate gritted his teeth and pushed up on the handles of one of his living room windows.

It didn't budge a millimeter.

"You're going to open," he said aloud.

Bear, lying a few feet away, raised his head, then laid it back down with a heavy sigh as if, in his opinion, before nine on a Saturday morning was far too early to be tackling a home-improvement project.

"Sorry to disturb you." Even if it interfered with Bear's sleep, Nate didn't want to waste the morning. It was too early, though, to call Abby to offer to help her clean up last night's mess.

And so he'd decided to tackle the windows. The air conditioner in his bedroom was struggling. The high for the past three days had been 98. He needed another unit in the living room, which was impossible unless he pried a window open.

Yesterday, Hank at the hardware store had recommended that Nate try a box cutter. Nate took it out of its packaging and slid the blade between the window frame and the sill, cutting through the paint. It looked like two different colors sealed the window. Couldn't his landlady, Neva, have left bad enough alone? Did she really need to "freshen things up" by adding more paint, reinforcing how the last paint job had sealed the window?

Nate ran the blade all along the edge of the window frame and tried again.

Still stuck. He slammed the box cutter down on the window sill and stomped away. Useless. Just as useless as he'd been so far in fixing this park mess.

After last night, he had to come up with a solution.

Bear stretched and walked over to Nate. The big dog rubbed his fuzzy head against Nate's leg, a clear message that someone needed to forget about the window and scratch his ears.

When Nate did, Bear gave him a look of undying love.

"Ah, Bear. I thought the answers would be simple here. If my colleagues back at Spillman knew the trouble I've had, they'd never stop laughing at how I've botched things up." If he couldn't figure this out, if doing his job meant breaking Abby's heart, it might end his time in Abundance. How could he stand it if he had to see her every day, her eyes filled with anger? Or with pain? It would be bad enough when the deal was settled. It would be even worse when Rose Park was actually destroyed.

Bear gazed up at Nate and dripped a long string of drool onto his shoe.

"You believe in me, don't you?"

Bear gave a resounding woof.

"Do you think there's any way to make Abby happy and do my job properly?"

Bear didn't reply. Either the dog had his doubts, or the single "woof" was as chatty as he was going to be.

Nate picked up the box cutter and attacked the window again, this time working from the opposite direction. After a minute, he tried once more to open it.

It worked.

"Yes!" Nate punched a fist in the air in victory.

He was going to get both windows open. And he was going to make Abby happy—and do an amazing job for Redmond and Associates. He may have temporarily been off his game, been unfamiliar with the players here in Abundance, and he might have been a little too sure of himself, a little too focused on Abby instead of his job, but he hadn't entirely lost his legal savvy. Everything was going to work out.

Someone knocked at his door.

Maybe it was Abby. There was no reason for her to stop by, but… He pulled the door open.

"Surprise!" Jessica stood on the landing.

Nate froze, his brain suddenly replaced with fiberglass insulation.

Jessica wrapped him in a huge hug and then eliminated any space between their bodies and kissed him.

He extricated himself from her arms and backed away. "What, uh…?" What in the world was she doing here?

"I took off a week to visit!"

"You what?" Nate glanced down. Beside her on the landing was a large suitcase and a leather carry-on duffle.

She scooped the carry-on onto her elbow and gestured to the larger suitcase. "Can you bring that in for me? I'm worn out from getting it up the stairs." She walked past him into the living room and spun on one red high heel to face him, her long hair whirling out around her, dark and shiny. "I probably should unpack a few things so they don't wrinkle, but I want to hear all about—"

"Jessica, you can't stay here. I only have one bedroom, and my couch is too short for either one of us to sleep on." Besides, Nate was pretty sure that, despite his stern admonishments, Bear slept on it every night.

"Naa-ate." She drew his name out to two syllables, moved closer, and ran a hand down his chest. "I'm sure there's room in your bed for me. There always used to be." She walked past him, pulled her suitcase inside, and shut the apartment door.

A sick feeling gurgled in his gut. Getting involved with Jessica had been a mistake. He'd figured that out when he was in rehab. She was fine as a colleague but not the right woman for a relationship.

Now being involved with her felt wrong on a whole different level. He had a pretty good idea that Abby Kincaid didn't sleep with someone simply because it was convenient. That her way of living would sit a lot easier on his conscience. And that even if he read the whole Bible, he wouldn't find a single verse that said sleeping with Jessica would bring him peace.

But she could sweetly steamroll over the top litigators

in New York. She wouldn't even see getting back in his bed as a challenge. He was going to have to be flat-out rude.

"Jessica." He ran a hand through his hair. "I don't really know why you came here. You know our relationship is over."

"There's no reason we shouldn't get back together. We were a great couple. I just know I can convince you to come back to New York. You simply need to see what you're missing." She undid the top two buttons of her shirt.

"Jessica, STOP!"

Her hands fell to her sides.

"We are not going to bed. You are not staying here. And I am not moving back to New York."

"But it's where you belong, Nate."

"No. Not anymore."

Jessica caught her lower lip between her teeth, looked away, and walked toward the kitchen. After a second she pointed at the fridge, at the picture Emma had colored. "I thought you had one little cousin, Kira. Who's Emma?"

"The daughter of a friend. She and Kira play together."

"Oh. Very sweet." Jessica glanced down for a moment, then returned to the living room. "Okay," she said in a voice he recognized as her final-offer tone. "Let's talk about this." She took a step closer to him. "There's a chance I might be willing to move here as well."

Move here? That meant—

The truth slammed into his chest and trickled down to sit uneasily in his stomach. Jessica had spent years working toward partner at Spillman, Hector, and Associates. Had she made some monumental error? Lost an account? Gotten fired?

He tried to imagine such a thing.

And couldn't. Jessica was as likely to get fired as she was to pull an apron out of her suitcase and start baking cookies.

No, she wouldn't be offering to move to Abundance unless....

Shame rushed into his stomach like sewage backing up a drain. He took her hand and led her to the couch. "C'mon, we need to talk."

This was going to be ugly.

How had he been so self-absorbed, so ignorant of what was going on around him? How had he not realized how seriously he needed to make amends with Jessica? Turns out, in addition to getting hooked on pills and seriously injuring a child, he'd also used this woman.

A woman who all along had been in love with him.

Half an hour later, Jessica's cheeks were mottled and her eyes red.

Even in their worst fight, even the time she'd been beaten down by the political games at work, Nate had never seen her like this. He leaned forward in his chair, closer to where she sat on the couch. She'd stopped crying, and for the last twenty minutes, hadn't spoken, just sat there seething, ignoring his repeated attempts to apologize. Surely there was something he could do. "Um, would you...would you like me to get you a cab to the airport in Kansas City?"

"Now you're throwing me out on the street looking like this?" She grabbed her purse and strode down the hall to the bathroom.

"Jessica, I—"

The door shut behind her with a bang.

Nate shifted on the couch. Normally comfortable, the cushions felt as if they were made of granite, but maybe that discomfort came from his conscience.

Bear came out of the bedroom, where he'd hidden, and walked over beside the couch. Nate ran a hand over Bear's back. The dog's show of support was rather late, but Nate couldn't blame him for hiding earlier. If Nate could have left the room while Jessica screamed, he would have too.

At last, she emerged from the bathroom. Her makeup was repaired, her hair smooth. She surveyed the apartment with her chin high. "I must have been insane, thinking even for a moment I could live in this dump. This pathetic backwater, that mutt shedding everywhere, it's all too sad." She sounded repulsed, and she slung her duffle over her shoulder.

Nate jumped up and reached for the handle of her suitcase.

Jessica jerked it away. "Don't even think about it. You've made your feelings very clear. We're nothing. And that's exactly what I want from you." She dragged her suitcase toward the door.

He followed her. "Jessica, I really am sor—"

She slammed the door in his face and went down the stairs.

Thud.
Thud.
Thud.

He wouldn't be surprised if her suitcase left a dent in each metal step.

What a morning.

Chapter Nineteen

Abby nestled the new petunia plant into the planter at the base of her porch steps. "What do you think?" She brushed some dirt off a soft blossom.

Emma looked up from the porch swing, where she was doing a dot-to-dot book. "They're beautiful, Mommy. Even prettier than the pink ones before."

"I like these better too." The deep violet petunias would stand out so well with the yellow shop behind them. Especially since her cousins Earl Ray and Jack had come by bright and early and painted over the spray paint. Hank had brought over the paint, a gift from his boss, old Mr. Porter at the hardware store, and had already replaced her window. Her parents even called and offered to come back early from their second honeymoon in Alaska, but she'd told them it wasn't necessary. She was going to get past this vandalism. She was not about to let a bunch of baseball-fanatic teenagers bully her into dropping her fight to save Rose Park.

All morning people had been stopping by as they ran their Saturday errands, giving her hugs and making it clear they were shocked by the actions of the four high school boys—boys whose identities and motivation were now known by the whole town, thanks to the Abundance gossip mill.

Emma stretched down one foot and pushed off the porch until the swing began to gently creak back and forth.

Abby's thoughts turned to Nate and how protective he'd been last night, charging to her defense with a baseball bat. If she hadn't already thought she was falling for him, the thought of him chasing away those kids would have sealed the deal. Simply knowing he was close by made her feel safe. Protected. Dare she say, loved?

She patted the soil around the petunia and loosened the next one from the plastic tray.

"Oh, hello." Beautiful red, high-heeled pumps appeared a few inches away from where Abby knelt. "I didn't see you," a dark-haired woman said.

Abby rose. "Not a problem."

The woman's eyes looked so sad, and the suitcase she was pulling seemed almost more than she could manage.

It was none of Abby's business, but— "Are you okay?"

"Sort of." The woman let out a long sigh. "I just ended a relationship. I'm trying to get my mind wrapped around the fact that it's really over."

"Oh, I understand. It takes a while to accept a big loss. Would you like a glass of water or something?"

Abby pointed to her shop. "I could run in. I'm Abby, by the way, and this is Emma." She gestured toward the porch swing.

"Emma?" An odd expression passed over the woman's face.

Emma looked up.

"Pretty name," the woman said quickly. She turned to Abby. Something had changed in her eyes, as if Abby's little bit of kindness had given her a spark of energy. "If you're serious, water would be lovely."

She parked her large suitcase, set a leather duffel on top of it, and peered in the newly replaced window. "That wouldn't be milk glass I see inside, would it? My aunt collects it."

"It most certainly is," Abby said. "Let's go in. I'll wash up a bit, get you some water, and show you what I have in stock. Antiques in Abundance is quite well known for its milk glass." Judging by those red shoes, this woman could afford all collectibles in the store.

Ten minutes later, Abby was gift-wrapping a large box with a pricey Fenton Hobnail urn inside. "Your aunt is going to love this! It's very rare."

The woman, Jessica, as Abby had learned, patted the box. "I can't believe I found the perfect gift for her birthday here of all places. And you've been so nice. It makes it a little easier to accept that things have ended with Nate."

Every nerve in Abby's body went on alert. "Nate?"

"Nate Redmond. Have you met him by any chance? I used to work with him in New York."

Abby managed a tiny nod.

"Well, more than work with him." Jessica gave a delicate shrug. "Until a couple of weeks ago, we were practically living together." She scratched her nose with the back of her hand.

Heat poured through Abby's body. With effort, she kept her polite-business-owner smile in place.

Jessica didn't seem to notice Abby's unease. "Between you and me, one woman to another," she said in an embarrassed tone, "I still hope he'll return to New York and we'll get back together."

Abby tied a ribbon around the package and trimmed off the ends, keeping her head down, as if she was focused on her task. Because, as upset as she felt, her cheeks must be bright red. How had she been so gullible? So naïve? Nate had been "practically living" with Jessica and less than two weeks later kissing Abby and acting like their time together was special.

"You know," Jessica said, "in some ways, things between us haven't been the same since the wreck."

"He told me about that." At least one part of his story hadn't been a lie.

"Did he?" Jessica's eyes narrowed. "I'm sure you agree that he can't let it ruin his life. Spillman, Hector, and Associates is more than willing to excuse the time he spent in drug rehab afterward."

Abby's mouth went dry, her body numb, and she looked Jessica in the eye. "Dr—drug rehab?"

"Yeah." Jessica checked her phone. "You know, those issues he had with amphetamines that caused the wreck. I'm sure he told you how he'd tried to quit cold-turkey and was half-asleep at the wheel." She slid her phone back in her purse. "Sometimes I think I'm the only attorney at Spillman who's not taking something to stay awake." She let out a high laugh. "But I do drink a lot of diet soda."

Abby could barely breathe.

She'd gone out with someone who used drugs.

Kissed someone who used drugs.

Thought she was in love with someone who used drugs.

Her whole body felt shaky, and nausea washed through her stomach.

"Well, I shouldn't keep you." Jessica tapped the corner of the package. "You'll insure this when you ship it to my aunt?"

"Uh, of course. I'll...I'll forward you the...the tracking number."

"Then I better get back to the airport and book a flight." Jessica sounded resigned. "Such a cute little shop you have. And you were so kind."

She left the shop, and the cowbell on the door jangled behind her.

Abby stumbled to the closest chair and collapsed.

Why wasn't Abby answering? Nate got up from his couch and clicked his phone off. He'd been calling since Jessica left. There was nothing more he could do about the mess he'd created by getting involved with her.

The mess those stupid guys had made at Abby's shop last night though? That he could try to fix. If she wasn't answering, he'd walk over. Maybe her phone was on silent.

Two minutes later, he stood in front of her shop. The window had been replaced, the graffiti painted over, a new flowerpot put in place of the broken one. Except for the fact that the new window was shinier than the rest and the petunias in the pots were purple instead of pink, he could barely tell the vandalism had happened.

As he walked in, the cowbell clanged, echoing in the quiet rooms. "Abby? I came over to help clean up. Is everything already taken care of?"

Abby came down the stairs, her eyes hard. "I don't need your help."

Uh-oh. Not this again. "What's wrong? Have the idiots in this town done something else?"

She stopped on the bottom stair and crossed her arms over a T-shirt advertising Porter's Hardware. "This morning the people from this town have been wonderful. It's someone from New York who's the problem." Her tone, normally so sweet, stabbed into him like a knife that had been left in the butcher shop freezer.

Nate backed up a step, running into the door. "What—?"

"I met your old girlfriend, Jessica. The one you were living with a couple of weeks before you took me out on a date that I foolishly thought really meant something."

Nate's breath came faster. Jessica? How on earth did Abby meet Jessica? No matter how much she loved shopping, he couldn't picture Jessica wanting to look at antiques after she left his apartment.

Abby's brows arched as if she saw his discomfort and took pleasure in it. "She also told me why you left New York. Including some information you left out, like the drugs."

Cold sweat covered Nate's body. "Abby, Jessica and I weren't, and you—you've got to let me explain."

Abby shoved her hands on her hips and stared at him. "Do you really think there's anything you could say that would help?"

Well, no, judging by the expression on her face, he didn't think anything he could say would help one bit. Because the woman wasn't listening. And there was a reason. If she'd take the word of someone she just met over his word after the time they'd spent together, she wasn't over her husband. She was looking for an excuse to avoid a relationship.

"Abby, you can't say anything to anyone about the drugs. In a town like this, by hiring me, Al's reputation could be—"

"Let me explain something to you, Nate Redmond. If you want someone to do something for you, like, say, keep your secrets, it's important to have a trusting relationship with that person." Her voice quivered with barely contained emotion. "Not to lie to them."

Nate's pulse throbbed in his temples. "I have *not* lied to you. Just because I haven't yet told you every detail of my past—"

She snorted.

"Have you told me every secret of your past? Every mistake you ever made? Or are you too perfect to ever make a mistake?"

"Oh, I've made a mistake all right. I made a mistake in thinking I could be involved with you." She pointed at the door. "It's time for you to leave. Now."

"Fine." He wasn't getting through to her. "But you

cannot"—he stood up taller and leaned toward her—"cannot ruin Al. No matter how incapable you are of believing me, you can't ruin his livelihood."

He left the shop and flung the door closed behind him with such force that the cowbell gave an odd clunk, as if it had bounced off the doorknob and hit the floor.

Sunday afternoon, Abby wandered down a gravel path at Rose Park.

A pair of doves cooed in a nearby tree, and a gentle breeze ruffled Emma's curls as she danced inside the concrete ring of the dry fountain. The sad, pathetic, dry fountain.

Abby knew the feeling.

Could she have been any more pathetic, imagining a future with Nate?

Not really.

Oh, the pain wasn't the same as when Eric died, but it still hurt. The scar tissue over her heart was tender, and Nate's lies had sliced right in.

Seeing him at church this morning had made her almost physically ill. At least she'd managed to slip out without speaking to him. Yes, church was for the broken, but his presence there had seemed so hypocritical.

For all she knew, he could still be using drugs, could have been using them while he took her to Kansas City, while he was in her home, while he played with Emma. Her pulse raced and she exhaled deliberately, trying to calm down.

She needed to focus on the park. She had more than a

hundred signatures on her petition. She'd keep asking people. Maybe go back and ask again with the people who had said they needed to think about it, like Frankie.

And she would focus on Eric. She needed to forget about any other man and remember her husband. Especially today, four years after the day he died. That horrible, horrible day.

Abby swallowed hard and walked a few feet farther, until she reached a yellow rosebush that stood all alone. This rosebush, unlike the others, received lots of sun. Full and healthy, it was covered in blooms. She moved beside it, stepping into the spot where she had been when Eric proposed.

It had been February, their junior year of college. The rosebush had been a shapeless blob then, covered, like everything in the park, in six inches of snow.

"I don't really know where the Army will send me, Abby." Eric had reached down and taken her hand inside his.

Her bright-blue glove had looked so small wrapped in his large black ski glove. And she hadn't known what to say. Even thinking about him leaving made it hard for her to swallow.

"I, uh...I don't want to do this alone, Abby," Eric said. "I know I'll be away for a long time, but I really want to know you'll be waiting for me when I come home."

She squeezed his hand and pushed the words out past the lump in her throat. "I will, Eric. You know I will."

"Not as a girlfriend," he said. He took off his gloves and pulled a ring box from the pocket of his ski jacket. "As my wife."

Tears sprang to her eyes and ran down her cheeks. She blinked them back and raised a hand to her open mouth.

"Abby Hamlin, will you marry me?"

Her *yes* had been instantaneous, her voice shaking with emotion.

Eric had pulled her close and kissed her, a promise of the vow to come, a pledge of love to last a lifetime.

A lifetime that should have lasted much longer.

How could she let the city cover this very spot with a store or a parking lot?

She had to fight for Rose Park. Just because someone had attacked her store, just because Nate couldn't be trusted to help her—none of that was a reason to abandon Eric and the park.

Would her petition, her arguments to the city council make any difference?

If only she could find a champion, someone who would fight with her. Someone with clout. Maybe someone in the media. Someone who took on hopeless causes. Someone like…

Shelly Dwyer on Channel Six out of Kansas City!

Adrenaline poured into Abby's veins. Yes. The idea was perfect.

She hurried back to the fountain and sat on the edge, then pulled out her phone and searched online until she found a number.

They transferred her and it rang and rang and—

"Shelly Dwyer."

Quickly, Abby mentioned how they had known each other. She explained about how the city was planning to sell a park that had been donated in honor of a woman prominent in the town history, a woman who had treated everyone with equality.

"And you're related to Rose?"

"Only by marriage. But my husband's grandmother is still alive. She's recovering from hip surgery, but she opposes the sale and—"

"Did she donate the land?" Shelly sounded interested.

"Her father-in-law did. And she wants the park saved. So do I." Abby sat up a little taller.

"That does seem like it would be a good story."

Abby rose and began walking around the fountain. It would be a *great* story.

"Hold on." The line went silent for a minute. "Sorry, my editor was yelling at me about something. If he'd check on his desk once in a while... Anyway, who's pushing for the development?"

"A bunch of folks who want a new park." Abby explained about the plan to sell one park and build another.

"This park story sounds promising. Exactly the kind that our 'Justice in the Heartland' series was made for, and—"

Abby could hear someone talking to Shelly, saying something about a feature.

"Hey." Shelly came back on the line. "I need to deal with something for today's broadcast. Can I call you back in a couple of hours?"

"Sure. You should also know that I'm speaking to the city council about this Wednesday night."

"What time?"

"Seven."

"I'll be there."

Abby gave Shelly her cell phone number and hung up.

This was going to work. Shelly would draw attention to what the city was doing. The city leaders would see how wrong they were. The youth baseball team would back off. Rose Park, a monument to Rose McFee Kincaid and a symbol of Abby's memories with Eric, would be preserved and probably upgraded with a new climbing structure purchased with the grant money. Nate Redmond wouldn't matter.

Getting a reporter involved would make everything turn out right.

Chapter Twenty

"Let me check a couple of things in Kira's chart," the orthopedic surgeon said. He scooted closer to the small desk in the examining room, pulled on the reading glasses that hung around his neck, and looked down at a laptop.

Frankie glanced around. The Columbia doctor's office was pretty much like all the doctors' offices she and Kira had seen in Houston. Same vinyl examination table. Same boring furniture. Same smell of antiseptic and dry air.

One thing was different. In her career in hospital public relations, Frankie had worked with a lot of physicians. She knew the indicators that a doctor was at the top of the field—graduating from impressive med schools, doing fellowships at the top hospitals, board certification. This physician had all those indicators—and more—on display on his office walls. Maybe this doctor would be the answer to her prayers.

Now that she saw how prestigious this guy was, she couldn't believe the nurse with Kira's pediatrician back in Abundance had gotten them in so fast.

"Look, Mommy." Kira held out a picture book, showing her a bunny in a pink dress.

"What a darling rabbit," Frankie said. Kira was being such a good girl. She'd been cooperative through the exam and answered the doctor's questions almost like an adult would have.

Probably because she'd been to the doctor as many times as most people had by the time they were adults. As always, the injustice of Kira's disability hovered at the edge of Frankie's heart, ready to move in and take up permanent residence. Most children saw a doctor only for colds and checkups. Sure, many kids had issues that were way more serious, but this was her girl, her sweet girl. It just seemed wrong. Frankie forced back the negative feelings and told herself to keep smiling.

The series of casts hadn't helped, but Kira had been wearing her leg braces exactly as the doctor in Houston prescribed. He'd assured them that those braces should help Kira's legs and feet become normal. In time, she should only need inserts in her shoes, and her mobility would be almost like every other kid's.

Once the doctor was done reading, Frankie could talk with him about the physical therapy. Her dad and Nate had offered to help drive Kira to her appointments in Columbia, but Frankie knew it was a huge imposition and also knew, that no matter what her dad hoped to do, his work would interfere. Probably not only in his plans, but also in Nate's.

This surgeon seemed nice, though. Maybe he could talk with the pediatrician and get him to agree to therapy back in Abundance, at least some of the time.

Frankie checked her phone. The surgeon sure was taking a long time to review the records.

He closed the laptop with a click. "I think we can really help you, Kira. I recommend that we operate as soon as possible."

Kira shrank back on the examination table.

Frankie stood and wrapped an arm around Kira's shoulders, then turned to face the surgeon. "Operate?" She'd asked the doctor back in Houston about surgery. More than once. Each time he had discouraged her.

The surgeon leaned in toward Kira, and his voice became warmer. "You won't even know the surgery is happening. You'll go to sleep and wake up and it will all be done."

He looked back at Frankie. "I know the orthopedic you saw in Houston took a more conservative approach, but in my opinion, it's not working." He launched into a lengthy explanation full of lingo that even Frankie, who was fairly comfortable with medical terms, struggled to follow completely.

She understood enough, though, to believe that he knew what he was talking about and to believe it could work. The more she thought about it, the faster her heart beat.

"If we operate soon," he said. "I think we can have Kira comfortably walking typically without braces in a matter of months. Shall we proceed?"

Frankie nodded.

Kira nodded as well, if a bit more slowly.

The doctor sat back in his chair, scrawled something on a billing form, and handed it to her to take up front. "My nurse will be in to go over the details. I'll have her tell the desk I want Kira scheduled for surgery as soon as possible." He left the room.

"Really, Mommy?" Kira said in a stunned tone. "No braces?"

Frankie wrapped Kira in a tight hug and stared over her head at the diplomas and certificates on the wall. "Really, Kira. I think so."

In spite of all Frankie's work in a hospital, in spite of all the articles she'd written about medical procedures, surgery was scary when it was one's own child. But this doctor's credentials were very reassuring. And Frankie's heart soared at the thought of Kira walking without braces.

Ten minutes later, after the nurse talked with them, they waited as the receptionist looked at the schedule.

She checked her notepad and then her computer. "Talk about good luck."

Frankie moved closer to the counter. "Yes?"

"An older patient had to reschedule because of a medication issue. We can get Kira in for surgery Thursday."

"This Thursday?" Frankie echoed, her mind spinning.

"Yes. The sixteenth," the receptionist said.

Thursday, July 16, was the day of the hospital's annual maternity fair. Frankie wasn't in charge, but it was an all-hands-on-deck event for the public relations department. If she missed the event, it wouldn't go over well. And she hadn't even thought to talk to the surgeon about where Kira would have her PT appointments.

Frankie didn't care. Her Kira, her darling girl, would be able to run and skip and climb anything on the playground, wearing shoes with the latest popular cartoon character on them, just like every other kid.

"Thursday would be perfect." She picked up a nearby pen to take notes on the back of the co-pay receipt. "What time should we get there?"

At twelve-forty Tuesday afternoon, Cooper scanned the tables of Cassidy's Diner.

There. At that booth near the back. Frankie looked amazing. Her glossy auburn hair was piled on top of her head, and she wore a bright-turquoise dress and sweater. But the plate in front of her was almost empty and, the second she spotted him, her lips thinned.

He made his way past the line at the register and scooted in across from her, positioning himself right under the AC vent. Unfortunately, in spite of how he'd rushed down the sidewalk in the heat, he was forty minutes late.

"I thought we were meeting at noon." Frankie's voice made it clear. Any mix-up about the time was not a mistake on her part.

"Sorry. I had to pull over to find some figures for a sub-contractor." It wasn't like he could ignore the call. Dad was depending on him. He'd texted Frankie as soon as he got off the phone, but—

"I have to leave in ten minutes or I'll be late for my

one o'clock. I ordered you a pop." She gestured to a cup that sat in front of him. "And a burger and onion rings like you had last time. Grace is holding your plate under the heat lamps." The words were understanding. Her tone wasn't.

"A burger sounds great." Although actually he'd been wanting a Reuben.

Her phone, sitting at the edge of the table near the wall, dinged with a text.

Frankie glanced at it and blew out a sharp breath. "My boss. I've got to answer this."

When she finished, he'd like to tell her about his meeting with Archie. It hadn't gone too badly. No measurable progress, but the man had listened and looked at the brochures Cooper brought to show him well-designed, accessible play equipment.

This afternoon Cooper planned to give the mayor some website links to vendors who made amazing play equipment that could be used by all kids, including those with accessibility issues. He'd include some ideas for simple accommodations in the restrooms, and he'd suggest that the city involve some community members with children who had more significant mobility challenges when they discussed the new park. Whoever Abundance hired to develop the park probably would know all that, but it never hurt for a client to know what to ask for.

None of that was worth mentioning to Frankie, at least not yet. Cooper had learned well enough in his business dealings that until something panned out, there was no use telling people about it and expecting them to be impressed.

His burger arrived. "This smells delicious," he said as she set down her phone. "Thanks for ordering it for me."

The tension in her face eased slightly.

Cooper added tomato, mustard, and ketchup to his burger, leaving the huge, floppy piece of lettuce on the side of the plate. He never had quite figured out the purpose of lettuce. Take a salad, for example. Unless you covered it in cheese and croutons and dressing and bacon, well, what good was a pile of lettuce? No real flavor and it sure didn't keep him full, not like a burger. He took a big bite of his sandwich. Not bad, even after sitting a while, but it too needed bacon.

"Sorry I had to deal with that text," Frankie said. "But I do have big news. Two pieces of big news. First, Mom's primary care doctor believes her seizure was a weird reaction to a new medication, something a specialist prescribed and she forgot to mention at first."

"If he changes her prescription, she should be fine?"

"That's what he thinks."

"Excellent."

"And yesterday I took Kira to an orthopedist in Columbia." Frankie sat forward with such excitement that she bounced on the booth cushion. "He thinks the braces aren't working and wants to operate." A bubble of laughter escaped her. "He says in a few months she'll be able to walk without them."

"That's excellent!"

"I know. You can't imagine how long I've prayed for this."

For a second, Cooper hesitated. For most children, the prospect of surgery would only bring tears. For

Frankie and Kira, though, it was an answered prayer. He didn't really have a clue how hard their lives had been or how brave both of them had had to be, but he was beginning to get an inkling. "When will Kira see this doctor again?"

"She'll have her surgery this Thursday."

"Wow. That's soon."

"I know." She explained what the operation would entail.

Cooper asked a question or two, but a lot of it was over his head. That didn't diminish how thrilled he was for Kira—and for Frankie.

"I was so excited that I even called Garrett, despite..." Frankie wadded up her napkin and dropped it on the table. "Well, you know."

Cooper knew. Despite how Garrett had failed to be there when Kira needed him. A bad taste welled up in Cooper's mouth, just thinking about the creep. Hard to believe they'd once been friends. As awful as his dad's punishment had been when Cooper flunked out, it had served a purpose. He'd grown up enough to realize that Garrett Parks was not the kind of person he wanted to be around.

Surely, though, even a creep would be excited at the possibility that his daughter might be able to walk without braces. "What did he say?"

"He said he was happy for her, but that of course, he wouldn't be able to be there—like I'd even ask—because any day now his new wife is expecting their baby."

Cooper froze. "New wife?"

Frankie took a drink of her iced tea. "Yeah, some

woman he started dating about a year ago. He had the gall to tell me"—she paused and her tone became soured—"that he expects *their* child to be perfectly healthy."

Blood pounded in Cooper's ears. Why, the lowdown...

"I mean, I want their baby to be healthy, of course." Frankie jabbed her straw at the ice in her nearly empty tea glass. "But the way he said it..."

If Garrett wasn't three hours away in St. Louis, Cooper would have slugged him. "Unbelievable. But I hope that, no matter what, he can be a more responsible parent this time around."

"Me too," Frankie said solemnly. "I almost think I should warn his new wife about how he treated Kira and me, but she probably wouldn't listen."

"She wouldn't. Any woman who's enough of a moron to marry Garrett Parks deserves what she gets."

Frankie's chin shot up. "A moron, huh?"

"Frankie—"

"Good to know what you think of my intelligence," she spat out.

"I didn't mean you." He leaned toward her.

She grabbed her purse, threw down a ten-dollar-bill, and stood. "I've got a meeting."

He reached for her arm. "Wait." There was no reason for her to be so hot-headed.

She glared at his hand and yanked her arm out of his grasp. "I don't have time for this. You can't imagine the pressure I'm under today, what with needing Thursday and Friday off for the surgery. You're late, and then you insult me."

She strode across the room with her heels making a *click, click, click* on the linoleum, just like at the hardware store.

Chapter Twenty-One

Nate walked into his office Tuesday afternoon, elbowed on the light switch, and dumped his messenger bag in a chair.

He'd spent two days on the road, driving deep into southern Missouri to take a deposition for Al, whose illness had turned into pneumonia. Nate had tried to tell him that Abby knew about the drug use in New York, but Vivian had intercepted the call and said Al was too sick to talk.

It had been a miserable road trip. The deposition had gone well, but the drive had been endless. Road construction, compounded by an accident, had stalled him in the middle of nowhere. He'd crawled along for two hours with no cell signal, the whole time on pins and needles, waiting to learn if his drug use had become public knowledge. At this point, though, it didn't seem it had.

Now, Nate found a bright pink sticky note from Jewel on his desk explaining that she was at the dentist. No wonder the building seemed so empty.

She'd positioned the mail and phone messages from Monday front and center on his desk. He scanned the messages, shoved the mail aside, and turned on his computer.

As soon as it booted up, it reminded him again to install updates.

He rolled his eyes at it. "Later," he said aloud. "Much later."

This afternoon, though it might be the last thing he did at Redmond and Associates, Nate was going to find an answer for Rose Park. A way to assure Al that he could solve problems and to show Abby that he wasn't working against her, that he was trying to help everyone involved.

He didn't expect her to forgive him. Couldn't even ask. But maybe if he honored her husband's family, she'd stay silent about the drugs and he could keep his job. And maybe, just maybe, he could find a way to win her back.

He pulled out his notes, dialed Cooper, and told him his idea. Half an hour later, Nate hung up and sat back in his chair, tension draining from his shoulders. He'd run by to get a sandwich at the diner, then flesh out the idea more.

The phone rang. Did Cooper have a question?

"Hello, this is Shelly Dwyer of News Channel Six. I'm trying to reach Nate Redmond."

"This is Nate Redmond."

"Mr. Redmond, I'd like to talk with you about the

development of Rose Park there in Abundance. Our viewers will be very interested to learn why a town would sell a park that had been donated to honor a very important woman. Would you have a few moments to discuss this?"

Shelly Dwyer. The tension returned to his shoulders. He'd seen her on the Kansas City news, on that series they promoted so much, "Justice in the Heartland." Not good, not good at all. First things first. He needed to talk to the mayor and Cooper, to make sure they all had the same story. And, while he got rid of this reporter, he needed to act like it was no big deal.

"You're catching me at a busy time here," he said, deliberately keeping his voice relaxed and even. "Can I call you back in a couple of hours?"

"Well, I don't think I'll be running anything until after the city council meeting tomorrow night, so that would work. I do want to get your side of the story, though. From what I hear from an old friend, this park is causing quite a controversy. How about I interview you in person after the meeting?"

"You're coming to Abundance?"

"My cameraman and I will be there tomorrow night."

Exactly what Nate didn't need. "I'll talk with you then." He hung up and pulled a hard candy from the jar on his desk. They were supposed to be soothing and distracting if he felt a craving for amphetamines. Hopefully the candy would be just as helpful now, as he felt a craving to pound his head against a wall.

Because if he and Cooper could get an idea worked out and get the mayor on board, that would mean the city, Sullivan Enterprises, and Redmond and Associates would look like they were honoring an admirable woman from Abundance history and improving the quality of life for people in the community.

If not, if the sale of Rose Park was portrayed negatively on "Justice in the Heartland," the town would hold Redmond and Associates—especially the newest associate—responsible. People would probably resent him so much that he'd be a liability to the firm.

And if Abby told the town that he was in recovery, things would be even worse.

He sagged lower in his chair.

If he'd known what he was coming back to in Abundance, he would have enjoyed that time stuck in construction traffic more. It might be the highlight of his week.

"I've got the information you wanted," Cooper said, as he went through the open door into Nate's office.

From behind several stacks of bulging file folders piled on his desk, Nate held up one finger and gestured to the chair across from him. With his phone tucked between his ear and shoulder, he murmured agreement with whoever was on the other end of the line and wrote something on a legal pad on his desk.

Cooper sat down and checked his own phone. No reply to his text to Frankie. She might be in a meeting though. She'd overreacted—way overreacted—today at lunch, but as he'd thought about it off and on over the past three hours, he'd figured out why. The fact that he'd been late to lunch and more than a little tactless had contributed, but neither of those things was the real issue. And, although taking time off her new job had to be stressful, that probably wasn't what got her so upset either. He had a pretty good idea that the real reason she was so stressed was that Kira was having surgery in a couple of days. Just talking about Dad's surgery made Mom edgy. It had to be worse if it was one's child.

After he talked with Nate, Cooper would call Frankie. He should have handled that urgent request from the subcontractor differently, and he should have kept his temper in check when Frankie told him what Garrett had said. If he could get Frankie to talk to him, he could explain that he made his "moron" comment not because of how little he thought of her and Kira, but because of how much. Garrett's insensitive words made him too angry to think straight.

Nate hung up and ran a hand through his hair. "We've got another problem. I got a call from a reporter."

"A reporter?"

"Shelly Dwyer from News Channel Six. I saw her for the first time the other night. She's the blonde who has a series on "Justice in the Heartland.""

"Tell me she wasn't calling about the park."

"She was."

Cooper groaned. "What made her want to do a story about Abundance?"

"She said an old friend had tipped her off."

"When did she call?"

"Five minutes ago."

Heat built in the center of Cooper's chest and spread

outward. He knew he'd made Frankie mad, but how could she have done this? He'd made one little slip of the tongue and she escalated things to sabotaging his business deal?

"What I wouldn't give to know who called the media." Nate shook his head.

"I think I know," Cooper said slowly. "I mean, I know someone who lives in Abundance who was friends with Shelly when we were in college."

"You know Shelly?" Nate leaned toward him.

"Only to say hello, but your cousin Frankie worked with her at a frozen yogurt stand at Mizzou."

"Frankie? Why would she want to stop the park deal?" Nate said. "The person fighting to keep Rose Park the way it is"—he stopped and his voice dropped an octave—"is her good friend, Abby Kincaid."

Cooper ran a hand over his mouth.

Nate rubbed his temple. "This is bad. Really bad. Abby's furious with me because I, uh…" Nate blinked. "Let's just say she's furious enough that she probably got Frankie to call Shelly."

"And I made Frankie mad when we were at lunch today," Cooper said. "She probably didn't need much convincing."

"Shelly's going to be at the city council meeting," Nate said.

"What if her story makes us sound racist or sexist for destroying Rose Park? Dad and I had no idea that Rose McFee Kincaid was a noted businesswoman who stood up against discrimination. I thought it was called Rose Park because it had roses."

"A logical assumption," Nate said under his breath.

"A news story like that could destroy The Main Place project. And it wouldn't even be true. Dad's a stickler about our hiring practices, not because he wants to avoid lawsuits, but because he believes that people should be judged for a job only on their ability to do the work."

With one elbow on the desk, Nate rested his head in one hand and stared down. After a moment, he looked up. "Abundance needs better park space," he said with determination.

"And Sullivan Enterprises needs this development to work out," Cooper said.

"Then we need an emergency meeting with the mayor, that lady over in finance—Paula, I think her name is—and Archie." Nate sat up taller in his chair. "And we need an amazing presentation for the city council tomorrow night."

Cooper got in his truck and cranked the air conditioning. Hot air roared out, only adding to the sweltering humidity. He turned back the fan and shoved the truck into gear.

Nate had offered him a ride to city hall to see the mayor, but Cooper said he wanted to take his own car. He needed a moment to think. And the more he thought, the more the blood heated in his veins.

He'd believed, really believed, that in spite of that disaster of a meeting where Archie stormed out, things would fall into place for The Main Place deal. People squabbled all the time over the details in negotiations.

Somehow, this deal could have been resolved.

But not with bad P.R.

If Shelly's TV station ran a piece about Sullivan Enterprises pushing a deal that would ignore the contributions of an early female entrepreneur, a woman who not only started her own business but used it to help others without any thought of their race or gender, it would kill this deal. And possibly the next one. And the one after that.

What a disaster! Both he and his dad believed that everyone should be treated equally, that race and gender didn't matter. Dad would be mortified to be associated in any way with racism or sexism.

He'd trusted Cooper to make The Main Place deal work. He'd certainly never expected Cooper to tarnish the name of the firm. No way would Dad go through with his surgery now. He'd postpone it indefinitely, so he could deal with the nightmare Cooper had created. All because Cooper had gotten involved with Frankie.

How could she have done this? Especially after he'd told her about his dad's heart condition and how he needed to prove that he was capable of running the family firm?

Yet, if he thought about the way she sent Garrett all that unwanted medical information, it made perfect sense. Frankie's revenge tactics weren't nearly as hilarious now as they had seemed before.

If he somehow got her to call Shelly back, was there a chance he could stop the story?

No. Reporters didn't work that way.

The only answer was to meet with Nate and the

mayor and try to find a way to build The Main Place and honor Rose McFee Kincaid at the same time. And now talking at the city council meeting tonight would be even worse than he'd feared. He hated addressing a large crowd. This would be a crowd, possibly combined with questions from a reporter. The type of situation that made his voice sound shaky and his mind go blank and his whole system rebel to the point where he felt like he might pass out. Probably because he forgot to breathe.

Somehow, he'd have to get through it.

He'd do his best to prepare.

And he'd deal with the root of the problem—Frankie McNamara.

He slowed at a stoplight and used Voice Dial to call her number.

No answer. Her voice mail picked up.

"Frankie," he said. "I can't believe how you've overreacted. I hope Kira's surgery goes well, but I think it's best if we don't see each other anymore." Harsh, but he didn't care. Not only had she hurt him, she had destroyed the efforts of her father and cousin. Not a person he wanted to be involved with.

No, the best thing he could do was stay far away from Frankie McNamara and focus on what really mattered, getting this park deal put into place.

For him, family was important.

Five minutes later he parked at city hall.

His phone dinged with a text.

He had a good mind not to even read her message but couldn't stop himself.

He looked.

And felt like he'd been punched.

It wasn't Frankie.

It was Mom.

Cooper's heart pounded as he stared at the words on the screen.

Dad headed to ER. They think he had a heart attack.

Chapter Twenty-Two

After meeting with the mayor, Paula, and Archie, and then stopping at the diner for a carry-out dinner, Nate hurried into the empty law office.

He set the warm bag from the diner next to the candy jar on his desk. If he had help, he could attend his regular support-group meeting at the hospital. But Jewel had texted earlier that she'd had a reaction to the antibiotics the dentist had given her. She couldn't help tonight and she wouldn't be in tomorrow. Al was too weak to even talk on the phone for more than five minutes. And Cooper was at the hospital with his dad.

Nate was on his own.

No support group. Tonight he'd have to be strong enough to handle his addiction by himself.

He, the mayor, Paula, and Archie had hammered out the details of a plan—a plan that even Abby should like. Thanks to an earlier conversation with Cooper, Archie had chipped in a cash donation in addition to the land and had agreed to two ball fields instead of three, even mentioned that improved accessibility would make it easier for grandparents to attend ballgames.

This could work. Nate dialed Abby's number.

The phone rang once, then clipped off, as if she'd seen who was calling and hung up.

He tried again.

Another hang up.

He really wanted to run this by her before the council meeting. The mayor had said she planned to speak to the council as well. If she could hear Nate's idea first, he was pretty sure she would agree that this latest plan was a good one. If she wanted some small change, he could take care of it without dragging it all out in front of the city council. It seemed, though, that Abby had no interest in talking to him.

Could he call the grandmother, Doris? No, she was in a rehab center. Even if Nate could talk with her, even if she loved the solution they'd come up with, she was probably on some sort of painkiller. Her endorsement wouldn't carry any weight. Besides, talking to her about a business matter while she was recovering from surgery seemed rude.

Should he call Hubert, get his brother's number, and talk to him? The brother didn't even live in Abundance. The person Nate needed to talk to was Abby.

He tried her once more, and this time, left a message. "Abby, please, I know you're mad at me, but we need to talk about the park before the council meeting tomorrow night. I think we have an idea you might like."

There. Eventually she'd listen. In the meantime, he needed to figure out this online design software Cooper had sent him a link for. It wasn't as fancy as what Cooper used, but it was supposed to be easy.

Easy was good.

Nate had a lot of appreciation for art, but anything that involved him doing art, well…easy wasn't only good, it was essential. And his presentation depended on a visual aid showing exactly how the new development could look. At the firm back in New York, they'd had staff to do projects like this, but here…

No whining. He'd manage. And hope that—even if Abby had told that reporter about his drug issues—he could make a presentation that would impress people so much that his past wouldn't matter.

At five-thirty the next afternoon, with plenty of time to pack up his presentation, Nate returned to the law office after a quick trip home for a shower. The stack of handouts for the council members sat on the corner of his desk, ready to go. He'd even picked up his dry cleaning and put on his favorite tie.

He'd thought of one tiny change to make to his PowerPoint, and then the presentation that he'd worked on all night would be perfect. Including the mechanical drawing of the idea he, the mayor, Paula, and Archie had come up with yesterday. That drawing alone had taken hours, but he was ready to go.

He turned on his laptop, made the quick correction, and moved his mouse toward the icon to shut the machine down.

Another annoying reminder about the system updates appeared.

He got rid of it.

Installing update. Do not turn off or unplug your computer. Doing so may render your system inoperable, the screen read.

"No!" He'd clicked *Remind Me Later.* He was certain of it.

He'd. Clicked. *Remind. Me. Later.*

Only apparently he hadn't. He shoved back his chair and glared at the machine. He should have known better than to try to work all night. It only led to disasters.

He had twenty minutes before the city council meeting started.

How long could this update take?

Standing along a side wall of the Abundance City Hall auditorium, Abby scanned the room. The place was packed, the meeting about to start. Rows and rows of plastic seats were filled with townspeople, all discussing the new park. In front, facing the crowd, the mayor and the city council members sat behind microphones at a long desk, looking slightly sweaty under the lights. Already, all the warm bodies that jammed the room were giving the air conditioning a run for its money.

From his seat three rows back, Archie Turner proclaimed that if the town had nice ball fields, local boys would have a better shot at playing college ball, maybe even making it to the major leagues. It was his way, he said, of giving back to the community. Having the ball fields named in his honor was too much, but he'd agreed when the mayor pressed him.

Abby reread her index cards and wiped one wet palm and then the other on the skirt of her peach flowered dress. This was her time to convince the council—and the town—to save Rose Park. It was what Eric would have wanted her to do.

The president of the city council rapped her gavel and called the meeting to order. The murmur of the crowd softened as the last few people standing took their seats.

Abby sat down in the front row and glanced around.

Nate wasn't even here yet. Maybe she'd get some points for punctuality.

Shelly slid in at the back, checking something on her phone. Abby hadn't seen her in person in years. Just like on TV though, Shelly's blonde hair fell in perfect curls. And she hadn't aged a day since college. Probably because she'd never missed night after night of sleep with a toddler.

Shelly looked up, caught Abby's eye, and gave her a little wave. "We'll talk after," she mouthed.

Abby nodded.

For a while, the council went through routine business matters, outlined on the agenda projected on the screen behind them. Time crawled by, and the audience began to fidget. Then, abruptly, the meeting moved into high gear.

"Mrs. Kincaid," the council president said, "would you like to speak now?"

Abby rose and ran a hand over her queasy stomach. Talking to the city council shouldn't be frightening. She never minded talking in front of people at church. But this meant so much. If she failed, the site of so many of her memories of Eric would be destroyed. She'd be disappointing Doris. And failing to preserve the family history for Emma.

Abby went to the podium and positioned her index cards.

The father of one of the boys who had vandalized her store sat right in front of her, his expression icy. Her father-in-law, Hubert, sat near the middle of the audience, his face hard to read. And she'd have thought Frankie would have been here, but she wasn't.

At least Abby had her family. Hamlins stuck together. Kristen sat with Emma in the back, along with Jack and Tess, Earl Ray and Stacey, Becky and Seth, and Hank. And though Mom and Dad were still on their way home from Alaska, they had called some of their friends, who sat scattered throughout the crowd.

But Nate still wasn't here. If he never showed up, it was certainly better for her, but his absence seemed really odd.

Shelly gestured with one hand as if to communicate that tape was rolling and Abby should start speaking.

She cleared her throat. "Hi, everybody. You all know I'm Abby Kincaid. My husband, Eric, was the great-grandson of Simon Kincaid and Rose McFee Kincaid. I'm here today because I think it's important that Abundance keeps Rose Park." She swallowed. So far, so good. "As most of you know, the land for Rose Park was donated by Eric's family.

"Eric loved the park, and I have many happy

memories of the two of us there, but my reasons for saving the park aren't only personal. That park is an important part of our town's history."

Abby straightened her note cards. This next part was easy. Just as she'd practiced, she explained why Rose had been such a special woman and what her example meant for Abundance. At last she came to the final bullet point, the part she had practiced the most. She politely asked the council, the mayor, and the townspeople to preserve Rose Park because of its historic value. "I have a petition here with signatures from two hundred and seventeen Abundance citizens who agree with me." Then, with her voice still sounding nervous, even to her, she offered her idea that some of the grant money be used to improve Rose Park.

She restacked her index cards. "Thank you."

Suddenly Nate walked in at the back. Barely in time to give his speech. Not looking like he'd spilled coffee down his shirt or developed hives or anything else that might be a reasonable excuse for being late. No, he simply was not polite enough to arrive in time to hear another opinion. How rude could the man be?

But what should she expect?

Good thing she hadn't been foolish enough to take his calls last night. This was the man who'd said he was helping her but had instead suggested that Archie donate his land and get a tax write-off. The man who'd acted like he cared about her, when two weeks before he'd been in another woman's bed. The man who'd let her fall in love with him and betrayed her.

Heat bubbled inside Abby, and her muscles tensed.

With one little comment she could—

"Is there something more you'd like to add?" the council president said.

Yes, yes there was. She'd like to tell the whole town that they shouldn't believe Nate, that he was not a man of integrity, not trying to help Abundance.

He was a drug addict.

The town needed to know. Had a right to know. She should tell the council, right now, where everyone would hear.

She took a deep breath and leaned toward the microphone, heart pounding. She was doing the right thing, protecting Rose Park and protecting the town from a lawyer who brought nothing but lies. She was—

No. Her breath rushed out. She'd gone through this at home. Gotten down on her knees and prayed about it.

Telling the whole town about Nate's drug use was wrong. No matter how much she wanted to.

She looked at the council president and shook her head. Her legs felt wobbly, but she made it back to her seat in the front row.

"Thank you," the president said.

Abby sank into the plastic chair. As far as she could tell, she'd done a fairly decent job of presenting her points, and she'd handled what she knew about Nate the right way, even if he didn't deserve it. She turned and glanced back at her family and Shelly. Her sister, Kristen, gave her two thumbs up. The rest of the Hamlins smiled encouragingly.

But Hubert's mouth was drawn into a line, and nobody else in the audience was smiling.

The truth landed hard in Abby's stomach, crashing down as painfully as the time she'd dropped an antique flat iron—the kind women would heat in the fireplace before tackling a pile of shirts—on her toe at the shop.

Rose Park was doomed.

She'd been given her chance—been given the perfect way to save the park with what she knew about Nate—and hadn't used it.

Nate watched Abby settle into her seat. According to the agenda on the screen, he was up next. Talk about cutting it close. Stupid, stupid updates.

At least he'd made it, although most likely, the minute the meeting was over, the reporter would approach him with cameras rolling and ask about his drug use.

If he wanted a chance to prove that he could be a vital member of the community, a chance to show he was someone the people of Abundance could count on in spite of what they might hear about him, this was it.

On the other hand, if things tonight went poorly, Nate wasn't sure what he'd do.

No pressure. Just his whole future.

Good thing he'd given up New York for the easygoing life in small-town Missouri.

"Mr. Redmond, would you like to address the council?" the president asked.

Nate set up his laptop by the projector in the back of the room and walked to the podium, then started his PowerPoint presentation. A map of downtown

Abundance appeared on the screen behind the council members.

"Ladies and gentlemen, my name is Nate Redmond. I'm here on behalf of Redmond and Associates. You probably know my Uncle Al."

The audience murmured in agreement.

"He's home recovering from pneumonia. Another person who wanted to be here tonight is Cooper Sullivan, of Sullivan Enterprises, the firm interested in bringing a new retail development to Abundance. But Cooper's father just had emergency heart surgery."

Whispers of concern ran through the crowd. Good, he had their sympathy. He needed all the help he could get.

"I have spoken with both Mr. Sullivan and my uncle, and I have ideas to share that we all agreed on. If I may?" He pulled out a laser pointer and used it to highlight Rose Park.

All too aware of Abby's gaze on him, he carefully explained the original plan. Sullivan Enterprises would buy Rose Park from the city. Abundance would build a new park at the Pine Street location, on the far west side of town, using land graciously donated by Archie Turner. On the next slide, Nate pointed out features of the park— two ball fields, a large play area with handicap-accessible equipment, a soccer field, a basketball court, a parking lot, and a modern restroom facility.

A ripple of approval went through the crowd.

Nate's chest filled and he stood taller. He explained more, describing the types of businesses that were interested in the retail space. "And in this plan," he said, "in addition to an anonymous donation and the grant money the city has received, all the proceeds from the sale of Rose Park, a total of about $1 million, would be used in building the new park."

He hooked his thumbs in his belt loops and looked out over the crowd. People were pointing to the drawing of the park and murmuring in tones that said they were impressed. They should be. This was a great plan. This new park would be everything the city needed. Everything a kid could want.

He glanced at Abby.

Her arms were crossed, her lips a thin line as if she was deciding what to complain about first.

He picked up the remote. *You just wait a minute there before you complain, Abby Kincaid.* He had more, which he could have explained if she'd taken his calls. "But the team members at Sullivan Enterprises highly value historic sites. They have also suggested a second option." Nate clicked the button.

Abby sat up taller, arms no longer crossed, staring at the screen behind him.

Nate looked at her face, waiting for her to study the drawing. Because he knew his plan was going to work. She was going to love the idea.

And him.

Chapter Twenty-Three

A second option?

Abby leaned forward with her hands clasped and her forearms resting on her thighs.

The screen at the front of the city hall auditorium went black.

"Sorry, I accidentally unplugged it," someone called from the back.

"That new development sounds wonderful, especially a Chinese restaurant that would deliver," said a nasal voice behind Abby. "If we had that, I'd order once a week."

"I like the idea of a phone store. Then I wouldn't have to go to Columbia every time mine acts up," another person said.

Abby almost agreed, but stopped herself. That phone store might be right where Eric had proposed to her.

At last the screen at the front of the room came back to life.

Except for the woman next to Abby, who sneezed, muttered about pollen, and then blew her nose, the crowd grew quiet.

Abby studied the drawing on the screen. What *was* this second option?

Nate explained that Sullivan Enterprises would leave a small green space in the middle of the shopping area that would be built on the site of Rose Park. A plaque and statue would be erected to commemorate Rose McFee Kincaid and would be surrounded by low evergreens and a few rosebushes.

Abby leaned forward. A statue? That sounded pretty nice, but—

"This second plan would require a slight decrease in the amount of money available for development of the new park on Pine Street, but think how visible this statue and plaque would be." Nate pointed to a small circle in the middle of the drawing of the shopping area. "The current Rose Park draws very few visitors. Even if we improve it dramatically, I highly doubt as many people will visit in one month in the summer as will visit one of these retail establishments. And even on snowy or rainy days, people still get their hair cut, still have questions about their phones, and still eat Chinese food. And according to my mom, any day of the year is the perfect day for a manicure."

The audience laughed, and the council president fluttered her fingers, showing off her hot-pink manicure as if she was already a fan of Nate's plan.

"I don't see how we can in good conscience spend hundreds of thousands of dollars to maintain the small existing park to commemorate Rose," the Fourth Ward representative said. "I don't go to the park, and my kids are grown and live in St. Louis, but think about when you're trying to hire a new employee from out of town. If you could show them a big, fancy new park with ball fields and play equipment that all kids can use, and then drive by the new shopping area—it might help convince them to take the job." He turned his palms face up in a why-not-go-for-it gesture. "I like this last idea."

Abby wrapped her arms over her chest. The man made a good point. A nice park would help entice potential new employees. She'd heard that it was hard to convince some people to move to a small town, and the green space with a statue wasn't a bad idea. And of course the town needed play equipment that was accessible for all kids, but that play equipment could be put at Rose Park.

The council president adjusted her microphone. "Having play equipment designed for children with all levels of physical ability adds up fast, but I do believe accessibility needs to be a higher priority than a historic site." She pulled out a sheet of paper and read off prices of climbing structures and swings.

Prices Abby could hardly believe.

People who had signed her petition turned to look at her, their lips thin, their eyes hard. A murmur rose in the room, and whispered criticisms of her—perhaps made by people who thought their soft voices couldn't reach her ears—were all too easy to hear.

The uncomfortable feeling in her stomach, which had seemed bad when she addressed the crowd, was back, and it felt even worse. She'd had no idea how much play equipment cost. The way the people behind her were talking, it sounded as if she was against disabled kids. And she wasn't.

She swallowed.

Now she understood what Hubert had meant when he said the town needed the money from the sale of Rose Park. She understood why Frankie had seemed so uncomfortable when Abby asked her to sign the petition, why she'd mumbled that she'd think about it.

Had other people tried to tell her the financial issues when she asked them to sign the petition? Had she ignored them because she was so busy talking about the history of Rose Park? She wouldn't be surprised. She sank lower in her seat. Normally, she was a good listener. People even said so. But the park had meant so much to her and the whole topic made her so emotional because of Eric. Maybe she hadn't been a good listener this time.

Maybe she'd been a horrible listener.

What had she done?

Now that she knew all the facts, she could see that Nate's solution was a good one.

She raised her head, ready to say so, but the council president had already called for a vote. The meeting was moving forward.

The time for public discussion was over.

Frankie's boss was an idiot.

No, that wasn't quite right. But he was all too happy to push a mountain of details related to tomorrow's special event onto her, despite the fact that she was new.

Keeping one hand on the steering wheel, Frankie stretched her shoulders against the seat of her SUV. At least this trip to Columbia was nearly over, thanks to her shortcut through the back roads. Oh, the scenery was pretty much the same as if she'd taken the highway—field after field of soybeans and corn, broken up by the occasional clump of trees by a little creek. The shortcut, though, saved fifteen minutes on the drive back from Columbia. About twenty more miles and she would finally be back in Abundance. Granted, it was almost eight and she still needed to stop by the hospital to drop off the navy-blue balloons and napkins. Balloons and napkins they easily could have ordered and had delivered, eliminating the need for this emergency trip to a party store. Those details, though, should have been taken care of weeks ago, before Harris shoved the project onto her.

Which is why Frankie had to make the trip. And she'd had so many other similar issues to deal with that she hadn't been able to leave for Columbia until after five. Now the sun was slipping toward the horizon, and she was racing back to pick up Kira from her parents' house, so she could get her snuggled into her own bed. Kira needed a good night's rest before they got up early the next morning for her operation.

Frankie jabbed the radio power button, cutting off an ad for tires. All in all, she had more than enough to think about, what with Kira's surgery and the details of the maternity fair and that voicemail she'd gotten from Cooper yesterday.

Her chest grew hot. She'd overreacted? How could he

even say such a thing? He was the one who'd dumped her over one little comment she made at lunch. When she'd been majorly stressed. And what kind of man breaks up with someone by voicema—

She looked at the road ahead, and her heart jumped into her throat.

A large piece of metal, possibly part of a muffler, lay right in front of her. She scanned the road ahead. No one was coming on the other side of the two-lane.

She changed lanes and went around the metal. Whew.

Back to Cooper. Okay, she'd admit she hadn't been her most charming self, but when she thought he'd called her a moron, it only repeated what she'd told herself a hundred times before.

Which wasn't his fault.

That didn't excuse what he'd done.

She'd been an idiot thinking things might work out between them. Stupid. Stupid. Stupid. She was better off being alone. Better off not being disappointed. Not being hurt. Because it *had* hurt that Cooper had been late for lunch, despite his good excuse. She'd heard too many excuses from Garrett. She could imagine if she continued a relationship with Cooper, if things went so far that they got married. Would his late arrival for lunch lead to late arrivals for dinner and some nights never even coming home? Like Garrett? With her wondering who he was in bed with? With her learning that once again, she wasn't enough, she didn't matter?

Her eyes filled with tears. Better to let things end. Cooper could think she was unreasonable. Think she overreacted. And—if he did ever have the grace to call her or talk to her in person—she could tell him that things wouldn't work out. She'd focus on the one thing she could do well, being a good mom. She fumbled in her purse for a tissue.

As she was wiping her nose, a huge buck launched himself from the brush at the side of the road and planted himself in front of her. Her pulse raced. She blared the horn and slammed on the brakes, but she was still going too fast.

In a split second she scanned the road ahead.

Nothing coming.

Just like before, she jerked the SUV into the other lane, ready to zip past the buck.

But this time the SUV started to spin, like one of those commercials where a professional driver shows off the handling of a vehicle, all the time in complete control.

Only she wasn't.

She was skidding off the road.

Her heart began pounding so fast she thought it might explode.

She ground the brake pedal into the floorboards, her whole body clenched, every ounce of energy focused on somehow stopping the car.

Her SUV slowed, but not enough. The spin continued and her tires slid over the gravel at the edge of the road.

Down she went, off the slightly raised highway, past a thicket, and toward a clump of trees. She kept braking, kept trying to steer. But suddenly the car was rolling and—

There was a crunch, and then everything went black.

Chapter Twenty-Four

This was the weirdest dream. There was a boulder on top of her chest and—

Frankie opened her eyes.

The thing on her chest wasn't a boulder. It was an airbag, a deflating airbag. And the window of her SUV looked wrong, like it belonged to a different vehicle.

Her heart sped. It wasn't a different vehicle. It was her SUV, only it was upside down. And so was she, hanging in her seatbelt.

She gulped for air and tried to remember what had happened.

She'd...she'd been on her way back from Columbia, almost to Miller's Junction. And she'd been upset.

Then antlers, lots of antlers, came right at her. She'd swerved and gone off the road and passed a thicket and...

She couldn't even see the highway with all the brush. Which meant no one could see her.

And she needed to get to her parents' house. Tomorrow was Kira's surgery.

She could do this. She simply needed to focus. She'd get out of the car, and then she'd call for help. She moved each of her limbs and flexed her hands and feet. Yeah, her head felt like she'd whacked it on something and her chest ached, but nothing seemed broken.

She coughed. What did they fill those airbags with anyway? Some kind of irritant dust?

No matter. She'd get out of the car, into the fresh air, and she'd take some ibuprofen once she was back in civilization.

It took a bit of maneuvering, but she managed to release the seatbelt, and she landed with a thump on her sunroof. Then she scanned the floor, uh, ceiling of her car. There. Her purse was less than a foot away.

She stretched a hand toward it. Every inch hurt, but she reached farther and farther, until she grabbed the little leather tag that promoted the brand. Yes. She drew in a deep breath and—

Pain shot through her chest. Bad idea. She took another, smaller breath and tugged on the leather tag. Inch by inch, her purse came closer until she was able to get ahold of the strap and bring it toward her.

She opened her door and climbed out just as thunder rumbled in the distance. A storm was coming, she'd lost a shoe, and the dry weeds poked at her bare foot, but at least she was no longer upside-down and disoriented.

On one side of the SUV, the side where she'd gotten out, the ground sloped up toward where the road must be. On the other side was a tree that must have kept her car from rolling farther.

She should be grateful. And be grateful that somehow the engine had turned off, and that she didn't smell gas. People probably called AAA all the time with little accidents like this. Some nice guy would come out with a tow truck and give her a ride and all would be fine.

She opened the front-driver-side door again and, after a few minutes of feeling around beneath the airbag, found her other shoe and slid it on. Then she reached in the little pocket of her purse where she always kept her cell phone.

It wasn't there.

She'd probably put her phone inside, instead of in the special pocket.

But she hadn't. She went through her purse three times. No phone.

It must have fallen out when the SUV rolled.

She set the purse on the ground and crawled back into her SUV from the rear door on the driver's side, slithering along the inside of the roof of the vehicle. She'd find her phone and call and—

Her phone sat in a pool of ice cubes and Diet Coke beside her drive-thru cup. She didn't see the lid or straw anywhere.

With shaking fingers, she grabbed her phone and backed out.

Once she was standing again, she pressed the power button.

Nothing.

She ripped off the plastic case. Maybe soda had gotten inside and if she dried it off—

She wiped the phone on her shirttail and tried again.

The phone stayed dark.

She took out the battery, dried it, and reinserted it.

"C'mon, c'mon. You've got to work," she said aloud.

Still dark.

Panic crawled up her throat. She was almost twenty miles from Abundance.

Twenty miles, and she needed to be there now.

Kira was waiting, maybe even worried, not knowing where her mom was.

Tears burned in Frankie's eyes, and her face grew hot. She was failing Kira. Failing her little girl.

She tried so hard to be a good mom, even moved back to Abundance to make a better life for Kira, but just like how Frankie hadn't been worth enough for Garrett to love, she wasn't enough for Kira to count on.

That last time Kira got her cast removed, when Garrett hadn't met them at the doctor's office, at least he'd told her where he was.

Working.

Frankie hadn't believed him. But he had texted. He had seemed apologetic.

Maybe that day, that one day, he had been telling the truth.

Maybe if she hadn't gone out in the hall, phoned him, and yelled at him, he would have gotten there in time.

Maybe the fact that he never showed up was partly her fault.

A sick feeling washed through her stomach and her throat grew tight. She'd been so furious that Garrett hadn't been there. Their girl had needed him.

She had needed him.

And she'd yelled. A lot.

Overreacting.

Just like Cooper accused her of yesterday.

She let out a ragged breath and a single sob. Tears poured from her eyes as she stared up at the sky. *Really, God? Am I so hard-headed that you have to let me run off the road and into a tree to knock some sense into me?*

To get me to see that it's time for me to forgive Garrett? To see that not everything was his fault? To see that my failures in life are not caused by something I lack, not by how I'm made, but by how I act? To see that I can change?

Frankie swallowed and gently rubbed the sore place on her forehead. Tomorrow, she would call Garrett, apologize, and accept part of the blame for their divorce. Not for the infidelity—no, that was all on him—but she hadn't always handled Kira's issues well. She'd put so much energy into making things right for their girl that it had taken a toll on their marriage. Oh, Garrett wasn't Husband of the Year. That day Kira got her cast off hadn't been the only time he'd failed both Frankie and their daughter.

But he wasn't the only one to blame.

So she'd call. She'd update him on Kira, and she'd start praying for the health of his new baby.

And tonight she would find a way to Abundance.

Frankie let out a long sigh, dug a tissue from her purse, and blew her nose. Then she wiped her eyes and started up the hill toward the road. Someone would come by.

If it was someone she knew, or some nice woman alone or with her kids, Frankie would ask for a ride.

First, though, she had to stop a car.

"I'm sorry things didn't turn out the way you wanted, Abby." Shelly unclipped her microphone and handed it to her cameraman, who tucked it in his bag and strolled away.

Abby stood up from the bench in Rose Park where Shelly had interviewed her.

"I appreciate you giving me a chance to say a few more words," Abby said. "Never in a million years would I want to make it harder to provide play equipment for kids with disabilities. I didn't know keeping Rose Park meant that."

"Oh, Abby, no one who knows you would think that of you. You've got such a kind heart. But if anyone has any doubts, your point will be clear in my segment."

"I hope so." Abby checked on Emma, who was playing inside the dry fountain, twirling and whirling in her own little world in the twilight, content at last. She hadn't been too happy about sitting through the council meeting.

Shelly followed Abby's gaze and rested a hand gently on her arm. "I'm sorry about the park, but she's so beautiful. Those gorgeous red curls."

"Thank you," Abby said.

Shelly tipped her head toward the TV station van. "We better head out. Are you coming back to the parking lot?"

"No. I think I'll stay here for just a bit."

"Okay. It's been good seeing you," Shelly said.

Abby hugged her goodbye, then Shelly turned away and walked toward her van.

The sun had mostly set, and a storm wasn't far off, but Abby needed a minute. She stared at the yellow rosebush that was covered in blossoms, the bush she and Eric had stood beside when he proposed. Behind her, she could hear Emma, now singing a little song, one she must have made up because it didn't make sense. Kittens didn't dance.

Shelly and the cameraman drove away.

Abby picked a clover blossom from the grass and rolled the thin stem between her fingers. Had she been wrong to try to preserve Rose Park? No. If the economy was better, if Abundance had more money, it would have been wonderful to not only provide a new park that could meet the needs of all children but also to upgrade Rose Park and preserve it as part of the town's history. But the solution Nate had come up with really was a good one. It wasn't exactly what she wanted, but it was best for the town as a whole.

A white car pulled into the parking lot, crunching on the gravel.

Nate.

Despite everything, Abby's pulse quickened.

He stopped and got out.

Nate wasn't the man she'd thought, wasn't the man she'd wanted him to be, but he was good at his job. Even when she hadn't seen the big picture, he'd found a way to respect her goals and offer the town a good solution.

"Abby." He walked toward her. "I'm sorry."

"Nate, I had no idea that saving Rose Park would

make it hard for the city to afford play equipment that would meet the needs of all kids."

"I know. I could tell by watching your face during the meeting."

"Your plan, the one the city went with, is a really good one."

"Thanks. I appreciate you saying that. And, uh—" Nate glanced at Emma and angled his head away from her. "Could we go over that way?"

Abby looked over at Emma as well. Hopefully she could be patient a little longer. Whatever Nate had to say, he didn't want Emma to hear. Together they walked about ten feet farther away.

Nate turned to face her. "Abby—"

Emma suddenly appeared at Abby's elbow. "Mommy, I found a caterpillar." She thrust her hand upward.

A small wooly yellow caterpillar sat on her finger.

"Put him gently back in the grass, Emma, and play in the fountain a little longer," Abby said. "And remember, you're not supposed to interrupt grownups."

Emma's lower lip stuck out, but after a moment, she returned to the fountain.

"Sorry about that."

"Don't worry about it." Nate's Adam's apple rose and fell. "I just wanted to say that I really appreciate that you didn't bring up my past drug use at the meeting or spread it to that reporter. When she interviewed me after the council meeting, I was expecting her to ask about it."

"Even when I was furious and called Shelly, I couldn't have done that."

"You called the reporter? Not Frankie?" Nate sounded a bit lost.

"Frankie? No. I called Shelly. She and Frankie were closer friends, but we all worked together in college."

"Oh."

"But I wouldn't have told her your private business. I mean, for a minute there I wanted to do something like that, but it would have been wrong."

"That wouldn't matter to some people." He shoved his hands in his pants' pockets. "I also want you to know two things. First, even though Jessica didn't accept it, our relationship ended as soon as I got out of rehab. We haven't been together in months."

Heat flashed in Abby's chest. "That isn't what she told me."

"Jessica lies when it suits her purpose."

"Oh." The flatness of his voice, as if Jessica had lied to him at times, made it impossible to doubt him. "What's the other thing?"

"I know it doesn't excuse what I did, but when I first took amphetamines, my intentions were good. I was trying to squeeze in a pro bono case and didn't have enough hours in a day. I thought if I could stay up a little later each night, I could get it done." Nate's words rang with self-disgust. "Those pills were the first step down a very bad path. They were prescription drugs, but no doctor ever prescribed them at the doses I was taking." His shoulders straightened, and his voice grew stronger. "I've been clean, though, every day since the accident. You're part of the reason."

"Me?"

"You. You gave me extra motivation. To stay clean. To do the things Pastor Corey talks about. To put God first. I thought...I thought they might make me more worthy."

Abby's muscles tightened. This was not a conversation she wanted to have. Especially not here. Rose Park was, in her heart, a memorial to Eric, a hero, a man truly worthy of her love. This was not the place she even wanted to think about a relationship with a drug addict.

"I want to be worthy of you, Abby," Nate said. "I'm in love with you."

Nate searched Abby's eyes, hoping for a sign, any sign that she might be able to look past his flaws, past his brokenness. Wasn't that part of what he'd read in the Bible? That everyone sinned? That everyone could be forgiven? Everyone—even people who had used drugs?

"I—I—" She took a step back. "I can't, Nate. Dating a lawyer was hard enough, but I can't be involved with you now that I know about the drugs."

An ache spread from the base of his throat down into his chest.

"Were you ever even going to tell me about your addiction?"

"I was. I was trying to find the right time. Isn't there any way we could move past this?"

"No," she said, voice low. "I'm not sure I could ever trust you with Emma."

His lungs felt as if they were collapsing. "I see," he

managed to say. He never should have gotten his hopes up, never should have told her how he felt.

Abby twisted her head away.

He couldn't blame her. How could she possibly respect him? He didn't respect himself. He'd made choices that, no matter how he lived today, would affect him the rest of his life. He had no business even thinking about a relationship with a woman like Abby. He—

Abby clutched his arm. "Emma isn't in the fountain, and I don't see her anywhere."

Nate spun around to look.

The fountain was empty.

Abby called out for Emma.

Somewhere in the distance, a dog barked once. A bird hidden in the trees filled the air with carefree chirps that echoed in the dwindling light.

But no little girl was singing. And no reddish-gold curls could be seen.

Adrenaline coursed through Nate. He turned back to Abby.

"Emma!" she called again, louder this time, eyes wide with fear.

No reply.

"Emma!" he shouted. "Time to come out. We need to see you."

The park was silent. Even the bird had stopped singing.

Abby glanced at him, her face now white, then turned toward the trees at the back of the park and yelled so loudly that her voice strained. "Emma!"

Chapter Twenty-Five

Abby had called and called and called. She'd run from one end of the park to the other in the last light of the sunset. She'd searched around the rosebushes, beside the rusty play equipment, and used the flashlight on her cell phone to go inside the smelly bathroom with the pit toilets, a place where Emma would never go. Abby had even gone out the big gate and looked up and down on Main Street.

She hadn't found her girl.

Emma. Was. Gone.

Abby's knees went weak and she sank down onto the low concrete rim around the park fountain, letting her purse drop to the ground.

Had someone lured Emma away? Taken her?

Surely, that couldn't be true. Wouldn't she and Nate have noticed?

It was too, too horrible to think about. With Eric

gone, Emma was her whole world. How could she lose her girl?

And it was all because Abby had been focused on everything but her child. If she'd never gotten involved in this park mess, if she'd focused on her most important job—being a mom, if she'd talked with Emma about the caterpillar she found instead of sending her away, if—

"Don't worry, we'll find her," Nate said in a reassuring tone as he walked toward her.

She glanced at him and— Past the playground equipment. What was that?

Over beneath that group of cedar trees, something that might be pink peeked out.

Her heart pounding, Abby leapt up from the fountain rim and ran, focusing the light from her phone on the cedars. That pink looked like, yes, it looked exactly like Emma's shirt. Maybe she was ill or she was playing some game and didn't understand the terror she was putting them through.

Abby threw herself on the ground in front of the low-slung cedar branches and crawled closer. "Emma! Are you okay?"

No reply.

The cedars scratched at Abby's arms and at the sleeves of her dress, but she shoved the branches aside. Anything to get to her girl.

Anything to—

It wasn't Emma.

It was a small blanket, something Emma might use to tuck in one of her dolls.

Abby's shoulders sagged, and her chest ached. She

struggled to her feet and blinked back tears. She spun one direction, then the next, not sure where to search.

Nate took hold of her arms. "Abby, take a deep breath." His words were gentle, but firm. "You've got to pull yourself together. Emma's probably fine, but the sooner we find her, the more likely she is to be safe. Call your family. We'll need them to help search. I'll call 911."

Abby gave a jerky nod. Yes. The police would know what to do. And even if, after the city council meeting, the rest of Abundance thought she was a horrible person, and thought those boys who vandalized her shop had the right idea, her family would help. Her sister, her cousins. Even—if it took that long—Mom and Dad. They should be landing in Kansas City any time now.

She dialed Kristen.

As soon as Abby said the words "Emma's missing," the tears she'd managed to hold back poured down her cheeks. She gasped for breath and tried to explain what had happened.

"I'll call everyone," Kristen said. "To see if anyone has seen her. And we'll all come help look."

"Thank you," Abby said, trying not to sob. She hung up and wiped the tears from her cheeks. "I'm going to check over on Pine Street," she said to Nate.

"Abby..." He grabbed her hand and squeezed it. "You need to stay until the police get here to tell them what she was wearing, and they'll want a picture. I'm sure you have one on your phone."

She did. And that made sense. Sort of. She wasn't thinking straight.

And then thunder growled and the sky grew even darker.

A shudder went through Abby and her eyes filled with tears again. Her Emma lost—or worse—in a storm.

"Go look by the group of rosebushes again," Nate said. "I'll check near the playground equipment."

It was hopeless. They'd searched both those areas twice before. He was simply trying to keep her busy to stop her from crying. She was a mom. She knew how distraction worked. But she aimed the flashlight of her phone at the ground and stumbled toward the roses.

No Emma.

Just sad, straggly rosebushes with a few small blossoms.

A minute later a police cruiser pulled into the parking lot.

Abby ran toward it.

Cooper sank into the chair that he'd come to think of as his in the ICU waiting room.

Mom sat down beside him. Despite their difficulties trying to sleep in these chairs last night, despite their long day today, the light was back in her eyes.

The surgeon had been very positive after the operation. "Your dad came through fine," he'd said.

Throughout the day, Cooper had clung to those words, repeating them over and over in his brain. Even so, when he and Mom had first been allowed in to see Dad, Cooper's entire body had gone rigid. All those machines. And Dad had been so pale.

But a minute ago, at their last visit… Cooper glanced over at his mom. "He looked better, didn't he?"

"He did," Mom said almost immediately, as though she, too, had been thinking Dad seemed better but had been afraid that she'd imagined it. Suddenly, she stood up.

Mitch and Eileen Peterson, two of Mom and Dad's oldest friends, had just come in.

Cooper let out a sigh of relief. Other friends had stopped by today, but if anyone could help the time pass and comfort Mom, it would be the Petersons. And with them coming so close to when visiting hours ended, hopefully Eileen planned to convince Mom to go home and get some sleep.

So many blessings today. Dad was going to recover. And, according to a text Nate had sent after the city council meeting earlier this evening, the development at The Main Place would go ahead with the green space he and Nate had discussed. At long last, Cooper would be able to earn his father's respect in the business world.

Why didn't it feel better?

He ran a hand over the edge of the vinyl seat of his chair. He knew why.

There was more to feeling good about himself than simply getting a deal to work and earning his earthly father's respect. Cooper was pretty sure that his heavenly father wasn't impressed. Not after he left that message on Frankie's phone. What if Frankie hadn't been the person who called Shelly? The more Cooper thought about it, the heavier his stomach became. He moved toward the door. "Excuse me, everyone."

A few minutes later, in the shadows near an outdoor light, he sat on a bench by the hospital entrance. Lightening crossed the sky, and as he dialed Frankie's cell, thunder rumbled.

No answer. Chances were slim that she would listen to another message if he left one, and she didn't have a land line.

He wasn't going to let any of that stop him. One way or another, he was going to apologize.

He'd show up on Frankie's doorstep tomorrow if he had to, but first he'd try one more way to get her on the phone. He looked up Al's home number.

"I'm sorry," a woman answered. "Al's finally asleep after all that coughing keeping him up. I'd hate to wake him. Could I take a message and have him call you tomorrow?"

"Mrs. Redmond, this is Cooper Sullivan. I'm actually trying to reach your daughter, Frankie."

"Frankie?" Mrs. Redmond's voice wobbled.

"Is something wrong, ma'am?"

"She went to Columbia to get supplies for some event at the hospital tomorrow. She was supposed to be here to pick up Kira over an hour ago. I've been calling and calling her cell, but there's no answer."

"Maybe her phone is on silent and she stayed late without realizing it."

"I don't think so. She didn't even want to make the trip because she was so determined to get Kira in bed early the night before her surgery."

"Oh." He'd forgotten. The operation was tomorrow.

And the operation would be all Frankie was thinking

about. If she had car trouble, she'd be out of her mind, wanting to get home to Kira.

But if she'd had car trouble, she would have called.

He rechecked the time on his phone. It was long past what seemed like a time for getting a five-year-old to bed early. Things at the hospital were stable. Could he sit here another hour until visiting hours ended, not knowing if Frankie was all right? Judging by the way his stomach twisted, probably not. "Ma'am, how about I drive the route Frankie would have taken?"

"Would you?"

"I'd be happy to. In the meantime, if you hear from her, you call me." He gave Mrs. Redmond his number.

"Thank you. I...I really appreciate this."

"She'd go through Moberly and take Highway 63, right?"

"That's how I'd go."

"Okay. I need to take care of one thing here, and then I'll be on my way." Cooper hung up. A quick run upstairs to hug Mom and make sure the Petersons could stay with her, and he'd hit the road. Because this didn't sound like Frankie.

Didn't sound like her at all.

Nate pointed his flashlight at a bunch of shrubbery near the end of someone's driveway.

No sign of Emma. He and Abby had been to the police station, had talked with a detective, and a search was ongoing. Nate was doing his part, looking where he'd been instructed.

He shone his flashlight toward a large tree across the street, then took another step and caught his shoe on a buckle in the sidewalk. He landed hard, scraping the heels of both hands on the rough concrete.

Slowly, he picked up the flashlight and got back to his feet. He wiped his hands on his pants and checked to see if his palms were bleeding. Not enough to worry about.

If only he wasn't so tired. What with getting up early yesterday to drive back to Abundance and staying up all night last night to prepare the presentation for the city council meeting, he'd been awake for almost forty-eight hours.

It didn't matter. All that mattered was finding Emma.

Logically, he knew that the situation wasn't all his fault, but he had drawn Abby's attention away from Emma at the very time she got lost. He had asked Abby to step away from her child because he was ashamed of his drug use and didn't want Emma to overhear. As if it couldn't wait until she was asleep in bed. As if Emma could even understand.

Would he ever get to a place where his past didn't haunt him?

Not if something happened to Emma.

Suddenly, his light landed on a treehouse at the back of one of the yards.

Nate called out Emma's name once more.

No answer.

"Emma, come on out. No one's mad. We only want to know that you're all right."

No answer.

All he heard was a car a couple of streets away and

the voice of the nearby officer, calling out Emma's name.

"Are you in the treehouse?" Nate shone his light up in to the tree. He didn't see anyone, but the structure wasn't completely open. He shoved the flashlight in his back pocket and grabbed the ladder. The boards were worn and wet, slick under his dress shoes.

At the top of the ladder, he shone his light all around the treehouse, but found only the remains of a peanut-butter-and-jelly sandwich.

No Emma.

He put the flashlight back in his pocket and worked his way down the ladder.

His vision blurred with fatigue. He rubbed his hand over his eyes, but it did nothing to sharpen his focus. His feet moved as though slogging through water as he stepped to the ground. He leaned against the tree, inhaling great gulps of cool air. It was vital to find the energy to go on if he hoped to find Emma, and right now coffee just wasn't going to cut it.

One pill, one little pill would make all the difference.

Early on, when he hadn't been using so heavily, he'd been able to stay in control.

Tonight, well, surely he could handle one pill. He could text Thornton. Thornton had gotten hooked on narcotics right here in Abundance. He had connections. And the situation was an emergency. Thornton would understand.

Maybe even Abby would understand.

If he found her daughter.

He was doing this for her. He was—

In an instant, his throat thickened and nausea welled

up inside him. How could he be so spineless? So pathetic? This horrible situation was just an excuse to him, a reason to give into a craving. He'd thought he'd made progress, thought he had things under control.

But no, here he was lying to himself again.

All the weakness that he thought he was moving past was still a part of him.

He stood there, riveted by his realization, until thunder ripped through the sky, the wind picked up, and the rain, which had been threatening for hours, poured down.

Nate hunched over and let the water pound his back, every sheet of rain another lashing of shame.

Chapter Twenty-Six

There had been one car, right after Frankie discovered that her phone was dead.

She'd scrambled up the hillside, yelling at the top of her lungs.

And been too late.

There hadn't been another car since.

She'd been walking and walking and walking, through the rain and the wind and the dark, picking her way along by feel and by the illumination of lightning strikes. Her hair and her dress, long since soaked, were plastered to her skin.

And her pointy-toed flats, barely comfortable enough to wear for a whole day of working at the hospital, had given her blisters on both heels. She was pretty sure that at least one of them was bleeding.

How was it possible that no one was driving on this road? Lots of people knew about this shortcut on Highway F.

But she'd walk all the way to Miller's Junction if she had to. Or swim, if it kept raining this hard, and—

The gravel beneath her right foot gave way, and her ankle bent.

She crumpled to the ground, sucking in air.

Why—oh, why—hadn't she gone more slowly? Or waited for another lightning strike or the storm to pass and the skies to clear?

Tears ran down her cheeks as she tried to get back up. How was she going to get to Miller's Junction and—?

Wait—

That sounded like—yes, it was a car!

Adrenaline slammed into her veins. She scrambled to her feet and, fighting past the pain, hobbled to the middle of the road. This was her one shot. Her one chance to get to Abundance. This driver was either going to rescue her or run her over.

The pickup truck slowed, then pulled to the side and parked with its lights still on.

Frankie's heart leapt. As fast as she could, she limped the rest of the way across the road, trying to make out the vehicle behind the lights.

"Frankie!"

Cooper. The relief hit so hard she almost felt dizzy.

The door of his truck slammed, and he ran toward her, through the beams of his headlights, through the rain with no umbrella. "What happened?" he shouted.

"I rolled my SUV. My phone's ruined." She took another step toward him, put too much weight on her ankle, and winced.

He closed the distance between them and pulled her

into his arms, supporting her weight and encircling her with warmth. "I can't believe I found you. I've been looking and looking."

"You have?"

"Yeah. I called your parents' house. Your mom told me where you'd gone and how late you were. She's pretty worried." His eyes were full of tenderness and concern.

"You've got to take me to Kira. I need to get her home in bed."

"You need to see a doctor." Gently he peeled her wet hair off her forehead. "You've hurt your foot. And you've been bleeding. Did you hit your head?"

"Yeah," she said slowly. And there was that time that seemed a little fuzzy right after she went off the road.

"You might have a concussion." He put a hand under her elbow. "Let's get you out of this rain and into my truck, and you can call your mom. Kira's probably already asleep."

"But —"

"No 'buts,' Frankie," he said in a firm voice. "Your mom can watch Kira. I'm taking you to the hospital, and I'm going to apologize for those horrible things I said in my phone message. And tomorrow, we'll take Kira in for her operation. Together."

"We will?" A tingling sensation filled Frankie's chest.

"Yeah, we will," he said. There was no maybe-if-its-convenient tone to his voice. Only certainty.

She turned toward him and pressed a hand against his chest. For a moment she just stood there in the rain, feeling his heart beat beneath her fingers.

This man, who she'd dismissed as a failure, who

she'd gotten all snippy with at the diner, who had said he never wanted to see her again, had come looking for her. And he was apologizing and offering to be there with her during Kira's operation.

This man cared for her in spite of her mistakes.

Tears mingled with the rain on her face.

He gazed into her eyes and then helped her to the truck.

Close to midnight, Nate got in his car to drive to his next assigned location to search—Elm Street.

He was so tired.

He needed…

No.

Not drugs. But he needed strength from somewhere. Anywhere.

He stared up into the sky, and the rain rolled down his cheeks. What was that verse Al had given him?

Something about a victorious right hand.

Nate dried his hands on a drive-thru napkin from the glove box, pulled his phone from his pocket, and opened a search engine. He typed in *Bible* and *victorious right hand*.

Less than a second later, it popped up. The top result.

Do not fear, for I am with you, do not be afraid, for I am your God; I will strengthen you, I will help you, I will uphold you with my victorious right hand. Isaiah 41:10 (NRSV)

Strength. Not coming from inside him, but coming

from God. That sounded pretty good.

And the other verse? Oh, he remembered the reference for that one, at least part of it, because it was symmetrical. 1 John 1.

After a minute, he found that verse on his phone as well.

If we confess our sins, he who is faithful and just will forgive us our sins and cleanse us from all unrighteousness. 1 John 1:9 (NRSV)

He liked the idea in that second verse too. His sins forgiven and washed away.

But did he believe either one of them? The first one— yeah. Nate could pretty easily see God helping someone he loved, being with them and giving them strength.

That second verse was harder. Confess his sins and be forgiven and purified? It was easy to see it applying to someone closer to God, someone with smaller sins. Abby, for instance.

Could that apply to everyone, even him? A month ago he would have said no. But he'd read that section of Luke about the woman who was a sinner, even read a few other things in those emails about peace. God didn't seem to limit his forgiveness to small sins.

Al believed he was forgiven, and he was in AA. And Thornton believed. Nate knew from his meetings at the hospital that Thornton had done things a lot worse than shooting up his neighbor's fish tank.

It couldn't hurt to ask God for help, could it?

Nate pushed back his damp hair and wiped his palms

on his pants. Then he bowed his head, rested his elbows on the steering wheel with his head on his clasped hands, and spoke in a hoarse whisper. "God, I don't think I'm worthy to ask, but please...please protect Emma. Please give me the energy to keep searching for her."

Should he continue? Did he have the right to ask for more? To ask for forgiveness? Probably not. But maybe it wasn't about how worthy he was, maybe it was about how loving God was.

"God, I made so many bad choices when I lived in New York—choices that used Jessica and that caused that wreck that injured Ashley. Please forgive me. And please give me the strength to stay clean. Amen."

Nate lifted his head.

The space around his heart felt warmer, and his chest felt lighter, as if his breath could now spread to parts of his lungs that had been closed off.

He gazed up through the windshield at the rain. "Thank you." Then he glanced down at his hands. There should be more to say, but he didn't know what.

And he'd better get over to Elm Street.

He reached for the ignition, then stopped. Why hadn't he thought of it before? He pulled out his phone.

Pick up, Vivian. Pick up.

After the fourth ring she did.

"Have they found the little girl?" she asked.

"No, not yet. That's why I need to speak with Kira. I'm hoping she might have some idea where Emma is."

"You know, she might. She's so smart for her age. Wait one minute." In the background Nate heard Vivian waking Kira. "Here she is."

"Hi, Nate."

"Hi, Kira." How to word this? She might not know what had happened, and he didn't want to alarm her. "You know Emma pretty well, don't you?"

"She's my new best friend." Kira sounded indignant that Nate didn't realize the obvious.

"Well, her mom can't find her. I was thinking, since you know her so well, maybe you'd be able to help us. What do you think? Where would she have gone?"

Kira didn't hesitate a second. "To see the kittens."

"Kittens?" Nate's heart sped. "What kittens?"

"The ones that belong to the man who lives next door to her grandma and gave me my kitten."

"Can I talk to Vivian again?"

Vivian knew exactly who Kira meant. A minute later, after she tucked Kira back in bed, she found Quentin Waller's address.

Nate slid his car into gear. The detective at the police station had asked Abby about relatives in town. From the way he'd talked, Nate was sure the police would have searched her grandmother's house, even though Abby had told them she was in the rehab center.

But would they have checked Waller's place? Was it right next door or were the houses there more spread out? Could they have missed her?

He had to find out.

Nate parked his car in Quentin Waller's driveway, climbed out, and clicked on his flashlight. The rain, at last, had ended.

Waller's house was dark, as was the ranch-style house next door where Emma's grandmother lived. Either Waller was asleep or he was one of the townspeople searching for Emma closer to Rose Park.

Which was almost certainly a better place to look.

These two houses were the last on Eleventh Street, with nothing but trees behind them and no houses across the street. They were so close together, though, that the police would have searched around Waller's house too.

And Nate couldn't imagine Emma going all this way by herself. This place was too far from the park. He needed to quit kidding himself and go to Elm Street, where the police expected him to be searching.

Five minutes. He'd check here for five minutes.

"Emma," he called out.

Nothing. This was a waste of time.

"Emma," he yelled even louder.

A pitiful "help" echoed through the night.

His pulse shot up. "Emma!" He raced toward the sound, deep into Waller's yard. "It's Nate. Where are you?"

"I'm stuck," she called. "In the barn."

He ran the beam of the flashlight across the yard. There, far in the back, near an outdoor light, was a barn.

He bolted toward it, splashing through a low place in the yard where the rain had pooled. "I'm coming," he shouted. "I'll get you out."

The door of the barn swung open easily, and Nate raced inside.

No light switch. He shone his flashlight around the dark space. Empty stalls on both sides and a space in the middle below, where Nate supposed a tractor might once have been parked. But where—?

"Up here," Emma said with a sniffle.

Nate swung the flashlight beam upward. Where a light fixture might have been, instead hung a bare leg and a little tennis shoe.

He gulped. She'd fallen halfway through the floor of the—what was it called?—the hayloft. "Are you hurt?"

"No." She sniffled again. "But I can't get my leg out."

If he went up in the hayloft, where the floor hadn't been able to support her weight, there was no way it could hold him. And he couldn't reach her leg, where it dangled down, to push her upward.

"I'll call your mom to get help," he said.

Abby answered halfway through the first ring. "Nate?"

"I've found her. She's in Quentin Waller's barn."

Abby let out a sob. "Oh, thank you. Mom and I will be right there. We were already in the car going—"

"Abby, I think we need the fire department and an ambulance. Emma seems okay, but she's fallen halfway through the floor of the hayloft and I'm not sure how to get her out."

"Oh." Abby's voice shook. "I'll have Mom call them while I drive."

"I'll do the best I can until you get here." He hung up and raised his head toward Emma. "Your mom's on her way with help."

"Good," Emma said.

Her voice sounded so thin.

There had to be a way he could help her now. He

307

didn't want to make any injuries she might have worse, but what if she fell through before the fire department arrived?

"Emma, how long have you been like that?" he said.

"Forever. Since right after I came up here to hide when I heard the policeman looking for me."

"Oh." So the police had been here.

"I thought I was in trouble. And then I saw the kittens over in that corner, and after he left I went toward them and…" She started crying.

"Don't worry. You're going to be fine."

At least Nate hoped so. With jerky motions, he searched one stall, then the next. If he could find a ladder, some wooden boxes, anything he could climb on, he could help her. But he didn't see anything—

There—in the last stall—a hay bale. Adrenaline poured through him. This would work. The bale would be enough. He'd be able to push Emma up so that she could crawl back on the part of the floor that had been solid.

He grabbed the bale, positioned it under her, and climbed on top of it.

He stretched his body upward, trying to reach as high as possible, stretching, straining—

He still couldn't reach her leg. He sank back down, chest heavy.

But she said she'd been there forever. It sounded as if her position was stable. He hated to leave her, but without any equipment, it was hopeless. "I need you to hang on for just a little bit longer. I'm going to look around your grandmother's house and knock on Mr.

Waller's door to see if either of them has a ladder. I'll be back in two minutes at the very most. Will you be okay?"

There was a long pause. "I...I will," she said.

"You're a very brave girl."

Nate dashed to Waller's front door and pounded on it.

No one answered.

Nate looked around the back of both houses, but couldn't find a ladder.

He raced into the barn.

More of Emma's leg now hung down through the hole in the hayloft.

Should he stay here below Emma, where he could catch her if she fell?

Images of broken wood jabbing into her flashed in his mind. A chill encircled his heart. She could end up with a punctured lung, a serious eye injury.

With quick movements, he checked the hay bale from one side, then the other, to make sure it was centered under the spot where Emma hung. It was. She was a little girl, maybe forty pounds. If the worst happened, the hay should absorb the impact if she fell.

He tucked the flashlight in his pocket and began to climb the hayloft ladder, which was a few rough boards nailed together and running up the side of one stall.

At the top, he pulled out his flashlight again and shone it over the loft, adding to the light that came through a window from the yard fixture outside.

Here and there boxes rested on the floorboards, and in the far corner the mother cat curled around her kittens. Between him and the kittens, Emma lay, sprawled out, one leg disappearing into the floor, face pale, eyes huge. And although most of the loft appeared original, two parts looked as if they had been replaced—the floorboards around the ladder and one joist, leading to Emma.

Suddenly—though she hadn't moved—the floor beneath her gave an eerie groan and she fell a few inches farther into the hole.

Nate's heart rate skyrocketed. "Hang on!" he shouted. "I'm coming for you!"

Despite his wet clothes, despite the cooler air brought by the rain, sweat drenched his body.

He shoved the flashlight in his pocket and took one step onto the joist that looked newer, cautiously testing it. It held his weight. If he didn't lose his balance, he could safely get to her. If not…

Below, he heard footsteps.

"Emma!" Abby shouted.

"Mommy!" Emma moved and the floorboards creaked, sounding even more ominous than before.

"Emma, hold still!" Nate shouted. Then he yelled downward. "Abby, do you have any rope? Or a ladder?"

"No, but I have a flashlight."

"I'm trying to walk across a joist to get to her, but the floorboards are rotten."

"Emma," Abby called, her tone falsely bright, "Hang on, pumpkin. Hang on."

"You can do it, honey," someone else cried.

"Okay, Grandma," Emma called.

Nate took hold of the rafter above with one hand, held the other hand out to the side for balance, and took another step forward. The joist seemed solid.

A few seconds later, a light shone from behind him, reflecting off the tears on Emma's cheeks and the cobwebs that hung like seaweed from the rafters.

He didn't dare turn around. In the flashlight beam he could see that the hand he held out for balance was shaking. His blood seemed to have been replaced with pure adrenaline. How could he ever get to Emma without falling off the narrow joist?

Somehow he had to get to her.

Somehow he had to save her.

Somehow…

Help me, Lord. Just give me a little more strength, a little more steadiness.

He drew in a deep breath. He was almost there. Maybe a yard to go.

Suddenly, a piece of the rafter crumbled beneath his hand.

He lost his grip.

And wobbled.

Chapter Twenty-Seven

Abby gasped.

For a fraction of a second Nate swayed violently from side to side.

She scrambled up the last rung of the ladder and onto the loft floor.

Then, like a basketball player going for a slam dunk, Nate leapt up, grabbed the rafter a few inches closer to Emma, and regained his balance.

Abby's shoulders crumpled forward and she pressed a hand to her heart. If he'd fallen…

Nate eased forward the last few feet, then leaned down, wrapped one arm under Emma's arms, and carefully maneuvered her free.

"You've done it!" Abby cried out.

"Almost there," he said. He helped Emma onto the joist in front of him and held the rafter with one hand and her arm with the other as they inched back toward the ladder. He slowed as he reached the place where the rafter crumbled, but got safely past it.

Abby moved closer, staying on the lighter-colored floorboards, the ones that seemed newer, and trained the flashlight on the joist to help Emma and Nate. Emma had scratches on the leg that had fallen through the boards, but she seemed to be moving normally.

At last they stepped off the joist onto the newer floorboards.

"Mommy!" Emma rushed toward her.

"Oh, Emma." Tears ran down Abby's face, and she held her daughter as closely as she could. Emma was safe. Her sweet Emma was safe.

Abby raised her eyes to Nate's. "How—how can I ever thank you?"

A siren cut through the night and grew closer.

"Just let the EMTs check her out," he said.

Abby nodded and blinked back her tears, then had Emma wiggle all her fingers and toes. Her little pink T-shirt was torn, she had even more scrapes than Abby had realized, but she was fine. Abby went down the ladder before Emma, ready to catch her if needed, and once they reached the barn floor, Abby lifted her into her arms. Abby's mom, tears streaming down her face, wrapped them both in a hug.

Two policemen rushed through the door of the barn, one holding a huge flashlight.

Nausea welled up in Abby's stomach. From here at the base of the ladder, in the beam of the big flashlight, the distance that Emma and Nate might have fallen seemed even farther. And the floor—the floor was concrete.

When she'd come in the barn, she'd seen the hay bale that Nate must have placed under Emma. If she had fallen, the hay would have cushioned her. But if Nate had fallen trying to get to her, he would have landed directly on concrete.

She looked up at him, sitting at the top of the ladder, his feet dangling down.

"Thank you," she said. Her words were so full of emotion that, even to her, they seemed hard to understand.

But he nodded in reply.

For a moment, she stood, holding Emma, gazing up at him.

His dress pants were ripped, grass-stained, and smeared with dirt. His eyes looked as bloodshot as hers felt after hours of crying. And a tangle of cobwebs stuck to the top of his hair.

The longer she gazed at him, the more an ache grew at the base of her throat.

This man had risked himself to save her Emma.

No, he wasn't a hero like Eric, risking his life for his country.

But he was still a hero.

Despite nearly falling through the hayloft, despite being up late, Emma was awake bright and early the next morning, well before Doris's phone call at seven.

Even after a shower, Abby felt as if she needed four more hours of sleep. Emma, on the other hand, was full of energy, too full of energy for a visit to the rehab center.

Abby called Kristen to babysit and drove over alone. Doris wanted a first-hand account of what had happened to Emma. And Abby needed to tell her face to face about Rose Park.

"Abby?" Doris called from the common room near the front entrance of the rehab center. "Where's my girl, Emma?"

"Too fired up to bring here." Abby headed toward Doris. "You'd think she'd be tired, but it's just the opposite. Kristen's watching her and the shop for me." Abby glanced around the rehab center as she did every time she came in. Yes, as always, it looked spotless and it smelled clean. Good.

"Well, you give her a big hug for me."

"Gladly," Abby said.

The older woman stood and, skillfully using a walker, came to meet her.

"You've gotten a lot better with that thing in the last two days," Abby said.

"I know." Brightly dressed in lime-green pants and a yellow-and-green striped top, she raised her chest like a proud parakeet. "I'll be going home in two or three days."

"That's fabulous!" Abby gently hugged the older woman's shoulders, careful not to make her unsteady.

"Not as fabulous as when I heard last night that Emma was found." Doris led Abby into a small sitting room and lowered herself into a chair by a fish tank. "A group of us sat up, praying. You should have heard the cheers when we learned she was safe."

Abby let out a shaky sigh as she sat down. "I'm sorry. It's still so overwhelming to think about."

Doris patted her hand. "But she's safe now, dear. And she's bounced back fine."

"She has."

"I never would have dreamed she could find her way from the park to my house, but I do think we've commented from time to time, when you picked me up so we could go work on the roses together, that we drove straight down Eleventh Street."

"I thought of that too. And she is a rather determined little girl."

"Like her grandmother," Doris said proudly.

Abby grinned.

"I have more good news." Emotion rang in Doris's words. "Hubert was here this morning. He apologized for how he's acted since Eric died." She reached out and took Abby's hand. "You have your girl back. And I have my boy."

"Oh, Doris." Abby wrapped her in a hug.

Doris held her tightly, then settled back in her chair. "He said he'd be coming by your shop today to apologize to you as well. I mean, we both knew he was just so overcome with grief that he wasn't thinking right, but after my fall and the scare we all had last night, he sees it as well. He understands that Eric's death could have happened anywhere."

Abby could barely believe it. Finally, finally, the Kincaid family was healing. Except— "I couldn't save Rose Park."

"I know, dear. Hubert told me."

"I tried. I—"

Doris patted her arm. "Hubert explained how selling

Rose Park will allow the city to make sure the new park can serve the needs of all children. I think the statue and the plaque and the green space in the current park location will do a wonderful job of honoring Rose."

The tension drained from Abby's shoulders. "I'm so glad. I honestly think Rose would be proud of Abundance for building a park that all kids can use. That was really what she wanted, for everyone to be treated alike."

"I think she'd be delighted, and I think Zane would have approved."

Abby blinked. None of this was how she expected Doris to react. Not that Abby was complaining, but—

"She's right in here, Mr. Waller," an aide said, appearing in the doorway to the sitting room. "We were wondering when you'd be in after we were all up so late here last night."

"I knew I was too slow to be much good out hunting for little Emma last night. I was much better off here with my Doris, praying." Quentin sat down in the chair beside Doris.

Abby turned to Quentin. His Doris? When did she become *his* Doris?

"Quentin!" Doris said, her voice higher and her eyes shining. "How lovely to see you!"

Abby looked from Doris to Quentin and back again.

Quentin covered Doris's hand with his own.

And it all made sense.

No wonder Doris could accept change at Rose Park. Oh, Abby was sure the older woman would always love Zane.

But Doris's world wasn't all about the past anymore.

She'd taken a step into the future.

"I'm ba—ack," Abby called as she entered her shop.

"In here." Kristen's voice came from the kitchen.

Halfway to the kitchen, Abby met Emma, who hugged her legs.

Abby knelt down, pulled Emma close, and kissed her soft curls until she wiggled free and tugged at the hem of Abby's shorts. "Can I watch my show, Mommy?"

"Yes, you may," Abby said.

Emma headed up the stairs, and Abby listened for the TV to come on. She and Emma needed to have a major talk about how she'd wandered off on her own last night, and Emma might not be watching TV for a while after that, but Abby was waiting until after Kristen left to deal with the situation.

She walked into the kitchen and sank down into a chair at the table, shoulders still aching from the hours she'd spent tense with fear last night.

"I'm just cleaning up. Emma had a little snack, half a banana and some milk," Kristen said as she put a small plate in the dishwasher.

Which didn't explain why the dishwasher was completely rearranged from earlier this morning. No, that was all Kristen, making things better by doing them her way. *Not really needed, but hey, Kris, knock yourself out reloading if you want.*

"How did it go with Doris?" Kristen shut the dishwasher and leaned against the counter.

"Surprisingly well," Abby said, and she explained

about Quentin.

"Imagine that—Doris Kincaid seeing another man, after all these years," Kristen said. "And you dating Nate."

"Well…"

"Abby, with how he saved Emma last night, you've got to forgive him for whatever he did that made you so mad," Kristen scolded.

Abby did want to talk to Nate. From the bottom of her heart she wanted to thank him. She'd known last night that she needed to say more than those few words she mouthed as he sat at the top of the hayloft ladder, but more police had arrived and the paramedics and Dad and the rest of her family. She'd been caught up in making sure Emma really was okay, determining that she needed a tetanus booster, and answering all the police officers' questions. When she'd looked for Nate again, one of the officers had said he'd gone home.

Maybe Nate didn't want to talk to her. Maybe the things she'd said, the fact that she couldn't forgive him for his drug use, had hurt him too deeply. Still, she had to try. "I was going to stop by his apartment later to thank him."

"Now, you know I'm not one to tell people what to do…" Kristen leaned in.

Abby smoothed her hair back and began to redo her ponytail. Her sister was in major denial here.

"But you need to tell him how you feel about him," Kristen said.

Abby let her ponytail elastic snap back into place. "How I feel about him?"

"How you're in love with him."

"Kristen! I am not in love with Nate Redmond!"

"Really?" Kristen's voice dripped with disbelief, and she gave Abby a who-are-you-kidding face.

Abby's stomach tensed. Who did Kristen think she was? An expert on romance? Her, the woman who hadn't mentioned dating anyone for the past year?

Kristen crossed her arms over her chest and stared at Abby.

Abby sat back in her chair and ran a hand back and forth along the side of the wooden seat. She couldn't be in love with Nate, not after the drugs. It would be the worst possible betrayal of Eric's love.

It didn't matter that Nate said he'd ended things with Jessica as soon as he got out of rehab.

It didn't matter that he was going to church and trying to follow Christ.

It didn't matter that he'd found a way to give the town a beautiful park and honor Rose.

It didn't matter that he'd risked his own safety to rescue Emma.

But...it did.

He'd made a mistake, taking drugs.

A mistake she considered unforgivable.

But after rehab, he'd left his job and his friends and what was probably a fancy apartment to get away from the things that tempted him into drug use in the first place.

Not many people would do that.

Only those who were really serious about staying clean and really wanted a second chance.

Maybe…maybe she should give him one.

And give herself a second chance as well.

A second chance at love. With Nate.

Her heart sped and she felt like some of Emma's bubbles were bouncing into her, popping with little tingles.

"Maybe," Abby said tentatively. "Maybe I am in love with him."

"Maybe?" Kristen said.

Abby pressed her lips together and slid her wedding ring from her finger.

There. Did that seem right?

No. Her hand looked odd, with that dent of paler skin on her fourth finger. She felt…unsettled, as if a thick fog was swirling through her with no path or pattern.

She placed the ring on the kitchen table, closed her eyes, and pictured Nate's face. Pictured him laughing with Bear, pictured him playing pretend with Emma, pictured him right before he kissed her in the courtyard at the restaurant in Kansas City.

As if the sun had broken through, the fog thinned. Her brain relaxed.

"I'll do it," she said. "I'll tell him." A zing of anticipation filled her veins.

"Good." Kristen said. "All that's left now is for you to forgive the man who shot Eric."

Abby sat bolt upright, all excitement and happiness gone. "Enough already, Kristen." There was no way she was forgiving the man who had murdered Eric. That scum hadn't turned his life around, hadn't done anything to redeem himself. All he'd done was kill.

"As Christians we're supposed to forgive. It's right there in the Lord's Prayer. You know that's not only to help the other person."

Abby crossed her arms over her chest. Why did she have to have such a know-it-all little sister? Why—

"You'll never find peace until you do."

Heat built inside Abby. She'd had all the advice she could take from Kristen. "What makes you think you know what I should do?"

"I know you need to forgive. This isn't rocket science, Ab. You know as well as I do that holding onto anger doesn't help anything."

"Anger doesn't help anything," Abby repeated in a sing-song voice, then clenched her jaw and dug her nails into a rough place in the bottom of her chair seat. Easy for Kristen to say. She was the person who tended to make people angry. Not the other way around. She wasn't the one who'd lost her husband to—

A small piece of wood chipped off the chair from where Abby had dug her fingernails in.

She looked at the tiny fragment of wood, blinked, and flicked it onto the floor. Then she crossed her arms over her chest again. What was she doing, getting so angry she damaged an antique chair? What was she letting anger do to her? Kristen loved her. She was probably trying to help. And Abby hadn't listened when Hubert tried to help her. Was she really listening now? Or was she blocking Kristen out?

Abby let out a sigh. "I'll...I'll pray about it."

"Good. I better go. I've got to deal with a major disaster of a chapter in this Algebra One book I'm editing."

"Thanks for watching Emma and the store. And for talking with me, I guess."

"Anytime." Kristen called goodbye to Emma and left, the clang of the cowbell echoing through the showroom.

Abby lingered in the kitchen, thinking about what Kristen had said.

Maybe she *did* need to forgive the man who shot Eric. Maybe it wasn't her place to judge him, to say he should have done something to redeem himself. He may not have had as many opportunities as Nate or as much of a support system to help him. Maybe, if he had, he could have turned his life around too.

She walked over to the counter and picked up his letter from the corner where she'd tossed it, not entirely sure why she hadn't thrown it away. She wriggled a finger beneath the flap and ripped it open, then pulled out a single sheet of paper, smudged with ink on one corner. The pressure of the pen had made deep indentations in the paper, as if each word had been agonized over.

Dear Mrs. Kincaid,
I wanted to tell you how sorry I am for what I done. I beg your forgiveness.
Sincerely,
Charles Radford

Abby's face grew hot and tears poured from her eyes. She stumbled to a nearby chair and sank into it. How much clearer could the message be? God had tried again and again to get through to her. Through Kristen, through the Sunday school lesson about Joseph—which was not about moving on but about forgiveness—and through bringing Nate into her life.

Everyone deserved a second chance.

Everyone.

She laid the letter aside, bowed her head, and asked God to help her forgive Charles and to help her fully forgive Nate. And she asked God to forgive her—for her intolerant spirit and for her arrogance in believing that she was worthy of judging someone else's sins.

At last she raised her head, wiped her face, and got a sheet of paper and a pen from the desk drawer.

She would write back to Charles to tell him she had forgiven him.

After Nate got off work, she would thank him for saving Emma.

And hope he might forgive her.

Chapter Twenty-Eight

Alone in the quiet law office, Nate sat down at his desk.

Time to get to work.

But once more his mind filled with the expression on Abby's face last night when she knew Emma was safe. That expression that had been the last thing he saw as he collapsed into sleep and the first thing he thought of this morning.

Abby's eyes had held tremendous gratitude. Nothing more. Not acceptance and understanding. Not the promise of the relationship he wanted. Not love.

She couldn't be involved with him because of his addiction.

No matter how much his heart ached, he needed to accept that and move on.

Yet another thing he'd need to ask God to give him strength for.

He straightened his shoulders and turned to his

computer. He had phone calls to make, emails to write, and a million details to take care of to make sure the park project went forward.

After checking his calendar, he glanced at the clock in the corner of the screen.

It was past nine, and still no sounds of Jewel arriving. She'd texted late last night to congratulate him for finding Emma, and she'd assured him that she had recovered from her dental visit.

Not sure what to think, he opened his email. Near the top, he found a message, auto-forwarded from the account he'd set up to anonymously handle Ashley's medical bills that exceeded the insurance cap.

The email began with a photograph of a note, written in fat, grade-school printing, with a flower drawn to dot the *i*.

Thank you for the chance to go to college. I am going to be a nurse.
Ashley

Below was a note from Ashley's mom.

Dear Trust Administrator,

Thank you so much for my daughter's scholarship. No one in our family has ever gone to college. Ashley's teacher says she has already seen an improvement in her reading skills. Apparently, after she learned of the scholarship, Ashley started working harder. She told her teacher that nurses have to be good readers.

She was discharged from rehab and seems completely recovered.

You have turned the darkest of days, the day of the accident, into a blessing that will last her whole life.

Thank you,

Miranda Watkins

Warmth radiated through Nate's chest. He could never make up for the physical pain he'd brought to Ashley, but he had done one thing right. The scholarship—his long-term investment—would help her.

And last night, yeah, he'd had a craving. It happened. At least he'd recognized the lie he told himself. Today he'd be back at his support group, and he'd keep doing the best he could, one day at a time.

"Doughnuts are here." Jewel's voice rang out as she knocked and opened his office door.

Nate eagerly accepted the jelly doughnut she held toward him. "I thought Friday was doughnut day."

"Any day is doughnut day for the hero who rescued Emma Kincaid," Jewel said emphatically, and a glittery gold bow jiggled in her hair.

"I'm not a hero."

"You are in my book." Her tone left no room for dissent. "Do you want me to take back that doughnut?"

"Well, no." It smelled delicious. Nate took a quick bite. Tasted delicious too.

"Then hush." She spun on her heel and left.

Gooey red filling oozed out of his donut.

Nate caught the filling with his finger before it dripped on the desk, and chuckled to himself.

He still wished, might always wish, for a future with Abby, but even without her, maybe he really could create a good life here in Abundance.

After all, God had given him a lot of help. Al, a man Nate had always respected, who knew the path Nate needed to walk and was willing to help him. The support group meetings. The friends there, like Thornton. Even though she couldn't love him, the blessing of the friendship of a decent woman like Abby who, when she had the opportunity to destroy his future here, had kept silent about his past.

He wasn't going to waste all that. He had a good support system here in Abundance. He had God. And he had found the man he was supposed to be.

Outside, a bluebird flew to the maple tree, perched on a limb, and began to sing.

Nate finished his donut, pushed up his sleeves, and began the first email of the day, an email to help make the new park a reality.

"Do you want to get some breakfast?" Cooper angled his head toward the door from the hospital waiting room to the hall.

"No," Frankie said. "You go ahead."

"I already ate this morning, but Kira said right before we checked her in that you didn't. We can leave your number with the woman at the desk here, and you know the nurse said we wouldn't hear anything until after ten. That's when you told your parents to come."

Frankie shook her head.

"You should eat something. Toast? A cup of coffee?" Decaf. The woman looked shaky. And chilled, despite the fact that she was wearing long pants and a sweater. Why did hospitals have to be so cold?

"Could you get me some kind of juice?"

"You bet." Cooper got up quickly. He hated to leave her alone in the waiting room, but she needed to eat. He'd get her juice and food. After being here most of the past twenty-four hours because of his dad's surgery, he knew the cafeteria would have something tempting.

Frankie twisted her hands together, jaw tight.

"Didn't you tell me the doctor is really good?"

The tension in her face eased slightly. "Yeah, I did."

"Kira's going to be fine."

"Thank you."

"I'll be right back."

Poor Frankie. He'd tried earlier this morning to take her mind off the operation by telling her the ideas he'd discussed with the mayor for accessibility at the new park. She'd seemed impressed, but it had only held her attention a few minutes before she started worrying again. She seemed so fragile. Maybe breakfast would help.

As soon as Cooper got through the cafeteria line, his phone dinged with a text.

Dad moved to a regular room. Wants to talk to you.

Cooper sat the bag of food on a windowsill and dialed his mom. "What's going on?"

"Your father thinks—"

Muffled voices came through the phone. Cooper strained to listen. Should he go to Dad's room now? No, Dad was improving, and Frankie needed him.

"Cooper?" Dad's voice came over the line.

"Dad. You sound better."

"I feel better. I'll be in the office Monday, and I'll go with you to that meeting in Moberly."

Cooper's pulse sped, and his chest grew hot. Still? Dad still couldn't trust him? Was he always going to be considered a failure? Was he—?

Wait a minute. After he'd found Frankie on Highway F, he learned he had in fact misjudged her, blaming her for a phone call she'd never made. What if he was looking at this wrong as well? What if there was something Dad wasn't saying?

"Dad? Are you—okay, this is going to seem crazy— but are you afraid I don't need you?"

The line was silent. Not filled with denial.

How long had this been the real problem, that Dad thought he wasn't needed? How long had Cooper been letting his failure back in college cloud his view of today? "You're not being replaced, Dad, just taking the time you need to come back even stronger."

The silence grew, and then Dad let out a grunt. "Okay, I'll admit you can take that meeting in Moberly alone. But don't go moving into my office."

"I wouldn't dream of it." Cooper let out a silent chuckle. "As long as you'll stay home until the doctor says you're ready to come back."

"Hmph. All right," Dad said. "What?" His voice sounded far away. "Wait a minute," he said into the phone.

Cooper stared at his phone. Was everything all right?

"Your mother just showed me the Facebook post. I guess if people like how you handled The Main Place project that much, you'll do all right without me." Dad paused. "For a week or so."

Facebook post? What Facebook post?

"You've really made me proud, son."

Cooper stood taller, chest expanding. "Thanks, Dad." He wasn't quite sure what was being said on Facebook, but someone must be happy about how The Main Place project worked out.

And Dad was proud of him. The thought echoed in Cooper's mind until his throat grew thick.

"Got to go," Dad said. "The nurse just came in."

Cooper swallowed back his emotion. "I'll be back up to see you as soon as Kira's out of surgery."

Dad hung up.

"Bye, Dad," Cooper said to the dead connection. "And thank you." For a second he waited, soaking in Dad's approval, then he grabbed the bag of food. As soon as he took it to Frankie, he'd see what was on Facebook.

Two minutes later, he was back in the waiting room. He handed Frankie her orange juice and pulled a hot, fluffy biscuit and packets of butter and honey and jam out of the cafeteria bag.

Just as he'd hoped, Frankie perked up when she saw the biscuit. It smelled so good he was tempted to go back and get one for himself. She slathered it with butter and honey and took a bite.

Cooper clicked over to Facebook on his phone and began to read.

A minute later he found a post thanking Sullivan Enterprises for helping Abundance plan a new park that would fully accommodate disabled children and adults. Already it had been liked by more than fifty people and

333

had eight comments, all of them glowing. As he watched, someone appeared to be typing a new comment. He refreshed the screen. Another positive comment, another ten people had liked the post, and three had shared it.

He scrolled up and down the page once more. If he had paid some expensive ad agency, he doubted he could've gotten better publicity for the firm.

He glanced over at Frankie, who was wiping her fingers on a napkin.

He laid a hand on her arm. "Here I thought I was doing something nice for you by getting you breakfast. Turns out that while I was gone you did something even nicer for me." He raised his phone and turned it so she could see the Facebook post.

"Oh." Frankie gave a quick shrug and took a sip of juice. "I was just so impressed by what you told me while we were waiting. I thought you were only interested in proving yourself to your dad. I didn't realize how much you'd been doing to help people with disabilities."

"I didn't do that much. ADA compliance is kind of a special interest of mine. I think people don't always see how it actually can benefit lots of people. The elderly, someone who breaks a leg. Not only people with disabilities." He pointed to his phone. "But this—well, we couldn't buy better advertising."

"I am rather good at my job," Frankie said.

"And you're making me look awfully good at mine, even to my dad. That means a lot. You...you mean a lot."

"Oh, Cooper, you mean a lot to me too. I'm so grateful to have you here with me today." Her eyes shone.

His heart beat faster. "Frankie." He took her hand in his. It was too soon. He should wait. He should plan. He should take her somewhere romantic. But—

She reached up and brushed her fingertips down his cheek.

"I love you," he blurted out. "And I love Kira. I want to be there for both of you—today and every day."

Tears welled in Frankie's beautiful brown eyes and her lower lip trembled. "Oh," she whispered. "I love you too." She melted into his arms.

He drew her close and breathed in deeply, chest filling with joy. She loved him. Him! For the rest of his days he would treasure this woman and treasure her child. Whatever they went through, he would be there for them. He would protect them. And he would surround them with love.

Footsteps neared. "Ahem. Mrs. McNamara?"

Frankie leapt to her feet. "Yes. Sorry. Is she—?" Her throat grew tight.

"Kira did beautifully in surgery. Even better than I'd hoped. The operation was a real success." Pride rang in the surgeon's words as he explained what he had done.

"Oh." Tears flooded Frankie's eyes, and she blinked repeatedly. "Thank you." She pulled a crumpled tissue from the pocket of her cardigan and wiped her eyes.

"Someone should be out to get you soon so that you can go see her." The doctor disappeared through swinging double doors.

Cooper turned to her, beaming. "I'm so glad," he said

in a husky voice. "This truly is an answered prayer."

Frankie's shoulders relaxed and she reached for his hand, steadying herself with his strength. The surgery was over. It had been a success. Her darling Kira would be able to walk without braces. It hardly felt real. She'd prayed so hard, for so long. And God had answered her prayer.

She wiped away a tear and looked up at Cooper. "You know that line in the Bible where it says that God blesses more than we can ask or think?"

"I can't tell you where it's from, but yeah, I know that scripture."

"It's from Ephesians. I think that's what God's done today." She paused, for a moment too overwhelmed by the fullness in her chest to speak. At last she let out a heavy breath and brushed away another tear. "He brought me to Abundance, where Kira's doctor would send her to this amazing surgeon. And he brought you into my life."

Cooper gazed down at Frankie, his own eyes shining, and pulled her into his arms and kissed her.

Chapter Twenty-Nine

Abby leapt up from the base of the metal stairs that led to Nate's apartment.

He was coming down the street from the law office, looking once again as if he'd walked out of a magazine ad, despite all he'd gone through last night.

She'd been waiting for fifteen minutes, here in her spot in the shade, planning how to apologize. Kristen was at the shop again, more than happy to watch Emma if it meant Abby would take her good advice.

"Hey, Nate." Abby smoothed out the skirt of her dress.

He looked up and seemed surprised. Perhaps surprised to see her, perhaps surprised to see her dressed up.

She would admit that the sleeveless aqua dress was not what she normally wore in the shop. In fact, she had dug it out of her ironing pile, a pile she most often ignored. It had only taken fifteen minutes, though, to get the dress crisp. She'd let out her ponytail and curled her hair—everything she could think of that might increase the odds that Nate would forgive her.

"Abby. How is Emma doing?"

"She's fine. Kristen's with her. I wanted to talk to you for a moment if I could."

"Sure. I need to let Bear out first, though."

"Of course." If Nate was letting Bear out, it would give her a chance to gather her courage. Because now that he was home, her confidence faltered. She'd said horrible things to him. Why should he ever forgive her?

And oh, how she wanted his forgiveness. How had she been so blind?

Bear gave a gleeful bark and galloped down the stairs, leash dangling loose behind him. Nate and Abby followed him to the lot behind the florist, where the grass tickled Abby's feet around the edges of her sandals.

"So, what's up?" Nate said.

Abby tried to ignore the butterflies in her stomach. "When I think what might have happened if you hadn't found Emma, if she'd fallen through to land on that concrete floor—" An involuntary shudder ran through Abby, and she squeezed her eyes shut.

"Don't think about that," Nate said. "It didn't happen."

"No. It didn't, because you saved her."

Nate glanced down.

"I was wrong to call you weak." She lightly touched his arm. "Leaving your apartment, your job, your friends to make a new start here in Abundance took real courage.

And I don't know anything about addiction, but I imagine every day takes an awful lot of strength."

Nate drew his shoulders back slightly.

Did that mean he wanted to leave? Or that her words weren't what he'd expected? Or...? She had to keep going, had to say what she'd planned. "Last night, when you rescued Emma... I can't imagine anything more heroic. When I said I couldn't respect you, I was so wrong." Abby looked over at Bear. "I don't know if there's any way you can forgive me, but if you could..."

She hesitated, waiting for Nate to speak, but he remained silent.

This was never going to work. If he was going to forgive her, he'd have said something by now. She'd ruined everything with her arrogance and pride and the foolish thought that she was perfect and could judge other people. She'd rejected him. She'd—

"Forgive you?" Nate sounded as if he didn't understand. "There's nothing to forgive. I was an idiot to start taking drugs. I'll always be ashamed of the wreck and how I injured Ashley and the way I hurt people. But with God's help, I am trying to change my life. I—I know you said there was no chance, but I still hope that someday, maybe you can learn to look past the drugs."

"Someday?" For someone so smart, Nate wasn't getting it. "Try now. I can. I have. I will. I'm—I'm in love with you."

"You are?" His eyes grew wide and a smile stretched across his face, a smile that radiated such joy, such love, that her heart felt as if it would burst.

"I am," she said solemnly. "I think I started falling in

love with you the day you introduced yourself as Prince Nathaniel Redmond."

"Abby." Nate drew her into his arms and gazed at her beautiful hazel eyes, at the line of her cheek, at her soft lips.

She looked up at him, her eyes shining, and wrapped her arms around him.

This woman, who had been through so much, was willing to forgive his past.

Heart pounding, he pulled her closer and kissed her. The sweet rose smell of her perfume surrounded him, and he knew this was where he was meant to be. With Abby. For the rest of his life.

At last she stepped back.

Her cheeks were pink. Her lips were now bare of lipstick, and her eyes shone. "Nate Redmond," she said softly. "I love you."

"I love you too," he said. "And I love Emma." He drew Abby against his chest and raised his eyes to the heavens.

He had come to Abundance broken, empty, seeking a second chance.

God had given him that chance and so much more. Grace and forgiveness. Hope and strength to help him face every day. Emma, who brought such joy and delight. And Abby, whose love was so unexpected and so undeserved.

Never before had his heart felt this full.

Epilogue

Eleven months later

Abby set the plastic bag from Emma's corsage on her bedroom dresser, pulled the long pin out of the wrapped stems, and inhaled the sweet scent of the pink roses.

Hold on—

She went to the top of the stairs and leaned her head down toward the antique showroom. "Emma! You need to come upstairs. It's time to fix your corsage."

No answer.

"I'll go find her," Kristen said, sounding ready, as always, to take charge. "I think she went to see herself in that big oval mirror you have near the dress dummy. Too many people crowding into the full-length mirror up here," she called.

"I can't blame Emma for wanting to see herself," Becky said. "The dresses for the bridesmaids and flower girls are perfect. And so are the flowers."

Abby had to agree. All the attendant dresses were in the same pale-blue satin. All the bouquets, even her own, featured the same pink roses and white lilies.

"I still wish you'd been one of my bridesmaids, Becky."

Becky looked down at her bulging tummy. "I couldn't even guarantee that I'd be here today, much less that I could walk down the aisle. I'm just grateful I'm no longer on bed rest."

"Me too." Abby had been worried. "Your doctor says any time now, right?"

"Any time." Becky sat on the edge of Abby's bed and ran a hand over her stomach. "I'll do my best to wait until after the ceremony."

"Are you having contractions?" Abby peered at her cousin.

"I don't think so." Becky pressed her hand against her left side. "Someone seems to be wedging her foot into my ribs."

"Oh, I know that feeling," Tess said, coming over with her daughter, Lettie, in her arms.

Frankie stepped closer and laid a hand on Abby's arm. "You are going to be the most beautiful bride of the year. Absolutely stunning."

"I think that honor will be yours in a few months." Abby tapped the diamond of Frankie's engagement ring.

Frankie chuckled. "Maybe we can call it a tie. I have to tell you, though, never in a million years would I have imagined myself engaged to Cooper Sullivan. I can't believe I found just the right person here in Abundance."

"That seems to happen a lot," Abby said.

Kristen appeared in the doorway. For a second the ever-present confidence in her eyes seemed to falter.

Abby's heart twisted. Had she made Kristen feel the way she herself had felt not long ago—like the odd man out? That would never do.

But...if Frankie could find love after she moved back to Abundance, maybe Kristen could too. Especially if Abby tried to help once she got back from her honeymoon.

"I found both girls," Kristen said, and she led Emma and Kira into the room.

"We were twirling in front of the mirror." Kira demonstrated, her full skirt rippling around her.

Abby pinned on Emma's corsage and Frankie took care of Kira's.

"Is it time, Mommy?" Emma said.

"Not quite. Grandma and Grandpa aren't here to drive us yet."

The jangle of a cowbell contradicted her.

"Anybody here ready to get married?" Her father called.

"Me!" Emma shouted and dashed for the stairs.

Abby followed her into the hall. "Princess Aurora, remember your royal deportment classes."

"Oh." Emma slowed and raised her skirt with one hand. "Come on, Princess Chloe," she said to Kira. The two girls glided down the stairs, their steps almost identical. If she hadn't known Kira had once worn braces, Abby would never have been able to guess.

Behind Abby, Becky gave a low whistle. "You

promise to give me parenting lessons after my little one's born?"

"If it's a girl," Abby said, "I'll even find you some royal jewelry."

Abby gazed out the window of her dad's car as he pulled up near the gazebo at the new park.

The park had been finished only a month before. In the distance the ball fields stood, ready for the evening's games. Beyond them, a soccer field and a basketball court awaited. The restrooms were in a small white structure with a green roof, and two large shelters protected picnic tables, running water, and barbecue pits. A paved walking path encircled the park, with benches placed here and there along it. A paved pathway led to a large play area full of equipment. All of it was accessible to those with disabilities. It was a park Rose McFee Kincaid, her son Zane, and her grandson, Eric, would have been proud of—a park where all children, boys and girls of all races with all levels of mobility, could play.

And then there were the rosebushes. Across town, in the shopping area, Sullivan Enterprises had planted a ring of rosebushes around the plaque and statue of Rose. But here, throughout the new park, in sunny spots where they could thrive, clusters of old-fashioned yellow and pink and red and peach and white rosebushes were covered with buds and blossoms. Nate had insisted that the bushes be transplanted from the old park, and the boys in the youth baseball league had provided the labor as community service for vandalizing Abby's store.

Community service that, when the judge had given them options of what they might do for Abundance, the boys themselves had chosen.

"Ready, sweetheart?" Dad turned back to face her, hazel eyes twinkling.

"I am." Abby unbuckled Kira and Emma.

Dad helped them from the car, and Mom enveloped Abby in a huge hug and gave her a kiss for luck. Mom's face glowed with a wide smile, the same smile Abby had inherited. "Oh, Abby," she said. "I just know you and Nate are going to be happy."

"And me too!" Emma said, bouncing up and down.

Mom and Dad chuckled, and Kira giggled.

"Yes, you too, pumpkin." Mom took Emma and Kira's hands and led them over to get their flower-girl baskets.

A few minutes later, Abby and her dad waited at the back of a white runner strewn with rose petals, a runner that led to the gazebo, with wedding guests seated on either side. The ushers, her cousins Jack and Earl Ray and Becky's husband, Seth, waited nearby to assist any late guests.

Then a string quartet, four of Becky's friends, began to play "The Wedding March," and the audience rose and faced Abby.

So many wonderful friends. Neva from the florist shop. Grace Cassidy from the diner. Shelly Dwyer, holding hands with her cameraman. And George Gilcroft, her dear friend Stacey's father.

Near the front, Quentin stood with Doris, now fully recovered from her hip replacement. According to Doris, while she was in rehab and later finishing her recovery at home, Quentin had cared for her garden and visited each evening to give her a report. By the time Doris stopped using a cane, she was wearing a new engagement ring.

On the other side of Doris, Hubert smiled bravely.

In the row closest to the gazebo, Abby's mom, Becky, Uncle T.J., and Aunt Patsy sat on one side. Patsy held little Lettie on her lap, and T.J. had Earl Ray and Stacey's boy, George, on his. Nate's parents, his two sisters, his Aunt Vivian, and Jewel and her husband sat on the other side of the row.

And on one side of the gazebo, Nate's attendants stood. His best man, his Uncle Al, and the groomsmen—Cooper, Nate's friend Thornton, and her cousin Hank.

Her own attendants—her maid of honor, Kristen, and her bridesmaids, Tess, Frankie, and Stacey—beamed at her.

Kira stood near her mother, looking down at her dyed-to-match blue shoes, which Frankie had told Abby would never have fit over Kira's braces.

Emma held Kira's hand and stared at Abby, cheeks pink, eyes wide.

And there, in the center of all the people Abby loved, was Nate, so handsome in his tuxedo with his brown hair brushed back and his dark-blue eyes on her.

Dad took her arm and, as music filled the perfect summer day, they walked down the aisle toward her future.

With every step that drew her closer to Nate, her heart grew lighter.

When they reached the gazebo, Dad tenderly kissed

her cheek and moved to the side.

Abby turned to face Nate, and he took her hands in his. Emotion pricked the back of her throat, and tears welled in her eyes, but she blinked them back. What an immense blessing God had given her. She was about to marry Nate Redmond, a man of strength, a man who loved her and Emma with all his heart, a man who had taken a second chance.

And given her a second chance at love.

Pastor Corey began the service, speaking of the gift of love. Then he turned to Nate.

"Nate, do you take Abby to be your wedded wife, to live together in marriage? Do you promise to love her, comfort her, honor and keep her for better or worse, for richer or poorer, in sickness and health, and forsaking all others, be faithful only to her, for as long as you both shall live?"

"I do," Nate said. His tone was solemn, but his eyes shone.

Then Pastor Corey turned to her.

"Abby, do you take Nate to be your wedded husband to live together in marriage? Do you promise to love him, comfort him, honor and keep him for better or worse, for richer or poorer, in sickness and health and forsaking all others, be faithful only to him so long as you both shall live?"

The tears Abby had managed to hold back earlier ran down her cheeks.

She had made this pledge before and "as long as you both shall live" had been too short for Eric.

But she knew, deep in her heart, that Eric would

approve of her marriage to Nate. And she knew, beyond any doubt, that second chances were a gift from God. Nate was the man she was now supposed to be with, for as many days as God allowed them together here on earth.

And she knew those days would be filled with love.

She gazed into Nate's eyes. "I do."

He squeezed her hands.

Warmth overflowed from Abby's heart, filling every inch of her with joy.

Then the pastor looked past them, out at the audience. "Will all of you witnessing these promises do all in your power to uphold Nate and Abby in their marriage?"

"We will," the crowd answered in unison.

And Abby knew they would. For here in Abundance, though she and Nate might face problems, though the community might at times seem divided, people always came together in the end. She and Nate would be supported by the love of their friends and family.

A soft breeze stirred, surrounding them with the sweet scent of roses.

What a blessing to be marrying this wonderful man. What a blessing to have a second chance. What a blessing to have a life filled with love and roses.

All of Sally's books are available in paperback and e-book from Amazon. For a complete list, or to sign up for her author newsletter and get a free novella, please visit her website at www.sallybayless.com.

A NOTE FROM THE AUTHOR

Dear Reader,

I've had so much fun with Nate and Abby, especially with bringing surprises into their lives. Most of all, I've enjoyed letting them each find love and each grow in their relationship with God. We are so blessed that He always, always loves us!

If you enjoyed this story, I'd be really grateful if you would write a review on Amazon or Goodreads. Those reviews are the best advertising around, and you wouldn't believe how fun it is to get feedback!

I love to hear from readers! If you'd like to say hello, please visit my website, www.sallybayless.com, where you can email me or find me on social media.

If you'd like a free copy of another sweet Christian romance set in the little town of Abundance, please sign up for my author newsletter at www.sallybayless.com. You'll get a link to download the holiday novella *Christmas in Abundance* for free in ebook or PDF!

A sample of the next book in the series, *Love Once More*, is provided in just a few pages, along with information about some of my other books.

May God bless you,

Sally Bayless

ACKNOWLEDGMENTS

This book could not have been written without the help of many, many people.

Thank you to those who answered my numerous questions. Danielle McGraw, physical therapist, not only answered questions about congenitally shortened Achilles tendons and pediatric physical therapy, she also beta read the entire manuscript. Clinical Pharmacist Joyce McCarthy, PharmD, RPh, BCPS, answered questions about medications and seizures. William Hauschild, LTC (Retired), assisted with questions about military awards. Brian K. Williamson, Chief of the Bullhead City, Arizona, Police Department, helped me understand how law enforcement operates when a child is lost. I can't tell you how grateful I am to each of these people who shared their expertise. Any mistakes that slipped in are errors on my part.

My friend and neighbor, Gretchen Stock, and my fellow writer Keena Kincaid helped me brainstorm ideas for this story early on.

My wonderful critique partners, authors Susan Anne Mason and Tammy Doherty, helped this book in so many ways. I can't imagine this journey without you!

And what a blessing it is to have beta readers! This story is much stronger thanks to the contributions of Betsy Anderson, Michelle Blackwell, Kristina Gerig, Leisa Ostermann, Carrie Saunders, and Stephanie Smith.

Sally Bradley was my developmental editor. She asked the questions that pushed me to go back, work harder, and finally get a manuscript I was happy with. The wonderful Christina Tarabochia copy edited this story, and made it so much better. I am incredibly blessed to have both of these women in my life.

Jenny Zemanek of Seedlings Design Studio created the cover. Thank you, Jenny, for making it beautiful and being such a joy to work with.

Thanks to my dear family—Dave, Michael, and Laurel—for all your support and encouragement.

And finally, thank you, thank you, thank you, Jesus, for my salvation and for walking with me every day.

ABOUT THE AUTHOR

After many years away, Sally Bayless lives in her hometown in the Missouri Ozarks. She's married and has two grown children. When not working on her next book, she enjoys reading, watching BBC television with her husband, doing Bible studies, swimming, and shopping for cute shoes.

We hope you enjoy this sample from the next book in the Abundance Series, *Love Once More.*

Chapter One

Anyone could—if he or she put half a mind to it—leave the past behind and focus on the future. At least that's what the self-help books all said.

It's also what Kristen Hamlin kept telling herself as she climbed the porch steps of her sister's antique shop.

And what she'd told herself for weeks, ever since she finished reading *A Better You in Ninety Days.*

But it didn't feel like anything about her had changed.

At least not yet.

She blew out a long breath and opened the door of the shop, forcing her mood to lighten. After all, her sister was back in Missouri after her honeymoon, and it would be great to catch up with her again.

She stepped over the threshold, entering the former Victorian home that was now a shop filled with antiques.

A blur of pink satin sped toward her.

"Aunt Kristen!" Five-year-old Emma, wearing a princess dress, long white gloves, and silver flip-flops, barreled down the hallway from the kitchen.

Kristen's heart swelled with love as she knelt and gathered Emma into a hug, pressing a kiss into her red curls. "Hey, there, cutie pie."

"Mommy and Nate are back!" Emma's blue eyes danced. "They brought me seashells and a T-shirt and—"

"And she's decided we should go on a honeymoon every June." Abby came around a display of milk glass. "I get the impression Mom might have spoiled her a little while we were away."

Yeah, Mom might have. Kristen might even have helped. But she wasn't about to confess that to Abby.

"I've been sworn to secrecy," Kristen said. "All I can report is that I watered the plants at your new house and kept the shop." Which she'd enjoyed. The store was soothing, with its artfully arranged reminders of a simpler time, faint scent of furniture polish, and the gentle tick of the mantle clock in the front. No wonder customers frequently stopped in simply to look once more at a beautiful dresser or peruse the glass cases of antique costume jewelry.

"But I'm here, as promised, bright and early Monday morning, to give you an update on how sales went," she said.

And putting her own work schedule on hold for a few hours while she did so. But since she worked as a freelance textbook editor, her hours were fairly flexible. If she couldn't make time for her sister, what was the point of having that freedom?

Abby straightened a set of milk-glass punch cups that surrounded a matching punch bowl on a large Demilune table.

Kristen peered closer at her older sister. Shouldn't Abby be glowing after a whole week alone with her handsome groom? And be happy that she and Nate and Emma had moved into their new house on the outskirts of Abundance?

Abby adjusted one more cup, then rested a hand on Emma's shoulder and smiled down at her. "Sweetheart, why don't you run upstairs and show your stuffed animals all your pretty new shells?"

"Okay, Mommy." Emma picked up a turquoise beach pail and scampered up the stairs.

Abby's gaze followed her, but her smile faded as the slap of Emma's flip-flops grew fainter. "We need to talk," she said quietly.

"Was there a problem on your trip?"

Abby's hazel eyes lit. "No, it was lovely. Really lovely, but..." She led the way to a small seating area near the front of the store, a spot designed for weary shoppers to rest. "I popped over to Cassidy's Diner to get us a treat." She gestured to a carry-out container and glasses of ice tea on the coffee table. "And I heard all the latest here in Abundance. Including some bad news."

Kristen sat on one end of a maroon velvet loveseat and picked up a napkin. "What is it?" She opened the carry-out box and put a cinnamon roll on a delicate, flowered plate.

Abby pulled her light-brown hair—almost blond after

a week at the beach—between her hands at the base of her neck and smoothed it over one shoulder. "It's about Gwen." She sat down next to Kristen.

"Gwen?" Kristen put her plate on the table. Her high school best friend had recently planned a trip to Hawaii for her family and parents. "Was it the flight over? Was it too exhausting for her mom? Too hard with the babies?"

Abby shook her head, glanced down, then looked back up at Kristen, her eyes troubled. "I don't know how to tell you this, sis, but Gwen…Gwen and her husband were both killed."

Kristen's mouth gaped. "What?"

"I'm so sorry." Abby rested a hand on Kristen's arm.

Kristen's throat tightened, and her eyes stung. She numbly wiped frosting off the side of one finger and onto a napkin. "Killed? How?" This had to be a horrible mistake.

"They were on a helicopter tour with her parents, and the helicopter crashed. Her parents and the pilot survived, but Gwen and John…didn't."

Kristen's eyes filled with tears.

Abby pulled her into a hug, holding her as teardrops streamed down her cheeks.

How could this be true? How could Gwen and John be gone? Just like that? She tried to recall her last words to her best friend. Maybe something like "Have a good time in Hawaii. Remember, I want a video of you trying to do the hula!" The last time they'd spoken, and she'd made fun of Gwen's lack of dancing skills? Why couldn't she have said how much their friendship meant to her?

After a few moments, Kristen drew in a ragged breath

and scooted back. "Did you learn anything more?"

"Grace at the diner said Gwen's dad broke both his legs. Her mom was pretty much okay. I mean, as okay as she was before."

Kristen nodded slowly. Mrs. Norris had multiple sclerosis and had been having more issues lately. Gwen had planned the trip because her mom had always wanted to see Hawaii but wasn't sure she'd have the energy or mobility to enjoy some of the sights for much longer.

"I—I—" Kristen dug a tissue from her pocket and wiped her eyes. "I can't believe Gwen's gone. What about the babies?"

"They're fine. Apparently Gwen and her family were staying with one of her mom's oldest friends. The woman was watching the twins while the rest of the family went up in the helicopter."

Kristen's mouth fell open. If the twins had survived and Gwen and John were both dead, that meant... meant...

Her pulse began to pound. Snippets of a recent conversation with Gwen swirled through her mind. Gwen had been so angry with her brother, Clay. So concerned about her girls' future after she saw a story online about a young couple who tragically died within two months of each other, both from rare medical conditions, leaving three children. With Gwen's being such a close friend, there was no way Kristen could refuse when Gwen asked. With her own history with Clay, with the way he'd broken off their engagement, Kristen could understand perfectly...but—

She swallowed, her mouth suddenly dry.

"Are you okay?"

"Yeah." Kristen grabbed a glass of iced tea from the table and took a drink.

"You've gone kind of pale."

"With good reason." She set the glass on the table and watched a rivulet of condensation race down the side. "I...I think I'm supposed to be raising Gwen and John's girls." She looked back up at Abby.

"You?" Abby leaned forward. "Why not her parents? Or Clay?"

"Gwen told me her mom's health is too unpredictable to ask her parents to care for small children."

Abby dipped her chin slightly, as if she understood. "But what about Clay? He's her brother."

"Gwen and John listed Clay as the guardian when they made up wills right after the girls were born. But lately Gwen's realized he's too wrapped up in his work to be a good parent."

"Oh." Abby's voice held an awkward note.

Even after ten years, it *was* awkward. Clay's obsession with work hadn't been a newsflash to Kristen. She, more than anyone, knew that Clay Norris cared more about computers than he did about people. But even for Clay, losing his sister and almost losing his parents had to be hard. The whole situation was simply awful.

"What about Gwen's husband's family?"

"He doesn't—I mean, didn't—really have any family. He was an only child, and his parents were both only children, and they died while he was in college."

"So she asked you to be the guardian?"

"Yeah." Kristen took another drink of her tea, put the

glass back on the table, and wiped the moisture from her fingers on her shorts. "About a week ago. And I agreed. I mean, I never thought it would matter. I just thought it would give her some peace of mind if I said yes. But she took it really seriously, talking about how they had a big life insurance policy and how I wouldn't need to worry about money for housing or clothes or food or college. She sounded as if they were going to make the changes immediately."

"Wow," Abby said, "that's a lot to ask of someone who doesn't already have kids."

"I was honored." Kristen sank back in her chair. "But it is a pretty big thing to wrap my mind around."

Abby grabbed her hands. "I'll help you. Mom and Dad will too. You'll do a great job."

"Thanks. That means a lot coming from you, the World's Most Perfect Mom."

Abby gave a soft laugh. "Hardly."

Kristen lowered her chin and looked her sister in the eye. The question wasn't worth debating. Abby was an amazing mom and the nicest sister a person could have.

If Kristen sometimes felt a little less than in comparison, if her chest had ached as she watched Abby get married last weekend, it certainly wasn't Abby's fault.

Besides, the inadequacies in Kristen's life wouldn't really matter now. She would be too busy managing her editing projects and figuring out how to take care of twins.

But how could Gwen and John be gone? John was such a nice guy, and Gwen... Gwen had been so special, the kind of person who lived life to the fullest, who believed in others and encouraged them to chase their dreams. Just being around her always made Kristen happier. And now she'd never get to talk to her again...

She sat up taller. Her grief would have to wait. "Gwen wouldn't have asked me if she didn't think I could do this. And I can. I can make sure those little girls are brought up with love and attention. Exactly how she wanted."

Abby squeezed Kristen's hand, her eyes filled with what looked like a spark of approval. "You'll be wonderful with them."

"Thank you." Kristen got up. One thing at a time. "The only number I know for Gwen's mom is their old landline from when they used to live here in Abundance. But I'm pretty sure a friend of mine has a cell number from when we were planning her shower. I'll text her."

Then she'd call Mrs. Norris and figure out what to do next.

Two nine-month-old girls were counting on her.

All of Sally's books are available in paperback and e-book from Amazon. For a complete list, or to sign up for her author newsletter and get a free novella, please visit her website at www.sallybayless.com.

MORE BOOKS BY SALLY BAYLESS

Love of a Lifetime
Prequel to the series (shorter novel)

When a woman who's starting over falls for a journalist trying to dig up her past, does the attraction between them stand a chance?

Cara Smith can't wait to put the first half of 1980 behind her and build a new life in the little town of Abundance, Missouri. If she can just avoid questions from that cute guy at the newspaper, no one ever needs to find out about her past.

Will Hamlin, editor of the local paper, has some serious questions about the mayor's new secretary. She's clearly hiding something—something that could be the big story the newspaper desperately needs to stay afloat. But after Will's initial queries find nothing, he grows less interested in Cara's past and more interested in winning her heart with slices of pie and stolen kisses.

When a crime is uncovered at city hall just as Will unearths Cara's secret, the repercussions shatter their romance. Can Cara ever escape her past? Can Will finally find a way to save the paper? And can they learn to place their trust in God and open their hearts to the love of a lifetime?

Love at Sunset Lake
The Abundance Series Book 1 (novel)

A caterer who's been burned by love.
An artist who's withdrawn from the world.
A property battle that just might heal them both.

When struggling caterer Tess Palmer inherits her great-aunt's home at Sunset Lake, Missouri, she thinks she's found the way to save her business. Selling the property can provide just the infusion of capital she needs to pay off her debts and move to a larger commercial kitchen.

Wildlife painter Jack Hamlin, who lives across Sunset Lake, wants the area kept exactly as it is—a place where waterfowl can thrive and where he can find peace and solitude to ease his troubled heart. Although he's drawn to Tess's honesty and beauty, he's appalled to learn she would welcome a deal with a developer, and he vows to stop her.

As Tess discovers the reasons why Jack is so passionate about protecting the lake, she finds him more and more attractive. She takes a tentative step past her own emotional pain to risk her heart again. But there seems to be no solution to the impasse over the property. As a sale becomes imminent, can Jack and Tess trust God—and each other—and finally find a love that will last?

Love and Harmony
The Abundance Series Book 2 (novella)

The first boy she ever kissed just walked back into her life—wreaking havoc with her plans.

For music teacher Becky Hamlin, every performance is important, a time for her choir to shine. But no performance has ever mattered as much as the upcoming benefit concert for the local food pantry. This concert is not just about music. It's a chance to make up for her lapse in judgment last summer, not to mention a shot at her dream job.

Seth Williams, the new interim high school principal, has barely unpacked when he realizes that the gorgeous local choir director is the same girl he fell for at church camp years ago. As soon as he gets his troubled sixteen-year-old brother on the right path, Seth hopes to pursue a relationship with Becky. With her in town, he's more determined than ever to convince the school board to make his position permanent.

But the faith Seth and Becky once shared is no longer common ground, and the logistics of her concert create a crisis in his job. Will their relationship be torn apart? Or can their renewed love, along with God's abundant grace, allow them to overcome every obstacle?

Love and Roses
The Abundance Series Book 3 (novel)

When a widow clinging to her past meets a lawyer running from his guilt, can the roots of pain and loss bloom into new love?

Young widow Abby Kincaid treasures the past, both the antiques she sells in her shop and the tender memories of her late husband. When she learns that her hometown plans to sell historic Rose Park, a place central to her marriage, she vows to stop the sale.

Nate Redmond, a former Manhattan lawyer, is eager for a fresh start in small-town Missouri. With his extensive background, arranging the sale of outdated Rose Park for retail development looks easy—the perfect way to help the town fund the larger recreational space it needs. His role in the deal might even impress Abby, the pretty new neighbor he feels so drawn to.

But as Nate and Abby clash over the park, more serious obstacles threaten their relationship. Mistakes that Nate had hoped to forget continue to haunt him. Abby comes face to face with her failure to forgive. And how can Nate compete with the memory of a decorated war hero? When the park battle brings on a crisis, can they each find the courage to believe in a God of second chances and a future where their love can grow?

Love Once More
The Abundance Series Book 4 (novel)

Two orphaned babies, one overwhelmed uncle, one former fiancée...

One way or another, freelance editor Kristen Hamlin will keep her word. She promised to raise her best friend's baby girls, should the need ever arise, and she meant it. Obviously, the twins should never be given to their workaholic uncle. After all, he's the same man who broke his engagement to Kristen so he could spend more time with his real love—computers. But when tragedy strikes, leaving the twins as orphans, Kristen discovers that the paperwork was never done. He's the legal guardian.

Entrepreneur Clay Norris has his hands full, taking care of his twin nine-month-old nieces, not to mention running his computer-gaming company. To make matters worse, his former fiancée claims *she* should have been given custody of the twins—not him—and has now suddenly moved in next door. Coincidence? He thinks not.

Once the demands of looking after two infants require a team effort, Clay and Kristen are inevitably drawn together. Old feelings rekindle, but the couple struggles to move beyond painful mistakes from the past. As circumstances conspire against them, can they learn to forgive one another, accept God's limitless grace, and find the courage to take a chance on love once more?

Christmas in Abundance
Companion novella (Fits at any point in the series)

An art teacher avoiding Christmas. A single dad planning a holiday light show extravaganza. A yuletide clash between neighbors that might spark a dazzling romance.

Lanie Phillips has a quiet holiday planned. So quiet, in fact, that the only sounds in the house where she's staying should be the clicks of her computer keyboard and the occasional bark from a chocolate Labrador retriever. No joyous choirs of angels, no jolly laughs from Santa, and no jingle bells—nothing to distract her from her master's thesis or bring up painful Christmas memories.

But for the single dad who's her closest neighbor, simple holiday decorations just won't do. Kyle Mattox is determined to give his five-year-old daughter the best Christmas ever—one that includes an outdoor display lit with fifty thousand lights, activated in time to music shared through four giant loudspeakers.

When Lanie comes to complain that she can't write with the lights flashing and carols blasting, Kyle realizes that—unknown to her—their circuits have crossed in the past. If he wants his daughter happy, he needs to keep that information to himself, keep the show running, and keep his distance from Lanie.

All of Sally's books are available in paperback and e-book from Amazon. For a complete list, or to sign up for her author newsletter and get a free novella, please visit her website at www.sallybayless.com.